SPINNING TIME
A TIME TRAVEL ROMANCE

D. F. JONES

JONES MEDIA

COPYRIGHT

Spinning Time, a time travel romance by D.F. Jones, © 2017 Dawn Frost Jones

The author and publisher provides this e-book and book to you for personal use only. It is strictly forbidden to make this title publicly available in any way. **Copyright Infringement is against the law.**

If you purchased or signed up for a free copy without the cover, be advise the book is stolen. It's been reported as "stolen or destroyed" and the author has not received any payment for the stripped book.

If you suspect this e-book or book you're reading infringes the author's copyright, please contact info@DFJonesAuthor.com

The novel is a work of fiction. Names, characters, places, and incidents are either the product of the author's imagination or used fictitiously. Any resemblance of persons, living or dead, business establishments, events, or locales is entirely coincidental.

Cover Art, by Jones Media, images provided by Shutterstock, © 2017

Editing by Alicia Street

Formatting by Jones Media

❦ Created with Vellum

PRAISE

"Author D.F. Jones Spinning Time is a fun read and a new departure from her previous books. I found her time travel romance to be inventive, fast-paced and enjoyable. Highly recommended!" Debbie Herbert, *RWA 2017 RITA Finalist, paranormal romance, Bayou Shadow Hunter*

"D. F. Jones does it again! Whether it's aliens or angels, the sky's the limit for her imaginative, engaging stories, and Spinning Time is no different." Allie Marie, author of the *True Colors* Series

"D.F. Jones delivers again! This story is a riveting page turner with a masterfully crafted plot." Lynn Sutton, author of *In Your Eyes*

DEDICATION

Mom, you inspire me every day.

ACKNOWLEDGMENTS

I have enjoyed researching time travel, space, and the universe with its billions and billions of galaxies nearly as much as writing the narrative for Spinning Time. While I don't delve in depth into the ongoing work of scientists and physicists, the possibility of time travel is moving from the fictional realm to experimental options.

First, I'd like to thank my husband who shares my passion for the concept of unknown space exploration and the possibility that other more advanced civilizations may exist. I credit him for ATTRA, Alien Time Travel and Research Agency and Klock, Spinning Time's alien dog. Brilliant!

Thank you, Alicia, my editor, for your insight, comments, and suggestions.

I want to thank my beta's, and the D.F. Jones team of readers who support my work. I need creative individuals to give me feedback. All of you who offer constructive suggestions and comments help me to grow as a writer. Your messages and emails uplift my spirit and encourage me to continue writing the next page. *You all rock!*

Thank you, Amanda, for designing my cover and marketing materials. You make my books look great.

And most importantly, to my readers, thank you for supporting and sharing my books. Your word of mouth referrals, written reviews, messages, and comments are fuel for my fire to write and create new characters and books.

PROLOGUE

*P*resent Day, ATTRA, Lunar City

Charlie watched Monica, the Commander of the Alien Time Travel and Research Agency (ATTRA) unsheathe a nine-inch, pencil-thin, razor-sharp knife. Monica casually walked around her desk to stand in front of the trembling new female recruit kneeling on the shiny black marble tile and slit the woman's throat.

Turning to face Charlie, Monica narrowed her eyes and said, "I caught Dedria hacking into my personal computer system. She denied it, but I walked in, and my screen was up."

Charlie stood at attention with her hands clasped behind her back. Her heart was pounding at the brutal death of the innocent woman. Charlie had been the one to hack into Monica's system, and she'd been summoned to the Gateway before she had time to replace the screen into the sleeve of the wall. Monica returned early from her mission and caught Dedria in her office and assumed the worst, slitting her throat before Charlie could confess to the crime.

Monica stepped over to her oblong glass desk. She pulled a tissue from her drawer, then wiped the blood off the knife and returned it to its sheath that hooked on the belt of her uniform. Taking a seat in the ergonomic white leather chair, she said, "Charlie, you have real potential. Are you up for a challenge?"

"Yes, Commander." Charlie stared out the wall of windows facing the Milky Way. She'd arrived at Lunar City shortly after tripping on acid at Woodstock in 1969. She apparently fell through a time portal on the farm.

Charlie wished she could remember what happened the day of the concert, but she'd been too wasted. Not that it mattered because she was on a permanent trip now, like something right out of a science fiction novel.

During Charlie's ATTRA training, she'd learned that after the Lord Supreme had created the Earth, the moon was brought in and placed in perfect orbit to stabilize the planet. The magnificent city within the interior structure of the luminous silver moon housed several thousand people working for the organization overseeing humanity, tracking Time Spinners, negotiating with alien interlopers, while deflecting debris catastrophic to Earth's existence. ATTRA worked to coordinate parallel universes and alternate realities to keep Earth's path on course to a future utopian society.

Charlie had been placed under Monica's authority, and with ATTRA's strict protocols, it made interference on the injustice she'd just witnessed impossible. Based on the Time Trackers' paradigm coming in from around the world, Earth was approaching a critical time shift.

Monica motioned for Charlie to sit in the white chair opposite of the desk. "Zane has informed me the Lord Supreme recently assigned Ruben to monitor a Spinner crossing the threshold on June 15, 1948, at fifteen hundred hours."

Charlie straightened her spine in the chair at the mention of Ruben, her friend, and mentor.

Monica picked up a report on her desk and briefly scanned the contents, and she said, "The Spinner's name is Julia Boatwright from North Carolina, born May 5, 1927. She'll give birth to a son, the first human physicist to break the barrier of the space-time continuum into the distant past. Ruben's assignment is to protect Julia. He's unaware of the child. Your assignment is to kill Ruben and bring me the girl."

Monica swiveled back and forth in the chair with a glazed look in her eyes. "The Plates of Prophecy state the time machine developed by Julia's son will travel into the far distant past. If I can train the boy, I'll control the historical events on Earth and use the information to barter with the more advanced civilizations in the galaxies. General Agriaous and I have set up colonization of a new planet, Veetreous, from the Andromeda Galaxy, and I need more Spinners."

Charlie's eyes widened. She leaned forward placing her right hand on the desk. "You're talking about the lives we've sworn to protect. And kill Ruben? He's one of our best Trackers."

With a wave of her hand, Monica scoffed, "For space sake wipe off that lovesick expression. I admit Ruben is very good-looking, and well, not bad as a lover. Oh, I'm sorry. I thought you knew we slept together. Do you want to end up on my marble floor, Charlie?" A slow smile crept across Monica's face as Charlie's cheeks reddened.

"No, ma'am. But if the Lord Supreme learns of you and General Agriaous using Spinners as slave labor, it'll be your head on the floor."

"Silence! May I remind you that you've sworn allegiance to me." Throwing her hands up, palms out, Monica said, "Look, Charlie, Ruben's a threat to me. He wants my job, and I won't allow it. That girl and her child are not only my ticket to a seat on the council but will also make me the Queen of Veetreous. If you play your cards right, you'll have more power than you've ever dreamed possible. I'm issuing you a direct order, Charlie. Be discreet and after he meets Ms. Boatwright, make Ruben's death look like an accident, and I'll consider making you the new Commander."

Charlie clenched her teeth and then replied, "Yes, Commander."

Monica motioned to the sliding glass doors. "Pick up the details of your assignment with Zane outside, then send him in to clean up this mess. You're dismissed."

Charlie turned on a dime and marched out of Monica's office. She grabbed the assignment chip and raced down the corridor, ducking into an alcove to gather her wits.

Charlie had to warn Ruben. But how? Last, she'd heard, Ruben had traveled in the Needle-Horn to 1950. Betraying Commander Monica Adams meant immediate execution, but Monica was out of control, and someone had to do something to stop the power-hungry maniac.

Charlie headed to the Gateway for a quick trip to 1950.

CHAPTER 1

*B*urkett Falls, North Carolina, May 1948

For a little extra oomph, Julia lifted and twisted the platinum blonde strands of hair before securing a diamond hairpin behind her right ear. She grabbed the silver hand mirror and glanced at her reflection. "Not too shabby."

Julia's little sister, Sloane, burst into her bedroom, out of breath. She and Sloane were only eighteen months apart and best friends.

"Julia, oh gosh, Julia." Sloane bent over and placed her hands on her knees to catch her breath. "Dad's coming down the driveway with your birthday present."

Julia stepped away from the dressing table and twirled around to feel the swish of the beautiful red-and-white, polka-dot skirt that cinched at her waist. She paired the new skirt with a short sleeve white cashmere sweater and a chic neckerchief.

Her twenty-first birthday party started in a couple of hours, and the entire house buzzed with activity. "Baby sister, breathe." She hooked her arm around Sloane's neck. "So, spill the beans. What am I getting?"

Sloane elbowed Julia in the ribs and dipped out of the headlock. "Let go of me, and I'm not telling. Dad made me promise."

The girls linked arms and jogged down the stairs until they reached Ethel, their housekeeper, who held an armful of linens. Ethel turned slightly on the stairway landing as the girls slipped past her down the stairs. With a raised brow, Ethel said, "Miss Bunny will want you to wear a cocktail dress this evening instead of your casual attire." Julia's mom was known as Bunny to her family and friends.

Julia leaned in and kissed Ethel on the cheek. "Oh, what mom doesn't know won't hurt her. Besides, she's too busy with the florist and the band director to worry about what I'm wearing. So, mum's the word, please, Mama Ethel." Her hands tented into prayer mode.

Ethel shrugged. With her lips pursed, she said, "Well, child, Mr. Joseph is going to see you first. If he doesn't say anything, then I won't." Julia and Sloane ran down the steps with Ethel yelling behind them, "Young ladies don't run in the house."

Julia slowed down as she slid to a stop on the slippery hardwood floors that had been waxed and buffed to a high sheen. "Wow, Bunny's gone all out."

Festive party decorations and flower centerpieces filled the grand foyer that boasted a broad staircase and an enormous glittering chandelier suspended from a vaulted ceiling. The elegant rooms on either side of the Corinthian columns had been cleared of furniture to make room for dancing.

Sloane leaned in, inhaling the fragrance of the pink peonies centerpiece on the dark mahogany pedestal table in the center of the foyer. "Mom's trying to find you a husband. Somewhere she's read there's a shortage of men since the war ended. She wants her debutante daughters married off to Southern gentlemen with substantial means before they're all snatched up."

Julia rolled her eyes as she pushed open the large white front door. "Utter gaga. I don't care if there's a shortage of men. I'm twenty-one and graduate college next week. I hate to disappoint Bunny, but the last thing I want is to be tied down to one man." She opened her arms with a broad sweeping motion. "I want to travel and experience everything in life and live somewhere they don't know me or the Boatwright name."

SPINNING TIME

Julia gasped as her father drove into the circular driveway in a brand-new Packard convertible with the top down. He waved and then laid on the horn. Julia scrambled down the front porch steps to greet him. The pale-yellow beauty with a cream-colored top was just simply divine. "Daddy, oh you didn't."

Joe Boatwright exited the driver door, and swooped Julia into his arms. "I most certainly did. Do you like it, tulip?"

Wrapping her arms around his neck, Julia planted a big smooch on his cheek. She took a step back. "I love it. May I take her for a spin to the Falls?"

Joe turned toward the front door. "Only if you and Sloane get there and back within the hour. Bunny will cook my goose if y'all aren't ready by party time." In his middle forties, Joseph Boatwright was everything a Southern gentleman aspired to be, confident, good-looking, and with the fashion sense of Cary Grant.

Plus, Joe did whatever Bunny told him.

The epitome of Southern hospitality, the Boatwrights regularly entertained family and friends. Often, the guests requested to drive on the farm's back forty to catch a glimpse of the majestic *Burkett Falls* with its impressive cliffs. Burkett Falls was named for the pioneer, Daniel Burkett, who discovered the Falls shortly after the Revolutionary War.

Julia's great-grandfather, Parker, had bought the Falls along with eleven hundred acres of prime farmland that continued to produce cotton and tobacco.

His grandson, Joseph, or Big Joe, coined by the locals, recently purchased an automobile company, and aptly named it, Big Joe's. The company sold cars, trucks, and offered a service station next door.

Samuel, the farm's manager, walked over from the barn, shaking his head. "Missy, that's more car than a girl like you needs." Frowning, he turned to Joe and said, "Are you trying to get the girl killed?" Sam and his wife Ethel had worked for the Boatwrights for years and were considered a part of the family. He had been deeded twenty acres with road frontage on the edge of the property during the depression.

Childless, Sam and Ethel thought of Julia and Sloane as surrogate daughters.

Joe waved a hand at Sam. "Oh, hogwash. My girl's all grown up, and she'll drive responsibly." Joe waggled his brows. "Right, tulip?"

Julia caught on quickly and nodded. "I promise to drive responsibly. Sam, you know me. When have I not been responsible?"

"Every day, young'un. Well, somebody has to work around here." Sam turned slowly, wiping his hands with a red bandana before walking back to the barn, he said, "Little girl, please drive safe in that big ole jalopy."

"Sloane and I'll be back within the hour. My sorority sisters are going to be pea green with envy." Julia did a spot-on imitation of Vivian Leigh as Katie Scarlett O'Hara's character in *Gone with the Wind*. Julia's parents spoiled her and Sloane almost as much as Rhett spoiled Scarlett.

Julia loved, and hated, the attention her family's wealth and prominence brought her. She tried to be grateful and appreciative, but sometimes being a Boatwright stifled her. And everyone on the farm seemed to treat her as perpetually prepubescent.

Sloane ran and jumped into the passenger seat. "C'mon, Julia. I gotta take a bath and get dressed for the party. "

Julia untied the neckerchief and wrapped the scarf around her hair. "Don't be such an eager beaver." She slid behind the wheel and cranked the engine. Before Julia pulled out of the driveway, she blew Big Joe a kiss and mouthed the words, *I love you*. Then she honked at Sam and waved as she sped past the barn, driving down the tractor lane leading to Burkett Falls.

Sloane fiddled with the radio until she picked up Bing Crosby's velvety smooth voice crooning, "The Very Thought of You." Sloane glanced sideways at her sister. "Bunny's invited every eligible bachelor within eight counties to your party, and she hired boys from Burkett Falls University to wait on the guests. In tuxedoes, no less."

Julia slammed on the brakes, and Sloane threw her hands out to brace herself against the dashboard. Julia tapped her head against the steering wheel and groaned. "Bunny didn't. Please tell me she didn't.

Oh, good lord, it's bad enough most of the girls in our sorority hate me, but now mom's trying to sell me off to the highest bidder." Rolling her eyes, she added, "And the boys at school... Uh, why does she have to humiliate me?"

Sloane settled back in the caramel leather seats. Releasing a deep breath, she said, "I think Bunny's trying to help you. But I thank God, every day I was born second. You're the firstborn, and with no son, you have to carry on the family tradition, my dear."

Julia yelled, "And you get to do whatever you want." She floored the gas pedal, spraying a cloud of red clay dust into the air.

Sloane giggled and shouted over the radio, "Don't snap a cap. The party will be fun, and there's always the champagne and the promise of meeting the man of your dreams."

Julia cut her eyes toward Sloane, gripping the steering wheel. "Fat chance." She flew down the well-traveled tractor lane passing several miles of farmland with rolling hills and dense forest. She eased up on the gas when she reached an opening revealing the magnificent waterfalls with a spray of mist rising off the jutting cliffs.

Julia parked, turned off the car, and leaned back in the seat. She threw her hands behind her head and sighed. The serenity of the clear blue pools, the natural rock formation of the cliffs, and the sandy rock beach created a perfect place to get away. The Boatwrights may legally own Burkett Falls, but in Julia's mind, the Falls belonged to no one except for maybe God. The Boatwrights were just the caretakers.

"I wish we could go swimming. But I promised Dad one hour. Sloane..." Julia paused and then reached over and squeezed Sloane's hand. "I don't know what I would do without you in my life."

Sloane playfully pushed Julia away, and teased, "Don't start getting all sappy on me or you'll have to redo your makeup, and you're sooo perfect as it is." She reached over and hugged Julia. "I don't know what I'd do without you, either. Let's come back tomorrow afternoon to swim. Just the two of us, okay?"

* * *

RETURNING TO THE HOUSE, Julia glanced up at Bunny who stood on the porch tapping her foot in agitation. "Young ladies, you have approximately thirty minutes to get dressed and be downstairs to greet our guests." She narrowed her eyes at Julia and said, "You're not wearing *that*. I've picked out a lovely light blue party dress for you, and I left you Grandmother Boatwright's pearls too."

Bunny turned to Sloane with her hands on her hips. "Darling, if you continue to dress like a boy, you'll never find a husband. Get in the bath, and for heaven's sake, clean your fingernails. I have a lovely dress for you too, and you can wear my diamond pendant." She kissed both girls, and they took the cue to run into the house to avoid further fashion critiques.

Thirty minutes later, Julia and Sloane stood at the front door greeting guests from the country club, Bunny's Women's League, Julia and Sloane's sorority sisters, and young men from all the best families in the area.

Champagne flowed like the Cane River, and Julia vowed to drink as many flutes as possible. Bunny knew how to throw a party. The orchestra played all the top hits of the day, and the ballroom filled with guests dancing and flirting as the evening wore long.

The dining room table was laden with an assortment of hors d'oeuvres and sweets along with the silver tea and coffee service set. Gentlemen stood in the breezeway smoking cigars, and ladies floated to and from the powder room.

Julia strolled through the rooms making polite conversation when she caught Sloane's eyes. She nodded then pointed to the gardens. The sisters met on the terrace and walked through the heady gardens filled with hollyhocks, pink and red hibiscus, and a variety of peonies in pink, red, and white. The full moon rose high in the sky as the big band orchestra music filtered softly through the warm spring air.

At the end of the garden pathway, Julia leaned against an old willow oak tree. "I'm almost drunk, and I haven't been kissed once. It's always the same boys at every party."

Sloane twirled her full skirts out and sat on the ground. "Brooks Davis is good-looking."

"He's a pompous ass and ancient history." Julia and Sloane giggled loudly.

"A good-looking pompous ass with the right qualifications." Sloane placed her gloved hands in her lap and glanced up at Julia. "You don't like him anymore, do you?"

"Ah, heck no. Brooks is a cheater, and the only person he loves is himself. He also has a bad temper when he drinks." Her gaze dropped to the dreamy look on her sister's face. "Sloane, not you. Please tell me you haven't…"

Sloane chuckled and said, "Nope. I just wonder what he looks like naked."

Julia bent over laughing while holding onto her sides. "You crack me up, and I wouldn't know. Don't look now, but one of the waiters is on his way over here with two flutes. Shoo, fly. This one looks like a keeper."

Sloane's eyes went wide. "Oh, no. Not the help. Bunny will have a stroke."

Julia narrowed her eyes and whispered, "Scram or I'll tell Brooks you're sweet on him."

"You're utterly foul." Sloane stood and brushed her skirts out, then left.

Julia called out, "I love you, Sloane."

Turning her attention toward the yum-yum waiter, Julia crossed her arms over her chest and waited for him to approach. Her gaze followed his long, graceful strides. The handsome man bowed and offered Julia a glass of champagne. With a raised brow, she said, "Hey, I know you. Don't you teach at BFU?"

He had an air of confidence about him. His shiny black hair was slightly longer on the top, slicked back with a side part. The night finally showed some promise. "Yes, Miss Boatwright. I teach at BFU." His thick black lashes surrounded dark golden-brown eyes that seemed to undress her.

Boy, oh boy, he spells trouble. Heat rushed into Julia's cheeks. "Do you have a name or are you going to keep staring at me like I'm not wearing clothes? And if you're teaching, why are you working here tonight?"

His deep rumbling laugh washed over her like spring rain, and she wanted to drink him in. He lifted the other flute and dropped Bunny's silver tray on the ground.

She giggled. Julia liked him already.

He clinked the crystal flute next to hers and said, "My name is Phillip Clayborn. I saw a sign posted in the Science Department about your party and only applied for this gig to meet you. I took a chance when I saw you walk outside."

Julia sipped champagne and stared at him over the rim of the glass. With a tilt of her head, she said, "You took the job to meet me? Pretty sure of yourself."

Phillip leaned in close, and she could feel his warm minty breath against her cheek. "Pretty sure. Was I wrong? Or do I need to go back to work?"

Julia swallowed hard, then slowly raked her eyes over his body before lifting her gaze to his eyes. "Nope, you're not wrong."

Phillip smiled in the moonlight and sent her heart into flutters. "So, are you bored with the fuddy-duddies inside?"

Julia hesitated, then nodded. "I am. How about we blow this joint?"

Phillip took a deep bow and replied in an elongated drawl, "Why after you, Miss Boatwright." He stood upright and gave her the sexiest grin.

"Where did you park?"

Phillip raised his arm and pointed. "Next to the barn." He grabbed her suddenly around the waist and placed a crushing kiss on her lips, one of his hands placed firmly on the small of her back and the other at the nape of her neck. Julia's knees went weak. His spicy cinnamon scent mixed with vintage leather and a hint of sunshine nearly made her swoon.

Hmmm, Phillip was the best present of the day. Julia's heart raced as she allowed herself to melt into the indulgence of his romantic kiss. It was her party, so propriety went straight out the window. She broke from the kiss and released a deep sigh. "Ahem, you're quick on the trigger."

"My apologies, but I couldn't resist." He angled his head and smiled that charming smile.

Julia relented. "Forgiven. Meet me at the barn in five. Oh, and take the glasses because I'm going to steal a bottle of champagne."

Julia lit out across the gardens to the outside kitchen where they kept the champagne on ice. The exterior kitchen hopped with the activity of the cooks and the waiters. No one noticed when she swiped the bottle. Julia slipped her shoes off, holding them by the straps in one hand and the bottle in the other as she raced to the barn.

* * *

PHILLIP TOOK off the borrowed tux and laid it on a chair in the tack room where the waiters had dressed for the party. He quickly changed back into his jeans and black dress shirt and slipped on his loafers. He'd spoken the truth.

Phillip applied for the waiter's job to see if Julia Boatwright might remember him. He'd watched her at BFU and knew she would be graduating next Saturday. So, tonight might be his only chance to get her alone. Julia ran in the high society pack and dated fraternity boys. Not the kind of crowd he ran in. Not that he had a crowd.

Phillip walked out of the barn and looked over to the exterior building next to the big house. Julia Boatwright was running to him. He leaned against the driver door of his Jeep. He didn't care he forfeited his paycheck for the night.

Julia stopped short of slamming into him and stared up at Phillip with emerald eyes which seemed to glow in the dark.

Hot damn. She's a beautiful woman.

Julia said, "Don't just stare. Let's get out of here before Bunny figures out I've flown the coop."

Chuckling, Phillip said, "I've met your mom. She's the one that hired me for the party. Why do you call her Bunny?"

"Dad said it's because mom jumps around as fast as a bunny rabbit. We've called her Bunny for as long as I can remember."

Phillip helped Julia into the Jeep and ran around the back before he jumped inside. He gave her a smile before twisting the key in the ignition, and the engine roared. He drove down the tractor lane with only the light of the full moon. "Where are we going?"

"Phillip Clayborn, you mean to tell me you've been teaching at BFU for what, a year or two, and never visited Burkett Falls?"

"No, ma'am. I've never been invited until tonight." Left hand steady on the wheel, he leaned his right arm on the back of her seat. His fingertips toyed with the silky strands of her hair.

Julia glanced at him and smiled. "Keep your eyes on the road, or you could pop a tire."

Phillip laughed, thinking he could pop more than his tire. "Jeeps are made for rough terrain. You just keep me going in the right direction, pretty lady."

The Jeep bounced over the bumps in the road as Julia held on to the door grip and pointed. "Turn, there to your left. The Falls are just beyond the open field."

Phillip's thoughts whirled. *She doesn't remember me.*

But he'd never forgotten her.

He drove through the opening and was rewarded with the panorama of the Falls rushing over massive cliffs while the moon rose behind the mountains in the starlit sky. It looked like something out of a motion picture. "Wow, incredible view. So where do I park?"

She giggled and replied, "Anywhere, silly. It's a Jeep. But don't drive into the water, it's deep."

Phillip pulled the Jeep to a stop, reached in the back seat, and drew out a quilt. "Wanna sit in here or out there?"

The smile left Julia's face, and she shook her head. With a hint of sarcasm, she said, "Well, it looks like you came prepared. I hate that I was a foregone conclusion." She jumped out of the Jeep in her bare feet and slammed the door.

Damn it. Julia had reached the beach before Phillip grabbed her hand. "I didn't think anything. The quilt has been in the Jeep since winter. It gets cold in there when the heater quits working."

She turned and tilted her head. "Promise?"

Phillip crossed his heart with his forefinger. "Promise. May I spread it out? We can just talk." She nodded yes, and he spread the quilt out on the soft grass. Sitting down, he patted the quilt with his left hand. "Come on, sit down. I promise I won't bite too hard."

Julia knelt and sat on her heels. "Did you really take the job to meet me tonight?"

Leaning back, he propped his upper body with his elbows. "Yeah, I took the job to see you. You don't remember me, do you?"

Looking down at him, she said, "Am I supposed to?"

"We went to elementary school together. I was in sixth grade and walking with my buddies to the jungle gym during recess. You were swinging on the playground and jumped in midair and fell to the ground on your knees and started crying. I ran to you. I-I—"

Julia interrupted and said, "You helped me into Mrs. Troop's room and fetched the first aid kit. You cleaned and bandaged my knees. That, was you?"

"That was me." His fingers brushed lightly against her gloved hands, and she didn't pull away.

"What happened to you? I never saw you again."

Phillip took a deep breath and exhaled. He sat up and placed his hands on his knees. "My mom passed away. I came home from school and found a neighbor waiting on me. She held my hands and told me that Mom had a heart attack, and she was living in heaven. That night, my dad began to drink heavily. He dozed off in his chair, and I tried to take the bottle from him. He didn't mean to, but he jerked the bottle out of my hand and broke my arm."

Phillip swiped his hand over his face. "Talking about that day still brings back bad memories. My mom's twin sister, Aunt Doris, from Upstate New York, came down for the funeral and took me back to live with her."

Shifting positions, Phillip sat cross-legged. "Aunt Doris raised me. I visited Dad during the summers and holidays. He'd make trips to spend the long weekends with me. But I didn't move back here until after the war, and I enrolled at BFU to finish my Ph.D. I was lucky enough to land a position teaching and given free rein to run my experiments in the lab."

Julia squeezed his hand and said, "You're finishing your Ph.D.? Impressive. I'm sorry about your poor mother. How sad it must've been for you as a little boy. Did you serve in the war? And why didn't you ever come and see me? Why haven't you talked to me before now?"

Phillip nodded. "While I served in the Air Force, I became interested in theoretical physics. My unit teamed up with the Navy on a secret project, and I got to work with Tesla. When the war ended, I moved back here to re-establish my relationship with my dad, finish school, and..." His voice trailed off.

For a long quiet minute, Phillip rubbed her hands gently while they locked eyes. "I did see you around during the summers. But you were four years younger than me. Not that that's a big deal now, but back then, I would've been robbing the cradle. I saw you once at The Bijou when I was on leave. You were about eighteen and all grown up. I would've asked you out then, but you were dating Brooks Davis and knee deep with your sorority sisters."

Phillip released Julia's hands and stared at the Falls. "And I confess, I hadn't been able to let go of the feelings I had for the girl I'd fallen for as a kid." He paused and turned to Julia. "I thought if I could see you at the party that I'd finally get the nerve to approach you. Any chance you'd go out on a real date with me?"

Julia tilted her head to the side and said, "Hmm, I think I'd like to go out with you, Phillip Clayborn."

He inhaled, catching a whiff of Julia's lightly scented floral perfume. He resisted the urge to kiss her and began to remove Julia's long satin gloves, one finger at a time. "What do you want in life?" With each word he freed one finger, sliding the glove from her hand on the final word.

The sensual movements seemed to unnerve Julia. Her gaze locked with his eyes as he repeated the movements with her other hand. She took the gloves from his hands and placed them beside her on the quilt before answering.

"I want to move to New York and become a writer for a television show. Or maybe develop my own radio broadcast. I want to be someone other than a debutante on display, like I'm some prize heifer, just waiting to get married."

Phillip grinned and said, "Good for you." He reached over to caress her peaches-and-cream cheeks. "Julia, may I kiss you?"

She nodded yes and closed her eyes.

* * *

JULIA KNEW the moment Phillip's lips connected with hers that he was different than the rest. Time seemed to suspend. The mingling of his soft lips brushing against hers made her heart flutter. No French kissing, just a gentle kiss meant to woo her, and Phillip was wooing her. He cradled her face in his large, strong hands.

Julia opened her eyes and found herself searching Phillip's face. She became overwhelmed with emotion and felt intense chemistry for him. For the first time in her life, Julia didn't care what others thought. She reached up and cupped his face with her hands.

In an instant, Phillip's eyes flew open and locked with hers in a smoldering stare. He caressed her cheek with one hand while the other slipped behind her neck. Phillip leaned in and closed his eyes. He gently brushed his tongue over her lips and just inside her mouth.

Julia's stomach flipped. She'd never allowed anyone to French kiss her on a first date, and this wasn't even the first date. Nice girls never went to first base, but Julia wanted to bypass all the bases and go for the grand slam.

She parted her lips and released a moan. Her adrenaline charged and Phillip must've sensed it because his tender kisses became harder and more demanding. Julia slipped her tongue inside his warm, sweet minty mouth.

Heart pounding, Julia's want seemed to waltz with Phillip's obvious desire. She returned his kiss with such ferocity that Phillip pushed her back onto the quilt. He caressed the curve of her face and trailed his fingers along the column of her neck, down her arm until he intertwined his fingers with hers and brought her hand to his mouth.

Phillip kissed the back of her hand, then turned her palms over and pressed feather light kisses on the soft skin of her wrist. Julia's body came alive with warm sensations igniting her nerve endings with burning passion.

She broke out in a sweat when Phillip broke from kissing her wrists and trailed his tongue along the delicate pale skin of her throat, and she arched her back pressing her chest upward.

Phillip whispered, "Make love to me, Julia."

She replied with a hoarse whisper, "I can't. I'm saving myself for marriage."

Phillip's tender kisses trailed to the cleft of her breasts. Julia stiffened and pushed him away. "Don't, Phillip." She rolled away, sat up, and tried to make herself presentable. *Who was she fooling?* Breathing hard, she said, "You're just like every other guy I've met. You just want inside my panties."

He chuckled again. "Yeah, I want inside your panties and your bra too." His face sobered. "But unlike other guys, what I really want is to spend time with you. I can wait for everything else if you give me a chance. Don't you feel it? I know you do."

Phillip sat up.

Julia's gaze followed his movements as Phillip rubbed his hands along his very muscular thighs. "People live their whole lives without experiencing the fiery passion I feel for you. In the war, I learned you don't wait for things you want in life. Life changes in a split second. I knew the moment I saw you again that I wanted you. I'm sorry if I pushed you too fast. Forgive me?" he pleaded.

He moved quickly, wrapping Julia up in his embrace and nuzzling his face against the soft skin of her cheek close to her ear, giving Julia pleasant goosebumps on her arms.

She giggled. "That tickles, and if you behave yourself, then you're forgiven for a second time tonight." In her heart, Julia was screaming yes— yes—yes. But, she was also pragmatic. She'd give Phillip a chance, and then she'd decide whether she'd give him her innocence.

Julia tilted her head to the side and said, "I admit it. I've never felt this way. But it's too fast, and I don't know you. How am I supposed to agree to make love to someone I barely know? When the time comes for me to take the next step regarding sex, I intend to marry that person."

"Sweet, darling Julia, I'm crazy for you." Phillip kissed her again, and she melted into his arms.

* * *

MUCH LATER, after some spectacular necking, Julia breathlessly whispered, "I have to go home. My parents are going to be furious I left my birthday party. What time is it?" She stood and offered Phillip a hand, which he took.

Phillip glanced at his watch. With a look of surprise, he said, "It's three-thirty."

"Holy macaroni. I'm in big trouble. Hurry, please."

Running to the Jeep, Phillip stopped Julia before she opened the passenger door. He swirled her around and pressed kisses along the curve of her neck. He muttered, "Have dinner with me tomorrow night?"

Shivers ran up Julia's spine as she dipped out of his caress. "I have to work at Big Joe's tomorrow. But if I'm still alive after my parents get through with me, you may pick me up around six." She kissed him on the cheek.

With a smile, he replied, "Six, it is."

Moonlight peeped from behind the clouds as Phillip made his way down the old road and parked at the barn. With one last frantic kiss, he helped Julia out of the Jeep. Then she watched as Phillip made a clean getaway down the driveway.

Dreamy-eyed, Julia sighed, turned, and began walking to the main house. She'd heard the cliché "love at first sight," she'd just never believed it. Or well, that is until tonight. Julia took a deep breath, and out of the darkness, Sloane grabbed her arm. Julia yelped in surprise. "Geez, you scared the pee out of me."

Sloane said, "Oh, girlie, you're in big trouble. Bunny's waiting up for you, and she's livid. After everyone left the party, Bunny shouted at Daddy telling him you're just like him. He laughed, and that made Bunny even madder."

Walking back to the house, Julia couldn't stop smiling. "I don't care if Bunny is livid. She's not going to ruin my night." She stopped and turned to Sloane, grabbing her hands.

In breathless whispers, Julia explained they'd driven to the falls and necked. Her voice grew serious when she said, "I think I'm in love with Phillip. I can't explain it. It happened so fast. Is that possible?"

Sloane hugged Julia and chuckled. "Oh, you have to dish the details later, boy, I can't wait to see the look on Bunny's face when she finds out you're in love with the help. It's the best news I've had all evening. She's liable to disown you."

"He's not the help. Sloane, he teaches in the Science Department. Phillip only took the waiter's job to meet me. And what if he were the help, you snob. Love has no boundaries or class distinction. Phillip is finishing his doctorate. He's smart and funny and so sexy that I'm lucky I'm still a virgin. He's unlike anyone I've ever met. Meet me in my room after Bunny's tirade."

Julia opened the door to the screened-in porch, and Sloane ran inside the double doors to the main house, leaving Julia to face her mother alone.

A lone lamp lit the room while Bunny sat in her wicker rocking chair, reading a book.

Pressing her lips tight, Bunny took off her glasses, closed the book, and placed it on the little side table. "Young lady, please come in and sit down. I'd like to talk to you for a few minutes."

Julia didn't argue with her mother. She sat down in the matching chair adjacent to Bunny and placed her gloved hands on her lap. Julia lifted her chin in defiance. "Okay, let me have it. Give it to me with both barrels."

Bunny straightened her back and narrowed her eyes. "Don't be impertinent. It's nearly four in the morning, and you snuck away with that waiter for most of the evening. How dare you? Where were you? Are you ruined?"

Bunny twisted around to face Julia and gripped the armrest of the chair, so tight her knuckles were pale. "Do you even care about the time and expense we put into your birthday party? Or the scandal that'll surely follow? Behind my back tonight, I heard whispering and sneers about my daughter. Not only did you place your reputation in danger, but you embarrassed your father and me."

Julia crossed her arms over her chest while her fingernails dug into her skin. "I see how it is. It's not about me or my reputation. It's about yours. I'm a grown woman, and he's not just some waiter. His name is Phillip, and he teaches in the Science Department at BFU. Mom, I'm in love with him."

Bunny jumped from the rocking chair. She threw her hands in the air, and shouted, "You're in love. *You're in love.* You've ruined yourself over someone you don't even know, and you're in love. What if you're pregnant?"

"For your information, I'm still pure as the driven snow. Mother, I graduate next Saturday, and I plan to move to New York."

Bunny paced back and forth across the room, and yelled, "Who do you think pays for your bills, Missy? Do you believe we'll pay for New York too?"

Shaking her finger at Julia, Bunny said, "And you have responsibilities to this farm. The plantation needs you to marry a man who can assume the role of your father. He's getting older every day, and we must have somebody in the position willing to work with your dad to keep the farm intact. We can't take the chance that some money-grubbing young man is going to take advantage of you."

Julia walked over to face Bunny and placed her hands on her hips. "Mother, I love you, I truly do, but you're overreacting, and Phillip isn't a money-grubbing young man. Didn't you hear me? Phillip's a teacher at the school and completing his Ph.D. Have you always been so spiteful and petty? Did you ever love Daddy or did you just marry him for the money?"

Bunny smacked Julia hard across the face. "Don't you ever speak to me like that again, ever. Go to your room."

Julia rubbed the side of her jaw and glared at Bunny. "I'm not twelve. I'm twenty-one, and you treat me as if I'm still a child. I'm smart, and I'm a hard worker. Just ask Dad. I handle the books at Big Joe's and the farm. I overheard you talking on the phone with Dixie, and I know you want me to marry Brooks Davis. Did you know Brooks hit me when we were dating? He, he tried to..."

"Stop. I don't want to hear this." Bunny turned away.

Julia wiped the tears away with the back of her hand. She couldn't say out loud what Brooks did to her. "Did you know Brooks cheated on me with several of my sorority sisters? He's a drunk and a coward. But you don't care about those things. You only care that Brooks has the right pedigree, and believe me, he is a dog."

Shaking from head to toe with anger, Julia lifted her chin and walked out of the room. Then she ran upstairs to her bedroom and slammed the door.

Julia heard her mother shout up the stairs, "I can't believe you were eavesdropping."

Her mom was a piece of work.

A gentle knock on the door and Joe said, "May I come in?"

Julia opened the door and burst into tears when her father walked into the room. He placed his arms around her. "There, there, my buttercup. Please don't cry." He gently rubbed her back.

"Dad, I'm sorry if I embarrassed you and Mom tonight. I must tell you; there's something truly special about this man. I'm going to marry him someday."

She shrugged out of his arms and sat down on the edge of the bed, and he joined her. "It'll be okay in the morning, sweetheart. You know how your mother is, and I'm afraid she isn't going to change. Bunny loves you and Sloane. However, this is your life. I don't need you selling your soul for the farm, and Bunny exaggerates. Do you like Phillip? I play golf with his dad from time to time. He's a good man. It was a sad ordeal when he lost his wife and all. He never quite got over it. But for the times I've met Phillip, he seems to be a fine fellow."

Julia looked up at her dad. "Phillip is the best. I promise that nothing happened tonight. Mom always sees the worst in me. Nothing I ever do is good enough for her. I'm not sure why I keep trying to earn her approval. It's a waste of time. Mom's more afraid of what her friends think than what I feel. And why do you allow Bunny to walk all over you?"

Joe brushed a strand of hair behind her ear and said, "Your mother is the sweetest and kindest woman I've ever known. Growing up, Bunny had a rough time, and she just wants the best for you. That's what I see. Bunny is a little set in her ways. It all started when she wanted to join the club, and then she became involved in the Women's League."

Joe placed the palms of his hands on the bed. "Bunny puts on airs at times because she has deep-rooted insecurities, but at the core of her heart, she's still the same girl I married. She's trying to be the best mother she knows how to be even if she gets misguided sometimes. I'll take care of Bunny. You get some sleep. The sun will be up soon, and this old man needs his shut eye."

Julia hugged Joe and said, "I love you, Daddy. Thank you for always listening to me and respecting my decisions. Dad?"

"Yes?"

Julia straightened her spine. With a low-pitched voice, she said, "I want to be a writer. I want to go to New York after graduation and write for one of the new TV shows. Or maybe even for radio. What do you think?" She held her breath for his response.

Joe said, "It's a splendid idea, and I think you should follow your dreams because if you don't, no one else will."

Julia leaned in and kissed his cheek. "Do you think Bunny will get over tonight and give Phillip a chance?"

Joe squeezed Julia's hand. "She'll get over it. Bunny has visions of grandeur for your life. But as far as I can tell, Ivey Clayborn and his son are good people in my book. I wished you'd said something about Brooks. I believe he and I are going to have a coming to Jesus talk."

"Brooks will get what he deserves one way or the other."

"Yes, he surely will." Joe kissed Julia's forehead and walked out of her bedroom.

Stretching out across the canopy bed, Julia threw her hands behind her head.

Sloane stuck her head in and said, "Is the coast clear?" before walking into Julia's room and quietly closing the door.

With a faraway look, Julia said, "I want to drink martinis at midnight in the middle of Central Park, and dance naked under the full moon with Phillip. Then wake up at dawn in his strong arms in a cozy flat in Greenwich Village sipping on champagne until I'm silly as a goose."

Sloane giggled and plopped down on the bed. "Well, that won't take much."

Julia shoved Sloane off the bed with her foot. "That's what I want to do. But who am I kidding? Good girls don't act foolishly, and if I'm to have a prayer with Phillip, I'll have to follow Bunny's dating protocols."

Sloane shook her head in disbelief. "You're such a dope. If I had a man like Phillip, I'd elope. You give a man like him too much time to think about Bunny and dating protocols, and you'll be marching down the aisle with one of the county's bluebloods. And where's the fun in that?"

Julia rolled over on her side, propped on her elbow, and rested her cheek on the palm of her hand. "Tonight, was magical. Phillip and I lay on a quilt under the moonlight with the Falls in the background. His fingers brushed against mine, and then he kissed me." She covered her face with a pillow and screamed. "Oh, Sloane. I've never wanted to make whoopee so much in my life. His body was so close to mine."

Sloane's eyes grew wide. "Holy moly. Why can't I find someone like that? I'd do it in a heartbeat."

Julia sighed. "I wanted to. I want to make love to Phillip. I've been studying the temperature method since the war ended so I'm pretty in tuned with my cycles, and when the time is right, I'm going to give myself to Phillip."

Sloane rolled on her side to face Julia. "Are you scared? Have you ever seen a man's winny winny jimjam?"

Julia threw her head back and silently chuckled so she wouldn't wake the rest of the house. "Where in God's name did you come up with that? You're making my stomach hurt from laughing so much."

"Bobbie and I found a hole in the women's locker room back in high school." Sloane waggled her brows and said, "The hole worked both ways if you know what I mean. Bobbie gave the male member its name." Sloane and Julia laughed again. Using hand gestures to indicate sizes, Sloane said, "Some of the guys were gigantic, and some were nonexistent. Ugliest things."

Julia held onto her sides, wheezing from laughter. "Stop it, sis. You're killing me. I've only seen the male anatomy in science books. Besides, I'd rather be surprised with my first look instead of seeing it through a peephole which doesn't qualify as being romantic in the least. But I'm not too scared. When Phillip kissed me tonight, well, uh, I wanted him as bad as he wanted me." Julia blushed, and said, "I just have a gut feeling I'm going to marry Phillip someday. I just know it."

Sloane whispered, "I don't want to lose you, Julia."

Julia opened her arms to Sloane. "Aw, come here, tulip. I'm not going anywhere anytime soon. Wanna sleep in here like the old days?" She patted beside her and Sloane scooted under the covers. Yawning, the sisters wrapped their arms around each other, and Sloane hummed a tune they used to sing when they were small girls.

A lot happened to Julia on her twenty-first birthday. Before she drifted off to sleep, Julia had a moment of doubt, anxiety, and fear that maybe Phillip had used her. What if he didn't care for her as she did him? Everyone would assume the worst of her, and maybe they should.

CHAPTER 2

Phillip drove down the streets of Burkett Falls, passing the First Savings and Loan building where his father rented office space for Clayborn Insurance. Phillip had replayed last night a million times in his head. For years, he'd imagined different scenarios with Julia. But the real Julia far surpassed his imagination.

He'd been afraid she'd turn out to be a stuck-up rich bitch, but that was far from the truth. Julia was funny, honest and forthright, and so beautiful from the inside out.

Pulling into Big Joe's car lot, he felt apprehension. What if Julia changed her mind? What if her dad told him to get lost? He didn't know how well he'd take that sort of rejection.

Phillip nervously tugged at the full collar of the white short-sleeve shirt he'd bought with his last paycheck. He chose a pair of gray slacks and black loafers. He wanted to look his best without overdoing it.

Right before Phillip opened the door to Big Joe's, the man himself stepped out.

Joe reached out and shook Phillip's hand. "Hi, Phillip. I haven't seen you much since we played golf with your dad last year. Julia told me you were picking her up for dinner. You two have fun, but remember to get her home at a decent hour."

Phillip's cheeks reddened, and he replied, "Mr. Boatwright, about last night…"

Joe threw up his hand and chuckled. "No need for explanations. I was young once, but her mother was quite upset. If you want on the good side of Bunny, you better make it ten o'clock. Agreed?"

Phillip said, "Agreed."

"Good. Julia's waiting for you inside. Before I leave, I have to make sure all the cars are locked."

Before Joe could walk away, Phillip said, "I'll help you check the cars."

With a raised brow, Joe said, "Yeah, well, all right. You take the cars on the right of the lot, and I'll take the rows on the left. Just check for keys in the ignition before you lock the doors."

Phillip nodded and started at the end of the row and worked his way through each car. A few of the cars still had the keys tagged with the make and model. He kept them in his pant pocket until he finished. He stepped over to Joe and handed him the keys. "Only a few of the models had keys, but the doors are locked."

Joe smacked him on the back. "Well, done. Let's go see if your date is ready."

Phillip nodded and followed Big Joe through the door. A couple of newer vehicles were parked in the showroom. He spotted Julia behind a desk in the back.

Wowzer. *What a knockout.*

Her platinum hair was piled high on her head in a twist, and she wore ruby red lipstick that made knots twist in his stomach. Julia looked up at Phillip and waved.

"I'll leave you here. I have to wrap up a few things in my office." Joe smiled at Julia and winked.

Giving her dad a grin, Julia closed the ledger and placed it in the bottom drawer, then locked it with a key, and put the key inside a small black purse. "I like a man that's on time. Give me a quick minute to freshen up?"

With a sharp nod, Phillip said, "Sure thing. I'll just look at the new cars." He watched her walk through the double doors and leaned against one of the new Packards. He couldn't remember the last time he was nervous for a date. Maybe his first date back in high school. But his time with Julia was something different. Tonight, would tell the tale of whether last night was a fluke or something real. He prayed for the latter.

A few minutes later Julia walked out to meet him. "So, where are we going to dinner?"

"Whatcha in the mood for? Fancy or fun?"

Julia said, "Fun."

Philip held the front door, and before Julia walked through, she yelled back at her dad who was stepping out of his office, "Bye, Daddy. See you later." She blew her father a kiss. *What a sweetheart.*

"How about Burgers and Beevo's?" asked Phillip. Burgers and Beevo's was a diner at the end of town. They served burgers, sandwiches, malts, and beer. It wasn't a dive, but it wasn't the Ritz either.

"Sounds fantastic. I didn't eat much at lunch today, and I'm starving,"

"I love a woman with a healthy appetite." He chuckled and opened the passenger door to the Jeep, and she jumped inside. Several minutes later, he pulled into the gravel driveway of the packed diner.

The quaint restaurant, next to the Cane River, offered their patrons the option to sit inside at one of the red leather booths or outside at one of the wooden picnic tables. Phillip opted for the inside. "Looks like there's a table open in the back. Is that okay?"

Wrinkles creased in the corners of Julia's smiling eyes, and she said, "Perfect. I'll have you all to myself." She slid into the seat next to the back wall, and he slid into the seat across from her.

The waitress came over smacking bubblegum. "What'll you have to drink?" she asked, handing Phillip and Julia the menus.

"Two beers." Phillip answered for Julia and said, "Unless you'd rather have soda?"

"Phillip, you need to relax." She smiled at the waitress and said, "Two beers, Net."

"Sure thing, doll." Net left the table and came back with two beers in bottles.

Phillip took a long pull and sat the bottle on the table. "Hey, Net, bring two more."

Net laughed loudly. "Julia, you got this one sweating bullets." She went to the bar quickly, coming back and placing two more brews on the table. Net pulled a pencil from behind her ear and flipped the order pad to a clean sheet. "Burgers or the catfish special?"

Julia replied, "I want a cheeseburger with the works and French fries. Phillip?"

"The same for me."

Net jotted down their orders. "It'll be out in a jiffy. Just holler if you need me." She went back to the kitchen and pinned the order to the stainless-steel carousel.

Looking at Julia, he said, "I don't know why I'm so nervous. I guess it's because I'm crazy about you and last night was the best night of my life. I meant every word I said."

Julia reached over and placed her hand on the top of his. "I meant every word too. Something wonderful happened last night. I didn't dream it, and neither did you."

"Did you get in trouble?"

Julia released her hand and leaned back against the leather booth. "Bunny was in a tizzy, but she'll get over it. We might want to wait a few days before I invite you back to the house. I told my father how much I like you. Do you think I'm too forward?"

He grinned and immediately relaxed. "That's what I needed to hear from you. I thought maybe you drank too much and I took advantage. You're not forward. You're honest, and I like you too." Phillip more than liked her. "Oh, and your dad said I had to have you home by ten o'clock."

Julia laughed, and the couple in front of them turned around and stared. She waved at them, and they turned around. "Dad is the best. He's not conventional, and he trusts me. So, tell me, where were you stationed during the war?"

Phillip leaned in, placing his forearms on the table. "Several locations. Philadelphia, San Francisco, Hawaii, Guam, and the Philippines. Ugly business, war. A lot of my friends from New York died, and many were maimed for life. I still wonder why I was spared when so many weren't."

Phillip and Julia talked easily over dinner, like two best friends. Julia looked at the world with freshness, and everything to her seemed attainable. It seemed like the biggest difference between them. Julia lived a privileged life where everything was possible. He lived in a world where you had to work hard to achieve any dream.

The jukebox played swing music, and after paying the bill, Phillip and Julia walked outside. The people on the back patio danced under a string of bright lights. He placed his hand on the small of her back, then leaned down and said, "Do you swing, Julia?"

"Does a honeybee make honey?"

Spinning Julia onto the makeshift dance floor, Phillip placed his hands on the sides of her waist, and she put her hands on his shoulders. The two began a procession of fast paced moves between the twirls and lifts. At the end of the dance, Phillip and Julia were laughing and out of breath.

"It's still early. What do you want to do?" Phillip asked as he held Julia's hand strolling back to the Jeep.

"Sloane's best friend, Bobbie, is having a few friends over tonight. We could stop by for a few kicks."

Phillip didn't want to go to Bobbie's, Snookum's, or any of Julia's sorority sisters, but he plastered on a smile and said, "Sounds fun."

Julia gave Phillip the directions to Bobbie's house. She lived close to campus with two of Julia's sorority sisters, Alice and Miggy. Cars lined both sides of the streets and music filtered out into the front lawn. Classes for the graduating seniors were over, and the party overflowed with students.

Inside, Julia held Phillip's hand and introduced him to several of her friends. Amelia Grierson stepped over and kissed Phillip on the cheek. "Phillip, it's good to see you, but I didn't think you liked parties." Amelia looked at Julia and said, "Phillip and I dated for a while last year, and I couldn't get him to go anywhere near one of our parties. You are one lucky girl, Julia."

Dougy Hawthorne draped an arm around Amelia's shoulders and said, "Professor Clayborn, how the heck are ya?"

The noise inside was deafening, and Julia shouted, "Let's step outside. It's too loud in here. Amelia and Dougy, we'll talk to you later."

Phillip followed Julia outside where the noise level wasn't much better. She said, "You dated Amelia?" People were laughing, dancing and drinking on the backyard lawn.

"Briefly. Nothing serious. Amelia works part-time for my dad's insurance firm."

"Oh, yeah, I remember that now. You don't like it here, do you?"

Phillip frowned and said, "What gave it away?"

Julia looked down at the ground and then back up into his eyes. Shaking her head, she said, "Your body language. I caught you rolling your eyes at Dougy. You're clenching your jaw tight, and you're not smiling anymore. I'm sorry. I shouldn't have brought you here."

Sloane ran over and shoulder-bumped Julia. She looked up at Phillip and slurred her words. "Julia is in love with you." Julia elbowed Sloane in the ribs, and Sloane laughed and said, "She wants to run naked in Central Park with you under the light of the full moon."

Julia pressed her lips tight and shook her head. "Sister, I believe you've had too many cocktails, and I'd hate for you to regret your actions in the morning."

"I'm spending the night with Bobbie, so buzz off, big sis." Sloane turned to Phillip and smiled. "Guess, I better fly, beautiful."

Phillip chuckled and looked down at Julia. "So, you want to run naked in the moonlight. I kinda like that imagery." His body relaxed a bit.

Julia whispered into his ear, "Maybe one day. Hey, I'm going to the ladies' room. Then we'll leave." He nodded and watched her go back into the house. He waited for about fifteen minutes, and when Julia didn't return, Phillip went into the house to search for her.

Walking down the hallway, Phillip saw Julia pressed against the wall in the arms of Brooks Davis. His heart started pounding, and he took two long strides, grabbing Brooks by the collar. "Get your damn hands off her."

Julia had her eyes closed and seemed frozen in place. Brooks swung around, and Phillip ducked to miss the punch. Brooks was obviously drunk and yelled, "Julia is my girl, Hoss, not yours."

Phillip nailed Brooks to the wall and pressed his forearm against Brooks' chest. "If you lay another hand on Julia, I'll break your blasted neck." He released Brooks and watched him fall to the floor. Phillip grabbed Julia's hand and pulled her out of the party. He was breathing hard, and once they were inside the Jeep, he turned to Julia, and with a raised voice, he said, "Did you take me to this party to make Brooks jealous?"

Julia blinked several times before looking at him. She barely whispered, "It's not like that, Phillip. You don't understand."

He snapped, "Then by god, you better well explain it. I don't play games with little girls."

Tears rolled down her cheeks. "Please, let's leave, Phillip. I want to get out of here, please."

Phillip tried calming down, but he was too damn mad. He peeled out of the driveway and flew down the back streets of campus. His breathing became normal once they hit the Burkett Falls highway toward the Boatwright Plantation.

Fog shrouded the area, making it difficult to drive. Phillip pulled down a dirt road and stopped. Gripping the steering wheel, he looked at Julia. "I like you, Julia, but I won't allow you to make a fool out of me. You either tell me what happened back there or this thing between us will stop before it gets started."

Julia swallowed hard and turned in the seat to face him. Between intakes of breaths, she said, "I didn't do anything, Phillip. Brooks is like Dr. Jekyll and Mr. Hyde. When he's sober, he's a gentleman, but when he gets drunk, he gets mean. When Brooks and I first started dating, our relationship was picture perfect. But once he joined the fraternity he began drinking straight whiskey."

She turned away from Phillip and looked out the window. The dense fog made the Jeep feel like a tomb. Julia cried softly, and he went to reach for her but stopped. He waited for her to tell him what happened and he got a sickening feeling in the pit of his stomach.

"About a year ago, Brooks and I left a party like the one tonight. He told me his billfold was in his room at the frat house. I said I'd wait in the car, but Brooks convinced me to go with him to his room. Inside, he locked the door. I became terrified when he turned and looked at me. No, that's not the right word. Brooks leered at me."

Phillip held his breath. He had a feeling where this conversation was heading, and he didn't like it one dang bit.

Julia turned and faced Phillip, nervously biting her bottom lip. "I begged Brooks to unlock the door and take me home, but his switch flipped. He was a different person. He shouted at me, calling me vulgar names. Brooks pushed me onto his bed and ripped the buttons from my sweater. The harder I fought him, the more he liked it. He smacked me across the face and then ran his hand inside my shirt, pinching my breasts."

Julia stopped talking. Her downcast eyes broke Phillip's heart, and he vowed to himself to beat Brooks to a pulp the next time he saw him.

Tears filled Julia's eyes, and her voice quivered. "I gave up. Brooks overpowered me. So, I went limp on the bed and closed my eyes. I prayed whatever Brooks did to me would be over quick. When I quit fighting him, Brooks stopped. He looked at me and started crying like a baby. He begged me for forgiveness. I felt so cheap and dirty. When he pulled into my driveway, I told him I'd never go out with him again. I knew we'd still see each other because it's a small town so I said I wouldn't tell anyone."

Phillip wanted to embrace her. He wanted to tell Julia he'd make everything right, but a violation like that took time. So, he reached over and squeezed her hand. Julia sobbed and leaned her head on his shoulder. He let her cry until there were no more tears. He shook all over with emotion.

Julia moved slightly away from him and said, "Tonight, Brooks' switch flipped again. He saw me with you, and he was drunk. He grabbed me when I came out of the bathroom, and I froze. I froze,

Phillip. I was terrified of Brooks, all over again." She placed her hand over her mouth and sobbed.

"I've never told anyone, not even Sloane. Sloane likes him. What should I do? Should I tell her? I felt responsible. If only I had stayed in the car that night, things might have turned out different."

Phillip held her hands. "Julia, alcohol makes some people do insane things to those they love. Brooks is obviously an alcoholic. You're not responsible for his actions. Do you understand me? What happened in his room was not your fault. As for Sloane, if she were my sister, I would tell her. If he did that to you, I would bet he's taken advantage of others. I'm going to kill him."

Julia looked in his eyes with such tenderness, and he melted. "No, Phillip, I don't want you to get in trouble. Brooks isn't worth it. I'll tell Sloane, and I'll understand if you don't want to see me anymore. I'm sorry."

Phillip drew Julia into his arms and held her tight against his chest. Her face nestled in the crook of his neck. "It took me a long time to forgive my father. I resented him for years for not trying harder to keep me at home. He had to grieve my mom's death, and eventually, he quit drinking. That's when our relationship got better. I think someday you'll have to forgive Brooks to move on from the scars of that night. I'll be here for you anytime you need to talk about it. I will always be here for you, my darling, Julia."

Julia seemed so confident on the surface, but underneath the veil of strength, her vulnerability made Phillip want to protect her and make sure nothing bad would ever happen to her again.

In the stillness of the night, Phillip and Julia forged a bond, and their love began to bloom.

CHAPTER 3

After graduation, Julia continued to work at Big Joe's but mailed off her portfolio to every television and radio broadcast show in New York. She even sent a few of her scripts to Hollywood. She received several nice "thank you for your submission" letters, but most were rejections of her applications. In her cloud of disappointment, Phillip was the silver lining.

Over the next six weeks, Julia and Phillip were inseparable. After work, they went to dinner, to the movies, and on the weekends, she took him swimming at the Falls and horseback riding on the farm. Julia even caddied for Phillip when he played eighteen holes of golf with Sloane at the country club.

One evening, Julia returned from work and found Phillip, stripped to his jeans, helping Sam with the tractor. She slipped out of the car and stepped over to them, overhearing Sam giving Phillip step-by-step instructions. Julia placed her hands on her hips and said, "Well, what do we have here?"

Sam looked at her like he just got caught with his hand in the cookie jar. "Aw, Miss Julia, Phillip is just helping me. My back is down with the misery."

Phillip rolled from under the tractor. He stood up covered in black grease, and leaned in to hug her. She stepped back and threw up her hands. "Whoa, you're nasty."

Sam handed Phillip a red bandana to wipe his hands. Phillip grinned at Julia and said, "I'll go home and take a bath. Meet me in town?"

"Sure. What's cooking tonight?"

Phillip said, "I have a surprise for you. Oh, and I brought Bunny a bouquet of wildflowers I handpicked, and she turned her nose up. She's never going to like me, is she?"

Sam laughed. "Miss Bunny likes you all right. She just loves putting on a show."

Julia said, "What can I say? At least, you've captured the hearts of the rest of the family."

Sam nodded. "That's right. Ethel made Phillip a pan of her prize-winning banana pudding. It's only a matter of time before Miss Bunny caves in."

Phillip raised his hands in the air as he leaned over and kissed Julia's forehead. "I'll be ready in thirty minutes."

"I'll see you at the house. Is there a dress code for tonight?"

Grinning, Phillip said, "Comfortable clothes that you don't mind getting messed up."

* * *

JULIA WORE ANKLE-LENGTH jeans with a long sleeve pink shirt and sneakers. The last time Phillip suggested she wear something comfortable, they'd helped stock cans of food at the school's food bank for students on working scholarships. Phillip made Julia want to be a better person.

She pulled into Phillip's driveway where he lived in a two-bedroom brick house one street over from campus. Walking up the little sidewalk, Julia pictured herself married to Phillip. She envisioned flower beds and rose bushes in the landscaping with a little brown and white springer spaniel playing on the lawn.

Julia raised her hand to knock on the door, but Phillip opened it before she had a chance. He scooped her up into his arms and nuzzled his face into her neck. "I love you in jeans, and I promise I'm not putting you to work tonight." He placed her feet on the ground and reached for a telescope next to the front door and tucked it under his right arm. "I'm taking you out to the old Dyer farm to stargaze."

After placing the telescope in the back of the Jeep with the quilt, Phillip helped Julia into the passenger seat. Seconds later, he sat behind the wheel and cranked the engine to a roar. He waggled his brows and said, "I washed the quilt and aired it dry."

Julia threw her head back and laughed. "Uh-huh, looking to smooch under the stars tonight?"

"And then some, ah-ram-bom-bom."

Phillip drove out of town and made a right down a dirt road barely visible from the main highway. He pulled into an open field where he parked the Jeep and reached in the back seat for the quilt and the telescope.

He grinned and said, "I want to give you the stars and the moon, but there's a slight chance for thunderstorms close to midnight." Julia melted into a puddle of sappy happiness. The gods were smiling on her. She had a handsome beau that was sweet, kind, and full of compassion, and his romantic gestures were icing on the cake.

After exiting the Jeep, Julia spread the quilt on the ground as Phillip set up the telescope. Glancing over his shoulder, he said, "I became interested in the constellations during my time in the Air Force. You know, space is the final frontier. So, I bought this old telescope at a pawnshop after the war. It's not great, but if we're lucky we may catch a shooting star or two."

Julia sat down on the quilt and looked up at him. "I love looking at the stars. They're so beautiful and mysterious. You ever wonder if they're looking back?"

"Great question. I am a man of faith and science. If God created this world, why wouldn't he create another one? Come on over here. I want you to look at the stars because I can't be responsible for my actions if I join you on the quilt."

Julia dipped under his arms and placed her hands on the telescope, resting her right eye on the viewfinder. She bent over slightly, brushing her bottom against his belt.

Phillip took another deep breath as he placed his hand on her low back. "What do you see? Do I need to adjust the lens?"

"No, I can handle it. I see the moon. It's incredible." She raised her head and glanced over her left shoulder. "Want to see?"

"Julia?"

She said, "Yeah?"

"Did you read about an incident last year in Roswell, New Mexico?"

Julia turned and placed one hand on her hip. "Yep, the people from the area thought a weather balloon was a flying saucer."

Phillip rubbed his hands up and down her arms and took a deep breath. The look of intent in his eyes had the air backing up in Julia's lungs. He said, "A friend of mine from the Air Force worked the crash site. He overheard a man whispering to the local sheriff that he found a flying saucer. The man found materials made from chemical elements not found in our periodic table. He hid them on his farm. That was June 14, 1947, and on June 20, 1947, rocket program was initiated. Whether the two events are related is merely conjecture, but my friend contacted me yesterday and invited me to Cape Canaveral for a possible job." He paused and searched her eyes. "I want to take you with me."

Julia's eyes widened, and her mouth fell open. With a shaky voice, she replied, "You want to take me with you?"

Julia watched Phillip reach inside his pant pocket and take a ring out of a black box. His fingers trembled as he gazed into her eyes. With his other hand, Phillip caressed the curve of her cheek. "The touch of your lovely face, the flowery scent of your silky hair, and the promise of a kiss from your sweet, full lips makes my heart burn brighter than all of the stars shining above us. I want you in my arms every morning and every night." He leaned in and kissed her, then whispered against her lips, "I love you, Julia. Will you marry me?"

Julia's smile couldn't hide her jubilation. Her face beamed as she returned Phillip's kiss. She jumped up and wrapped her legs around his waist and her arms around his neck. "Yes, Phillip, yes, yes, and yes." Warmth radiated through her entire body.

Phillip twirled them in a circle again and again. "You've made me the happiest man on the planet. My heart is near bursting out of my chest."

He gently lowered Julia onto the quilt and reached over to brush the hair from her cheeks and slipped the ring on her finger. Leaning down, Phillip tilted his face to the right, then kissed her so slowly and sweetly that all of Julia's senses went into overdrive. Her breathing became deeper as billions of her nerve endings fired off rapidly. She craved Phillip's kiss under the stars and the moon.

Breathlessly, Julia swallowed the lump in her throat and squeezed Phillip's hand. "I love you, Phillip."

Phillip held her face in his hands, kissed her gently, and moved his mouth to her ear. "I love you too."

Julia's blood thundered through her veins as he gently traced his fingers along the outer part of her thighs. Breathing hard, she closed her eyes and enjoyed the incredible sensations of his touch.

"Oh, my angel. You're so sweet. So, soft and sweet." Phillip placed tender kisses down the column of her neck.

Julia's chest heaved up and down from breathing so hard. With hoarseness, she said, "Phillip?"

Phillip wrapped her in his arms and pulled her close. "Yes, my love."

"Make love to me, Phillip."

He chuckled. "I thought that's what I was doing."

She took another deep breath and said, "I'm serious. I want you to make love to me. You're mine, Phillip Clayborn, all mine."

* * *

THE NEXT DAY after church service, Julia ate lunch with her family in the dining room. The front doorbell chimed, and Ethel walked into the dining room seconds later. "Mr. Joseph, Phillip is at the front door and wants to speak to you."

Joe looked over his newspaper and said, "Tell him to come on in here."

Ethel nervously looked at Julia, and then back to Joe. "Well, Mr. Phillip says he needs to speak to you in private about Miss Julia."

Julia's eyes widened, and she straightened her back. Sloane spat out her coffee. Bunny stood and shouted at Julia, "Phillip Clayborn, over my dead body."

Julia smiled at her mom and looked at her father. "I love him, Daddy."

Bunny collapsed into the chair, and Miss Ethel ran to her. "Miss Bunny, Miss Bunny." Of course, Bunny was over exaggerating for the dramatic effect.

Joe folded his newspaper, placing it on the table, and smiled at Julia. "I guess I'll be in my study with Phillip."

As Joe strolled from the room, Bunny shouted, "She isn't marrying Phillip Clayborn, Daddy. You tell that young man I said, no siree."

After a half hour of hysterics, Bunny calmed down. She let out an exasperated breath and said, "Julia, I want you to be happy, I do. I just know how it is to live without, and I never wanted you to live that way, ever. I'm not sure Phillip will ever have the means you've become accustomed to."

Julia moved away from the table and went to her mom. She hugged Bunny tight, then released her and took a step back. "Mom, I love you with all my heart. But I won't marry a man I don't love, and I'm in love with Phillip. I appreciate everything you and Daddy have given me, but I don't need a fancy house, the country club or even a closet full of clothes. I need someone who'll love me, and Phillip loves me."

Bunny released a deep breath and placed her napkin on the table beside her plate. She pushed the chair away from the table, walked over to the buffet, and poured a small glass of sherry.

She took a sip and then took another one. "I fell in love with your father a long, long time ago, and he fell in love with me. Your Grandmother Boatwright, God rest her soul, hated me. She called me a whore and slut behind your dad's back on numerous occasions. I was adopted. Don't look so surprised, girls. I meant to tell you, but the time never seemed right."

Bunny sat back down at the table and sipped her sherry. "My birth mother, who I grew up thinking was my older sister, became pregnant out of wedlock, and the rich boy who got her pregnant refused to marry her. It broke her heart, but she refused to give me up. So, my natural grandmother adopted me as her daughter. Oh, they tried to be discreet and sent my mother away to relatives. But gossip thrives in a small town. So, we moved to Burkett Falls."

Bunny looked at Julia and Sloane. "I found a letter after we buried Mama, or well, my grandmother. My birth mother and I fought like two wild cats. I was embarrassed and afraid my friends would find out that I was a bastard. So, my birth mother left in the middle of the night. She left me alone with my grandfather. I haven't seen hide nor hair of her since the day she left. If I could go back and change that day I would because I missed the opportunity of knowing my real mother."

Bunny drained the rest of her sherry and said, "Granddaddy didn't know how to raise a teenage girl. But from the moment I danced in Joe's arms at the Harvest Festival, I was home. I told Joe everything, and he still loved me." She wiped the tears from her eyes with a napkin. Ethel left the room and quickly came back with a delicate handkerchief and handed it to Bunny.

Julia said, "Then why wouldn't you want the same for Sloane and me? Why did you put on airs? You judged me, you judged Sloane, and you judged Phillip. You're a hypocrite, Mother. I'm going to wait in the foyer for Phillip." Julia walked away without looking at Bunny.

But Bunny reached for Julia's forearm. "You're right. I am. I wanted better for you, and your sister. I never wanted the taint of my life to be yours."

"I can't, Bunny. I can't talk to you right now. I've lived my life trying to please you. Give me some time to process what you've told me." Julia left the room.

Sloane followed Julia out into the foyer. "You may have been a little hard on the old girl."

Julia shook her head and plopped down in the wingback chair next to the study where her dad talked with Phillip. "I know I was horrid, but how could Bunny put us through all of that superficial bull crap after what she went through with grandmother's mistreatment? It's crazy."

Sloane leaned against the wall and crossed her arms over her chest. "Julia, I know you're upset, but do you have any idea how hard it was for Bunny to tell us that? How hard it must've been to live a lie?"

The door to the study opened, and Phillip locked eyes with Julia and grinned. "Your daddy said yes."

Julia ran and jumped into Phillip's arms, kissing him all over his face. She tossed a glance over her shoulder. "Thank you, Daddy."

Sloane stepped over to hug Phillip and Julia. "Congratulations on this battle, but you still have to win the war." She pointed to Bunny in the dining room, and Phillip frowned.

Bunny walked into the foyer and looked at Phillip and Julia.

Phillip released Julia and went to Bunny, bowed and kissed her hand. "Mrs. Boatwright, I've asked your husband for Julia's hand in marriage, and he has agreed. Will you give us your blessing too?"

Bunny smiled at him with tears in her eyes and glanced at Julia. She placed her hand on Phillip's forearm and said, "I wish you both all of the happiness in the world."

Phillip picked up Bunny and twirled her around, and yelled, "Yahoo." Bunny giggled as he gently placed her feet back on the ground.

Julia ran over and hugged her mother. Holding Bunny's hands, Julia said, "I'm sorry, Mom, for being so ugly to you in the dining room. Please forgive me. Let's move forward and forget about the past."

Bunny nodded and reached up on tiptoe to kiss Julia's cheek, then went to Joe and circled her arm around his waist. With her hand over her heart, she said, "Why, there's nothing to forgive, my angel. Why don't y'all have some fun today? I'll help Ethel with the dishes." Joe smiled down at Bunny and kissed the top of her head.

Julia clapped her hands together. "Let's go swimming. Phillip, you left a pair of your swim trunks in the laundry room." She kissed Phillip lightly on the lips.

Draping an arm around Julia's shoulder, Phillip said, "I'd love to go swimming on a hot summer afternoon."

"Phillip, just so you know, Sloane is part of a package deal, okay?"

Phillip bowed before Sloane and kissed the back of her hand. "Then I'm doubly blessed." Sloane blushed and gave him a big grin.

* * *

STANDING with Phillip and Sloane on the sandy beach next to the blue pools of Burkett Falls, Julia said, "On the count of three, we'll jump in together."

Phillip yelled, "Three."

Phillip, Julia, and Sloane ran and jumped into the chilly water. Julia plunged head first, taking long breaststrokes toward the Falls while Phillip and Sloane swam behind her.

Once the trio made it to the cliffs, next to the Falls, Sloane pulled herself up on the flat rock and sat on the edge. She tilted her face to the sun. "I don't think you need to climb behind the Falls. The current is too fast from the storms last night."

"Aw, baby sis, let the good times roll. I want to stand under the Falls and wash my hair." Julia and Phillip climbed to the natural stone steps leading to the back of the waterfall. She turned and yelled, "Come on, Sloane. It'll be fun!"

Sloane shook her head no. Phillip held Julia's hand and said, "Maybe we should listen to your sister."

Julia shook her hand loose from Phillip and giggled. "You chicken?" Right before she stepped behind the Falls, Julia blew Phillip a kiss and said, "I love you." The water rushing over the cliffs felt harder and faster than she remembered. Standing directly under the Falls, Julia stretched her arms out and up toward the sky.

Then she slipped and fell onto the slimy moss-covered rocks.

Julia heard Phillip yell out, "Grab a rock, grab anything, I'm coming, Julia."

Julia couldn't hold on. The force of the rushing water cascading over the Falls made her plunge deeper and deeper into the blackness of the pool. She tried with all her might to swim to the surface, but it was no use, the Falls kept pushing her further down.

Nearing death, her lungs threatening to explode, Julia witnessed images from her past, present, and future seemingly paralyzed in what appeared to be a timeless state of mind. Julia didn't realize that time, or the essence of time manipulated around her. Julia fell forward into a prism of colored particles in reds, pinks, blues, and greens wrapping and bending in a spinning tunnel with no end.

Oddly, Julia could breathe again, which was strange in and of itself, as the brightly colored lights swirled around her. The vortex made her think of the tornado in *The Wizard of Oz*.

Then someone grabbed her hand, pulling her up—and out of the water.

CHAPTER 4

*P*resent Day, Burkett Falls

A man tucked Julia under his arm while swimming sidestrokes to the sandy rock beach. He placed her on a flat rock, and then pulled himself up beside her. Julia stared at him in disbelief totally shocked by her surroundings. She knew him, didn't she?

Julia openly stared at the man beside her. She couldn't believe her eyes. The man looked exactly like Phillip except with blond hair and blue eyes.

He gently touched her shoulder. "You're in shock. God knows how long you were underwater. Are you able to talk?"

In a split second, everything in Julia's life changed. The only thing familiar was the majestic Burkett Falls. Concrete picnic tables and wrought iron grills were located around their property and people were swimming in the water she didn't know. Phillip's look-a-like guided her to one of the maple trees and pointed to the patchwork quilt. Tears flowed from her eyes because the quilt belonged to Phillip. He said, "Please sit down. I have some bottled water."

Julia began to hyperventilate. *Bottled water?* Julia watched him rummage through what appeared to be a large purse or satchel but followed his request because her legs threatened to buckle any second. She trembled with fear and felt numb, completely numb, and at a loss for words. Her throat burned as he handed her the bottle of water. *Not glass, hmmm.* Her voice hoarse, she said, "Do you have a bottle opener?"

He reached over and twisted the top off with his hand and tilted his head. "What's your name? Are you here with someone?"

Julia turned the bottle up and greedily drank the water. The thumping of loud drum music made her glance over her left shoulder, and she saw a group of scantily clad teenagers. A young man loudly recited a poem of sorts to the beats and waved his hand up in the air. *Wizard of Oz....*

Maybe I'm dead, and this is hell.

Julia looked back at the man and said, "What's in the black box?" He held it in his right hand.

"It's a phone. You know, a mobile. Maybe, I should call an ambulance. You may have hit your head."

Julia shook her head no. *No, no, no. This isn't real. I'm dreaming. I'll wake up.* "That's a phone?" She closed her eyes and said, "Tell me, do the Boatwrights still live in the plantation house?"

"Boatwrights? Come on. You're kidding me. What's your name?" He took another bottle of water out of the bag and handed it to her. Julia twisted the top like he'd done. It worked, and the top screwed off. After finishing the bottle of water, she handed the empty bottle back to him.

Julia drew her knees to her chest and wrapped her arms around them. "I'm Julia Boatwright."

The man choked on the water he drank, spewing it out on the ground. He began to laugh. "Good one. Then you're a legend around these parts." Still chuckling, he shook his head in apparent disbelief.

With the tilt of her head, Julia said, "Do I look happy to you? Am I laughing? And why in the Sam Hill would I be a legend?" Julia watched his fingers rapidly tap on the bright light of the telephone. "What are you doing?"

"I'm googling you." He rubbed his eyes with his fingers. "It's really you! Fuuuck!"

What's googling?

Julia abruptly stood up and shouted, "Well, I've never in my whole life heard anyone use that kind of crude language. You, sir, have no manners."

He stood, panting, and suddenly became very pale. "Wait, I'm sorry. Look, and read this article. You'll know why you're a legend."

Julia frowned at him and grabbed the box out of his hand. There was a photo of her senior high school picture. The headline read, *Burkett Falls Annual Celebration of Julia Boatwright*. Under her photo, she read the date spanning her disappearance, 1948-2017.

Tears spilled as she read the rest of the article describing her disappearance into thin air.

Based on the article, her parents had passed away years ago.

The annual celebration brought folks in from everywhere. Psychics and séances tried annually to revive her spirit from the other side. "Are you saying that I've been missing for sixty-nine years?" Shaking her head in disbelief, she said, "What's your name?"

Julia had known before he answered, "You disappeared in the summer of 1948 and this is 2017. My name is Phillip Andrew Clayborn, the third, but my friends call me Andy."

Julia walked toward the cliffs with her arms wrapped around her waist. She couldn't believe it. Phillip must've married someone else and had a child. Andy walked up behind her and reached for her hand. She turned around and wiped the tears out of her eyes. "Sloane, is she still alive?"

"Yes. Sloane is still alive. She lives in Sunnyside Meadows, a place for the elderly. Please sit back down." Andy led her back to the quilt.

She ran her fingers through her hair in frustration. "Who did Phillip marry? Is he still alive?" Julia began to sob, and he rubbed her back.

"Phillip married Amelia Grierson, and sadly, both are no longer with us. Look, I'm freaking out so, I can only imagine how you must feel, but we'll figure something out. You got here. Surely there's a way to get back." Andy gently turned her shoulders around to face him, tracing the back of his fingers along her jawline. "I can't believe it's you. My grandfather loved you until the day he died."

Julia jerked away from Andy and interrupted with sarcasm, "I'm sure Amelia just loved that. What did he do, wait a month? A year? How long did he wait before he got married?" She became increasingly angry thinking about Phillip doing the same things to her sorority sister that he did to her last night.

It was last night, for crying out loud. She shouted, "Last night, Phillip asked me to marry him. Not more than an hour ago, he asked my father for my hand." She pointed to the pool of water. "We swam in there, minutes ago, and now, you're telling me that Phillip's dead. That he married one of my friends, and you're his grandson. My parents are dead, and—and my baby sister is an old woman." She pointed at the quilt. "That's Phillip's quilt. And you—you look just like him, by the way."

She shook her left fist to the sky. "Is this some cosmic joke? Life cheated me."

Andy picked her up in his arms and brought her to what she assumed was his car. "Get in. I'll be right back."

Julia got in and watched as he ran back to the tree, snatched up the quilt and his bag, and raced back to the car. He opened the driver side door and threw his stuff in the back seat before sliding behind the wheel.

Gripping the steering wheel, Andy turned toward her and said, "We can't tell a single soul who you are. Do you understand?" She shook her head no. "The discovery that you traveled through time would create a fuuu—well, a freaking media circus. Heck, the government would get involved. Mass hysteria and riots in the streets. You're living breathing proof of Einstein's Theory of Relativity. Sorry, I'm totally whacked out. I need a beer. Do you drink?"

With a slight upturn of her lips, Julia replied, "Yeah, I drink. But don't you think I need some clothes? Or do people today walk around half-naked like those people over there?"

Andy burst out laughing. "I'm sorry, it's not funny. But this is too crazy, and people today wear pretty much whatever they want. It's nothing like your day."

"My day? Oh, good lord."

Andy drove his spaceship-looking car through the farm, which looked the same as it did this morning.

Then Julia spotted her house, and she shouted, "Stop. Stop the car." The entrance sign read Boatwright Plantation House and Museum. "Pull into the driveway. I need inside the house."

Andy said, "It's closed. They only open the house on the weekends. It's Monday, so I'm pretty sure no one is up there."

Julia faced him with her chin quivering and begged, "Please pull up to the house. I know how to get in."

Andy parked his fancy spaceship car in the circular drive. Julia looked at the door for a second before pulling the lever. "You can sit here. I won't be long." She ran barefoot to the house trying her best to rein in her emotions. She needed inside the house and in her dad's study. *Think, Julia.*

Andy ran up behind her. "You're not going in there. It's called breaking and entering in today's world."

Julia looked at her home, but it wasn't hers anymore. The house seemed cold and empty. Her home had always been so warm and inviting. Julia stood at the bottom of the front porch steps she'd just walked down with Phillip and Sloane. She thought of her argument with Bunny, and how Bunny relented and accepted Phillip. All of it was gone.

Julia went to the side of the house, got down on one knee, and felt for the spare key under the first right pier. *Ha!* It was still there. She walked to the side door of the house near the kitchen, placed the key into the keyhole and turned the knob, then pushed the door open. "I told you I knew where they hid the key. Are you coming with me, or are you going to stand there with your mouth hanging open?"

He said unreservedly, "For a woman born in 1927, you're very outspoken. Let's pray the museum doesn't have security cameras or we'll both get arrested."

Julia turned swiftly and stared him straight in the eye. "I said I would go in alone. That's my house, regardless of what the sign reads at the entrance."

Julia's world turned upside down in a mere thirty minutes. Andy briefly explained that Burkett Falls was a public park, and her home had been placed on the National Historic Register. A museum for strangers and she was some mythical legend the town of Burkett Falls celebrated once a year.

Julia grappled with Phillip marrying her sorority sister, and they had a son. "What happened to your parents?"

"My dad took over Clayborn Insurance. He and my mother flew to the Caymans on a charter plane shortly after I was born. The small plane malfunctioned and went down in the ocean. We never found them."

"I'm sorry for your loss, Andy. Did Phillip and Amelia raise you?"

"Phillip raised me. Amelia was killed in a home invasion when my dad was an infant."

"Oh, my god. I can't believe this is happening."

Julia's mind reeled from one Shakespearian event to another. Too many people she knew and loved had died. It didn't seem possible she was walking into an empty house that only this morning had been filled with so much love and life, another tomb of devastation crashing down around her.

She glanced at Andy and closed her eyes for a second. The likeness to Phillip was striking. Opening her eyes, she noticed that Andy didn't look anything like Amelia.

Jilted by life, Julia walked inside the house, passing the living area, and stopped. A portrait of her family hung over the mantle, frozen forever in her mind, and she fought back the tears.

Shaking her head, Julia tried concentrating on more practical matters. She needed money. Julia prayed that her dad's secret safe still held his box of money. She strode into his study. It looked the same as it did this morning.

Stepping behind his desk to the bookshelves, Julia flipped the small lever under the lip of the bottom shelf. The false panel opened, and she held her breath as she reached inside, pulling out a black jewelry box with mother of pearl inlaid in the center in the shape of a diamond. She opened the box and exhaled.

Julia's mother's jewelry, gold coins, and a wad of cash were in the box. With an intake of breath, her hand flew to her mouth. There was a sealed letter with her name on it.

Stepping behind her, Andy said, "We have got to get out of here. This property belongs to the city, and if they find you with that loot, we're going to need real lawyers. Give me the box, and we'll go to my house. You can go through the jewelry box once we're safely inside."

Glancing up, she said, "I still need clothes."

Andy gently squeezed her hand. "First things first. We need time to think, or at least I do. We'll go to my house, and you can wear some of my clothes until I can go to Wally's World." He led Julia outside to the car. He started the engine, sped down the driveway and out onto the main road.

"What's Wally's World?"

Andy snorted with laughter. "It's a discount store that sells everything from underwear to sweet potatoes."

Julia wrinkled her nose and stared out the window. "This place has changed so much. Discount stores and half-naked people."

Andy said, "Hey, my grandfather kept a cedar chest full of journals about you, and time travel. I didn't believe him. I thought he had dementia or was delusional when he gave me the chest. He told me to read the journals and memorize the data. I humored him, but I never believed him. Boy, am I an idiot. I could've asked questions. Instead, I thought he was a dawdling old man."

"I can't think of Phillip as old, and it's extremely disconcerting looking at you. You look so much like him." Julia's hands began to tremble. "I want to read Phillip's journals. Maybe there's something in them to help me get home and make things right."

"Phillip was a theoretical physicist. He's the reason why I became one. I should've paid more attention. I let him down, but I promise I won't let you down."

Andy pulled into the driveway of a two-story colonial with an immaculate lawn and landscaping. "This house belonged to my grandfather. He left it to me." He turned off the ignition and faced Julia. "Let's go inside."

Before opening the passenger door, Julia placed her hand on Andy's forearm. "Okay, but I want to read the letter in my dad's box. I want a bath, and then I want to get smashed." She followed Andy inside the house through the foyer to the kitchen off to the right of the house.

In the kitchen, Andy motioned for her to take a chair. "Beer? Wine?"

Julia sat in the chair placing her elbows on the table. "After I bathe. Do you have sweet tea?"

Andy poured two glasses of tea and brought them to the table and joined Julia.

"Andy, tell me what happened to Amelia? How did she die?"

A large lump formed in her throat looking at the expression on Andy's face.

Andy clasped his hands, bowed his head for a second and then stared into Julia's eyes. "Granddaddy never spoke of Amelia or you very often, even when I asked him to. He blamed himself for your disappearance and Amelia's death, when neither of the events had been in his control."

Julia began to cry again. Andy pulled her into his arms, and she cried until there were no tears left. He brushed the hair away from her face and cupped her chin. "We'll figure out the mystery together. Why don't you take a hot shower? It'll make you feel better, and I'll pick up some take-out for dinner. Then we'll get smashed. Deal?"

She nodded, sniffled, and wiped the tears away with her fingers. "Deal. Do you think you could find me something else to wear?"

"Sure, come with me." Julia followed him down the hall to a huge bathroom. Andy said, "The towels and washcloths are in the linen cabinet. The soap, shampoo, and conditioner are in the shower, and the hair dryer is under the sink cabinet."

Julia shook her head. "Hair dryer? Like in a beauty salon?"

Andy opened the cabinet, plugged the hair dryer in the outlet, and demonstrated how it worked. "You'll find a couple of hairbrushes and combs in this drawer, and there's a new toothbrush in the cabinet. I'll leave you to your privacy."

Numb, dazed, and confused, Julia sat on the toilet seat for a good five minutes before making up her mind to go home. Bust, gut or die.

After showering, Julia quickly brushed through her hair and pushed the strands behind her ears. She brushed her teeth before proceeding to peek out the bathroom door. She found clothing folded on the floor with a note from Andy:

I've gone to the mall to buy you some clothes. I'll guess your sizes. I'm also picking up a pizza and something decent to drink. I'll be back soon. Sorry, but I have no undergarments for you to wear. The sweats may be too big, but it's all I have for the moment. Andy

Julia picked up the clothes and put on the pants first, then pulled the sweatshirt over her head and rolled up the sleeves. Andy's clothes were three sizes too big, but at least they were clean.

The hardwood floors in the hallway creaked under Julia's footsteps. She paused and looked at several old photos on the bookshelves. Phillip and his son fishing, and later Phillip with Andy at a baseball game.

How did I get here?

Her dad's jewelry box sat in the middle of the kitchen table. Julia pulled out a chair, sat down, and hugged the box close to her chest as if the box.

Closing her eyes, Julia said a prayer, "Please, God, help me find my way back home." Her fingers trembled as she opened the box. First, Julia pulled out her Grandmother Boatwright's pearls. She held them in her hand and wondered how in the world she ended up nearly seventy years into the future.

Next, Julia brought out Bunny's diamond pendant, bracelet, and teardrop earrings. She swallowed hard while holding her dad's gold initialed cufflinks. Julia left the wad of cash in the box. She'd count the money later.

Taking another deep breath, Julia opened the letter, and immediately recognized her dad's handwriting.

Dearest Julia,

I can't believe you've been gone for nearly thirty years. But then again, it feels like an eternity since I watched you leave with Phillip and Sloane to swim at the Falls. You, my sweet angel, left that morning so much in love with Phillip.

Poor Phillip, he's been ravaged by your disappearance and has searched tirelessly for the answers.

I'm writing to you in hopes that someday this letter will find itself in your hands.

Here's what I've learned as of this date, September 12, 1978.

After extensive study, Phillip discovered some secret agency handling inquiries of the unnatural and the unexplained. Alien Encounters and Time Travelers made the top of our list we know as, ATTRA, Alien Time Travel and Research Agency.

Phillip spoke with a couple of agents in 1950. If you're not with them, and by some miracle, you read my letter, be aware they have your disappearance in their records and often operate in secret ways.

Phillip's written many journals since your disappearance. He discovered there are time portals that open and close every day, and all over the world. We believe you were caught in a type of portal.

Phillip met with some of the top scientists in the country regarding Einstein's Theory of Relativity. He also did a study with a colleague of Tesla's. Phillip's journals may contain the information you need for your safe return to 1948, so you may live your life as God intended.

One last thing, Phillip's research revealed that time travel is possible into the future with little or no side effects, but time traveling into the past has complications and many risks. Paradoxes happen. Traveling to the past is dangerous, and an individual may die or may materialize not whole in body.

If you find my letter without Phillip's journals, search for physicists well studied in the Theory of Relativity. I pray God will lead, guide, and direct your path home.

With all my love,
Dad

Julia stared at the letter. "Oh, Daddy, I miss you."

The back door opened, and Andy came in toting an armful of shopping bags. "Hey, Julia. I bought you some clothes."

Julia pushed the jewelry box back to the center of the table. "Here, let me help you." She grabbed the shopping bags from Andy and sat them on the table.

"Thanks. I have more bags in the car." He turned and went out the door.

Julia stood on the back steps, and he threw up a hand. "Please stay inside. I have everything."

With a raised brow, Julia said, "Why?"

Andy held a pizza box with one hand and slipped another bag of groceries in the other hand. "I'll tell you inside."

He jogged up the steps and into the kitchen, placing the pizza on the table and the groceries on the counter next to the pantry. "I've been thinking. We need to change your appearance. The town celebrated your birthday and disappearance not long ago. You're a recognizable person, and it may attract unwanted attention. We need to make a plan of action before you go out in public."

Julia plopped down in the kitchen chair. "Huh? I don't understand." She was tired and upset as she placed her elbows back on the table.

A second later, Andy massaged Julia's shoulders. "I'm trying to create a mental checklist of things we need to do to protect you. Let me put up the groceries, and we'll eat pizza and drink a few beers. Relax a bit. It's not like we're going to figure it out in a night."

Julia nodded and replied, "I'll help you put up groceries."

Andy picked up one of the shopping bags. "Hey, why don't you try on your new clothes? The girl in the boutique helped me pick out a few items, a couple of pair of leggings, several tunics and two pairs of snazzy flip-flops. Just try them on and see if they fit. Once we transform your look, I'll take you shopping for clothes more to your liking."

Andy's kindness touched her heart. She wrapped her arms around his neck. "Thank you for helping me."

"I haven't done much yet. I've been turning the wheels over in my mind on the kind of propulsion it would take to send you home. We've made large strides in the space program, but only a handful of scientists are actively working on time travel, and they keep silent about their work. Tomorrow, I'll start researching Phillip's journals."

He motioned for her to move along. "Go and try on your clothes and then we'll eat and drink a couple of beers."

Julia made her way to the guest bedroom. She emptied the contents of the bag onto the bed. "Are you kidding me?" She picked up what looked like stockings with no feet. There was one pair in black and the other in white along with different pieces of lingerie.

The tunics looked more like oversized men's shirts. She slipped on the black leggings and opted for the multicolored tunic with a thin black belt attached. Bunny would've had a heart attack if she could see Julia now. Turning her back to the mirror, she glanced over her right shoulder. She liked the way the tunic fit, and the leggings flattered her long legs.

Julia looked at the sandals, or well, the flip-flops. She chose the black paisley pair. At least her toenails were painted. She leaned in toward the mirror and pushed her hair behind her ears. Andy wanted to change her appearance.

Julia noticed a smaller bag and opened it. "Bless his heart—makeup and lipstick." She opened the tubes of red and pink lipstick and sighed. Red was her signature color. She applied the ruby red lipstick, smacked her lips together, and checked her teeth.

Lifting her hair off her shoulders, Julia tried to picture herself with short red or brown hair or possibly black. "Yes. I'll do black." She'd get a hairdo like Elizabeth Taylor's. Surely that little telephone of Andy's could find a photo of Elizabeth Taylor. She'd get Andy to drive her to a beauty shop in Asheville. "Maybe no one will recognize me in another town." Julia felt a little better that she'd made at least one decision: short black hair.

Stepping out of the bedroom, Julia caught a whiff of pizza, which made her stomach growl.

Andy suddenly stood, knocking over the chair. "You're stunning. Do you like the clothes?"

Julia's cheeks heated in a blush, and she demurely lowered her lashes. "You're embarrassing me." Looking up with a grin, she said, "I love the clothes. They're very chic. Oh, I've decided to color and cut my hair like Elizabeth Taylor's. Or at least what she looked like before I traveled in time. The pizza smells heavenly."

Andy pulled out a chair for her to sit down. "Double meat lovers, thin crust with extra cheese."

Picking up a slice, Julia took a bite and moaned. She covered her mouth with her hand. "Oh, my goodness. It's excellent." She took several gulps of beer. "Now, that hits the spot."

Julia and Andy talked while they polished off an entire pizza along with several mugs of beer. He relayed some of the significant changes since 1948, like the end of the first Cold War, Neil Armstrong and Buzz Aldrin walking on the moon, and how the internet changed everything from commerce to social interaction.

Andy picked up the plates and raked off the leftovers into the sink, turned on the water, and flipped a switch that made a terrible grinding noise. She placed her hands over her ears. "What is that?"

"It's a garbage disposal. It gets rid of unwanted food instead of leaving it in the trash, which attracts critters, one of the many new inventions of the twentieth century. Hey, I'll look online later for hair stylists in Asheville. Maybe someone will work you in tomorrow. Oh, I'm not sure if contact lenses were available in 1948, but..." He grabbed a small box sitting on the kitchen counter and placed it in front of Julia.

"These are cosmetic contact lenses. You can change the color of your eyes. See the directions on the box: you position the contact on the tip of your index finger and hold your upper lid, then pull down the lower lid, look up to the ceiling and put the lens on the bottom part of your eye. I bought two colors, amber, and aquamarine. I could try and find violet like Liz's."

Julia's eyes widened, and she crinkled her nose. "Sounds painful. Should I change my eye color too? I'm not sure I have the guts to put that thing in my eyes. If I dye my hair, why do I have to change my eye color?"

Placing his hand on her shoulder, Andy said, "I promise it's not painful. I wore a pair once to a Halloween costume party. You don't have to do anything that makes you feel uncomfortable."

Julia reached over and opened her dad's jewelry box. "This letter is from my dad. Will you read it and let me know what you think?"

"Sure, but let's get a couple more brews and sit in the sunroom." Andy went to the icebox and pulled out two more beers.

Julia followed him down a different hallway through the double doors toward the back of the house.

Large palm plants, ferns, and peace lilies filled every crook and cranny of the huge sunroom. An L-shaped brown leather sofa backed against a wall of windows. Angled to the left of the couch sat an off-white chaise, and across the room in the corner was a shiny black baby grand piano with the top opened. "What a lovely and inviting place. Did you decorate it?"

Andy sat on the couch and pulled a lever on the side, which popped up a footrest. "My ex-fiancée decorated the room for entertaining before I caught her sleeping with a college student in my laundry room."

She gasped and said, "Are you serious? You caught them doing it in the laundry room?" Julia slipped off her flip-flops and sat cross-legged facing Andy.

He handed her another beer. "Sadly, it's true. I gave her the washer and dryer as a going away present. I completely renovated the laundry room. It's pretty sweet, and I don't want to talk about her."

Julia said, "Good. I'm glad you caught her if she's that kind of girl. But I would like to see how the washer and dryer work. General Electric had just come out with an automatic washing machine the year before I fell through time."

"I'll show you around the appliances tomorrow." Andy placed his beer on a wooden coaster on the end table.

He took the letter from Julia and began to read. After a few minutes, his brows creased. Looking up, he dragged his hand over his mouth and chin. "I've read about ATTRA in several of Phillip's journals. Of course, I thought Phillip was going nuts when I read it. But from what I remember, the agency is very mysterious, and to my knowledge, no single government in the world claims ownership or acknowledges its existence. Ah, I thought it would make you more comfortable for me to refer to my grandfather as Phillip."

Julia nodded and said, "Thanks. Yeah, it's a little more comfortable if there is such a thing in my situation. Do you think ATTRA would help me get back home?"

"From what I read in the journals, Phillip placed hope and trust in them in the beginning, but later several of his side notes mentioned a possible cover-up and stated some of them were dangerous."

"Do you think they're aliens, like in Orson Welles's rendition of the *War of the Worlds*?" Julia took another sip of beer.

Andy scratched his left eyebrow and then twisted it. "I have no idea. I've been thinking about the journals, though. We need to organize them by date and catalog the data. Before Phillip died, he told me to protect the journals with my life. At the time, I thought he was using a catch phrase, but after today, I believe he was serious. I'll start inputting the data into my laptop. Maybe from the information, we'll devise a plan to send you home."

He kicked the footrest down and swiveled around to face Julia. "I have a colleague and friend, Ruben Callaway, who works with me in the Science department. He teaches physics too, and I know he's been researching time travel. We'll pick his brain. I'll call him tomorrow and see if he can come over for dinner. We'll tell him you're an old family friend who's working on a time travel project for your thesis. I think he'll buy it."

"What's a laptop? You're going to have to train me on the new terms and inventions, at least a basic crash course. For instance, what's that big black frame over your mantle? It doesn't look like art." Julia drank the rest of her beer.

Andy laughed out loud, and said, "You got it. That's my baby, a sixty-five-inch flat screen TV with high definition." He picked up a small device, and the screen turned on.

Julia's mouth dropped open as she looked at the brilliant colors and clarity of the screen. It was better than watching a movie at The Bijou. "Wow. I knew I was onto something. After graduation, I wanted to move to New York to write scripts for television, and just look at that big beautiful screen."

"Oh, man, I have access to hundreds of TV shows, movies, music and the internet. Follow me. I want to show you my laptop in my office. With a few taps on my keyboard, I have access to billions of records, people, videos, social media, just about anything, I bet there's tons of information on time travel, but most of it's probably junk."

Julia followed Andy into a small office next to the sunroom. A black desk was pushed next to a large window with a view of the backyard.

Andy said, "Here, sit behind the desk, and I'll grab another chair."

Over the next couple of hours, Andy taught her how to operate his computer laptop. Thanks to many typing classes, she picked it up quickly. Today, people accessed so much information it was mind boggling.

Andy glanced at his watch and yawned. "It's past midnight. We'll pick up on your tutelage tomorrow when we get back from Asheville."

Julia said, "Would you mind giving me one of Phillip's journals to read in my room tonight?"

"Sure thing. Give me a couple of minutes. You can play on the computer a little while longer." He left the room.

Julia looked at the screen and typed in the search engine, Phillip Andrew Clayborn Sr. and several images popped up along with links to different articles. She clicked through several of the pictures. Placing her hand next to his face, she whispered, "Phillip, my darling, I'm going to find a way back, I promise."

Andy came back in the room with an old notebook in his hand. "I went through the journals until I found the first one. Phillip started this journal the night of your disappearance." He gave the journal to Julia, and she took it, hugging it to her chest.

Taking a deep breath, she said, "I think I'll retire to the guest bedroom to read if you don't mind."

"Look, this is your home for as long as you want to live here. You don't have to ask permission, and I'm going to call it a night too." Suddenly, he grabbed her into his arms, squeezing her tight. "Julia, my heart breaks for you. I want you to know that I'm here for you any time, day or night if you need to talk." He released her, and together they walked down the hall to the bedrooms in silence.

Julia stepped just inside her room, but before closing the door, she said, "Andy, I don't believe in coincidences. You were there today for a reason. Somehow, all of this connects. Thank you for making me feel welcomed in your home." Andy gave her a slight nod, then turned and stepped into the master bedroom.

Closing the door, Julia slipped off her flip-flops and removed her leggings and tunic. She decided to sleep in Andy's oversized sweatshirt. She turned on the lamp on the nightstand and then flipped off the main light switch. Pulling the covers back, she slid in between the crisp, clean sheets. Propping the pillows behind her back, she reached over for the journal and opened the book to the first page.

Julia, my love, I blame myself for climbing the cliffs to the Falls. Sloane was right. It was too dangerous, and I couldn't find you...

* * *

1948 BURKETT FALLS

Phillip climbed the cliffs behind Julia, leaving Sloane to sunbathe on the flat rock next to the beach.

Sloane yelled out, "I don't think y'all need to climb behind the Falls today. The current is too fast from the storms last night."

"Let the good times roll, baby sis. I want to stand under the Falls and wash my hair." Julia and Phillip climbed the natural stone steps leading to the back of the waterfall. She turned and said, "Come on, Sloane. It'll be fun!"

Sloane shook her head no. Phillip held Julia's hand and squeezed. "Maybe, we should listen to your sister."

Julia's hand fell away from his. With a smirk, she said, "You chicken?" Julia turned and blew a kiss to Phillip right before she stepped behind the Falls. "I love you." Julia walked into the rushing water and stretched her arms upward to the sky.

Then she slipped and fell.

Phillip shouted, "Grab something, grab anything, I'm coming, Julia." By the time, Phillip made it to the rushing waters, Julia had disappeared beneath the roiling pool of foamy water. He ran back to the edge of the cliffs, whistled loudly, and shouted, "Sloane, take my Jeep and get help. Quick, Sloane! She's caught in the undertow, and I can't see her." He turned and dove straight into the churning waters of the Falls. He swam down as far as he could, until his lungs nearly burst, searching for Julia, but she was gone.

Even with his eyes opened underwater, the water moved so rapidly it made it impossible to see his hands in front of his face. Phillip's lungs burned badly, threatening to burst from the lack of oxygen, so he swam to the surface for air. He frantically swam away from the Falls to get a better perspective of the landscape. He screamed, "Julia, where are you? Julia!"

Phillip swam back and forth across the width of the pools. He climbed the cliffs again and dove back into the Falls where he'd last seen Julia. He edged along the wall of the cliffs behind the raging Falls to see if Julia crashed into one of the jutting rocks or boulders, but she had vanished into thin air.

Breathing heavily, Phillip became dizzy, but he kept searching. He was hoarse from screaming Julia's name over and over. With barely a whisper, he cried, "Julia, oh God, Julia. Don't leave me."

Phillip's head lolled back, and he sank into the water. Seconds later, someone pulled him out. With blurred vision, Phillip looked up to see Joe. "Did you find her?"

Urgently, Joe said, "We can't find Julia. What happened to her, Phillip?"

Sloane held Phillip's head and said, "Daddy, he's in shock, and I told you what happened. Julia climbed the cliffs and stood under the Falls and slipped before Phillip could get to her. She fell. Julia never surfaced but disappeared."

Bunny released a loud outcry. "No one just disappears. He killed my baby. What did you do to her, you monster?"

Joe frowned and shook his head. "That's not helping, sugar." He turned to Sloane and asked, "Did Sam call the Sheriff's office?"

Bunny stood over Phillip glaring at him like he was the antichrist. "I called the sheriff, and that son of a biscuit eater is going to jail."

"Mother, stop it. I was here the whole time. Phillip didn't do anything to Julia except try and find her. Maybe she was swept into an undercurrent we can't see."

Bunny plopped on the ground next to Sloane. "Julia's not dead. I'm her mother. I would know if she were dead."

Phillip fought the tears, but the thought of never seeing Julia again hit him like a shot to the heart. He sat up and looked between Joe and Bunny. "I couldn't find her. I tried over and over. She's gone. She's not in the water. She's just…gone." He rubbed his hands over his face and then gripped his hair in despair wanting to pull it out by the roots.

Distant sirens grew louder and louder before stopping in the open field behind the beach. Within minutes, the perimeter of the pools and beach crawled with men from the Sheriff's office.

Sheriff Lamb stepped over to the family, took off his hat, and held it in his hands. "I'm sorry, but we couldn't find Julia. We've called in a diving team from Myrtle Beach."

Bunny cried out in grief, and Sloane hugged her.

Joe and Phillip stood with the sheriff. Joe asked, "You mean, as a recovery attempt and not as a rescue?"

"Yeah, Big Joe. We're sending the diving team in to search for Julia. I don't have anyone on my staff that dives. There are undercurrents, and to my recollection, a cave runs under the Falls. She may be where we can't see her."

Phillip paled, and his lip quivered. "You're saying she's dead. She's not. She just vanished. Don't you get it?"

Bunny sprang up from the ground and pointed to Phillip. "Arrest him, Tommy. He killed my daughter."

Sheriff Tom Lamb remained calm while placing his hand on Bunny's shoulder. "Bunny, now is not the time for finger-pointing. I'm not arresting Phillip. I'll have him and Sloane stop by the station tomorrow to make an official statement. Get yourself together and let Sloane take you back to the big house."

"My beautiful girl is gone. I can't believe it. My baby is gone." Bunny fell into Joe's arms, sobbing.

An hour later, only Phillip remained at the Falls, and he prayed, "Please watch over Julia. Keep her safe. If it's your will, Lord, send her back to me."

Phillip had tried to be brave all afternoon, but finally broke down and cried until dark, then drove home.

His father met him at the door. "Phillip, I'm sorry, son. Tommy called me."

"Please dad, not now. I need some time." Phillip went to his room and shut the door. Still suffering from shock, he grabbed an empty journal and began to write Julia a letter:

Julia, my love,

I blame myself for climbing the cliffs and walking behind the Falls. Sloane was right. It was too dangerous, and I couldn't find you. The Sheriff's office is bringing in divers tomorrow, but they won't find you either. I watched you disappear in the Falls. I don't know where you've gone, but I vow to find the answers for you, for your parents, Sloane, and for me.

Today started out fantastic, the best day of my life. Your father agreed to our marriage, and then everything went miserably wrong. I thought the world ended when I lost my mother. But nothing accurately describes the pain I feel from losing you. The world as I know it ended today. I will love you with every breath I take, every moment of every day, and somehow, I will find a way to you.

Until we meet again, I pray my words will reach you, and you'll know that you hold the strings to my heart.

I am forever yours,
Phillip

* * *

PRESENT DAY, *Burkett Falls*

Tears streamed down Julia's face. Phillip knew from the instant she fell into the pools of Burkett Falls that she'd disappeared. He'd loved her and searched for her for the remainder of his lifetime. She had no clue how she was going to get back to Phillip, but Julia intended to spend whatever time she had left on Earth trying. She thought of Andy in the next room. Where did Andy fit in this cosmic whirlwind? Why did this happen?

CHAPTER 5

The next day, Julia walked into Edie's upscale and very posh hair salon and two hours later emerged as Kaye Bailey. Her hair stylist, Joni had a warm and bubbly personality and set Julia at ease as she transformed her 1940s hair into a chic millennial look with a Liz Taylor flair.

Scanning the parking lot, Julia spotted Andy leaning against his Camaro with his arms crossed over his massive chest. She sucked in a breath when he spotted her. Andy looked so much like Phillip that her heart skipped a beat. Seeing Andy made Julia acutely aware of the pain of losing Phillip, and the growing knowledge that she may never see him again.

Andy moved toward Julia and spun her around. "I love the new you. Real frigging hot, and I can see why my grandfather fell in love with you."

Julia blinked away tears and said, "You really like it? Joni's an excellent stylist, but my hair is so short." She touched the back and side of the cropped hairstyle. "I cried when she cut my hair. I didn't mean to hurt Joni's feelings, but I've never worn my hair this short before."

Andy opened the passenger door. "You're movie star beautiful, my friend." He brushed his fingers along her jawline. "The contrast

She adjusted the thin belt around her waist. "Well, isn't that just the smartest little thing? Y'all have so many gadgets."

Julia thought back to the night of her birthday party and the conversation she and Sloane had about Brooks. "I knew Sloane felt an attraction to Brooks, but she also knew Brooks hit me on more than one occasion. God knows what he's done to Sloane over the years." Julia grimaced at the thought of Brooks hurting her baby sister.

Exiting the elevator, Andy held Julia's hand as they walked in silence down the luxurious corridor of Winthrop Hall. The wall coverings had bleached cotton fabric pastoral scenes with intricate designs. They stopped in front of Suite 250.

Julia looked nervously to Andy, and he squeezed her hand. He said, "It's going to be okay. She's your sister no matter how much time has passed."

Julia gingerly knocked on the door instead of ringing the bell. A young nurse with dark red hair and a smattering of freckles across her nose opened the door. With a smile, she said, "Welcome. Ms. Davis is looking forward to visitors. She's just through the door on the left in her private study." The lovely young nurse couldn't take her eyes off Andy.

Julia turned to Andy and placed her hand on his forearm. "May I speak to Sloane in private? Maybe you could stay and keep this lovely young woman company."

Andy already checking the redhead out, nodded and replied, "My pleasure, Kaye."

Sloane's suite was remarkable. Several valuable pieces of art hung on the walls. Julia recognized a Monet and a Renoir as she gently knocked on the door of the study and stepped inside.

Sloane sat in a tan leather recliner reading a book. She looked up and tilted her head and frowned. "Damn it, Jessie. I told you those sumbitches keep upping my meds. I'm hallucinating again. Jessie, oh Jessie."

Julia walked over and knelt before her sister. Placing her hand on Sloane's knee, she said, "Sloane, it's me. I'm not a hallucination."

Jessica ran into the room. "Ms. Davis, are you okay?"

Julia moved back as Sloane stood slowly with the help of a walking cane. Sloane turned to Jessica and said, "I'm sorry, darling. You startled me. I rarely see visitors anymore. I'm all right." Sloane turned back to Julia and said, "Would you like coffee or bourbon?"

Julia chuckled as she clasped her hands behind her back. "Both."

Sloane laughed loudly at Julia, then looked at Jessica and waved her left hand. "Go on, child. Bring us a cup of coffee, and I'll get my guest to pour the bourbon. And don't give me that look, Jessie. I haven't had a cocktail since last week. Please close the door behind you." Jessica left the room and quietly shut the door behind her.

Tears glistened in Sloane's eyes as she reached up with a trembling hand to touch Julia's face. She pushed a few stray black curls behind Julia's ear. "Is it really you? You haven't aged a day. Where have you been? Where did you go?"

Julia cupped Sloane's face and kissed her forehead. "It's really me, peanut. Yesterday it was 1948, and you were lying on the flat rock sunbathing when I slipped and fell. In an instant, I traveled in a time portal. Phillip's grandson, Andy, found me in the pools of Burkett Falls. You and Phillip were gone. Half-naked people danced on our beach listening to strange and deafening music. It's surreal, Sloane. Just yesterday, you were nineteen, and today you're eighty-seven. It's craziness, but I swear on Bunny's diamond pendant, it's true."

Sloane chuckled, shaking from head to toe with laughter. "The authorities report stated you were lost somewhere in the cavern under the Falls. But I knew you didn't drown. Phillip and I knew you disappeared from the face of the Earth. Nobody believed us. And don't rub the eighty-seven part in because I'm still your baby sister." She dropped the cane and reached for Julia.

Julia circled her arms around Sloane's shoulders. "I'm so glad to see you. I've been utterly terrified. This new world is too foreign and too fast for me. I can't believe Phillip married someone else, and that Mom and Dad are gone. I want to go home, Sloane." She laid her head on Sloane's shoulder and cried.

Sloane rubbed Julia's back and said, "There, there, tulip. We better sit on the couch. The old gray mare ain't what she used to be. Pour us a drink." Sloane pointed to a small cocktail table in the corner next to a tall window overlooking the golf course.

Julia opened the crystal liquor decanter and poured her and Sloane two rather large bourbons, neat. She walked over to the plush bright yellow sofa with patterns of pineapples and handed the cocktail to Sloane before she sat down.

Sloane laughed again and said, "By God, woman, I missed you. Now, that's a drink. Here's mud in your eye." Sloane knocked the glass back, drinking down the bourbon in three gulps.

"Geez, Sloane, should you drink so fast?"

"Honey, I could die any minute. Let the good times roll. Isn't that what you said to me before taking the plunge?" Sloane leaned back against the couch and closed her eyes.

"Are you mad at me? I need you, damn it. Open your eyes. And what were you thinking to marry Brooks? Did he hurt you?" Julia took a sip of her drink.

Sloane flashed her eyes open and narrowed them at Julia. "Don't you dare talk about Brooks. He was there for me when you disappeared. You just had to climb behind the Falls, didn't you? Phillip went off the deep end. Bunny had a nervous breakdown, and Dad drank himself silly during the first year of your disappearance."

Sloane paused a moment, taking deep breaths before she said, "Brooks was my friend, and then we became lovers. I didn't want to get married. I moved to New York to live your dream. It made me feel close to you, and Brooks followed me. And for your information, Brooks told me what he did to you in his fraternity room. He was eaten up with guilt after your disappearance. Get me another drink, and I swear I'll punch you if you mention my age again."

Julia went over to the liquor table and poured Sloane a smaller drink. "Here, drink it a little slower this time. I want to talk to you, and not have you pass out on me. So, Brooks never hit you?"

Sloane placed her drink on the French provincial side table. "No. Not once. We fought about you many times. I wanted to kill him for hurting you, and Brooks cried like a baby. He quit drinking liquor and rarely drank beer. We eloped to Niagara Falls and lived in New York for a year before moving back home. Brooks helped Dad manage the dealership, and I ran the farm. We moved into the mansion after Mom died. Dad and Phillip became very close. The two of them traveled the world looking for time portals."

Sloane sighed and said, "I sold the farm and house to the city when Brooks died. You live long enough, and everyone you ever cared about dies, Mom, Dad, Brooks, and then Phillip. I've been alone for years."

Julia reached over and squeezed Sloane's hand. "No children, Sloane? I'm sorry. I wished I could've been here for you. I didn't do this on purpose."

"I know you didn't. I couldn't have children. Brooks said we could adopt, but I think after you left I got afraid. What if a child got trapped in one of those time portals? I'm tired, and I'm old, and now I can die since I've seen you again. I think that's what I've been waiting on, for you to show up."

Julia slipped off her flip-flops and sat cross-legged facing Sloane. "Oh, honey. Please don't die on me. You've had years to deal with my disappearance. I'm only going on thirty-six hours. Sloane, how did Phillip and Amelia happen?"

Sloane took in a deep breath and exhaled. She looked at Julia and said, "Phillip was a ghost. He lived in a different world after you left. Many thought Phillip was crazy talking about time travel, but not me. He held to the belief, and now you've proven he was right. Amelia initially came around to comfort me, and then she started helping Phillip with research. I think it was a couple of years after your disappearance when I found out about Phillip and Amelia."

Sloane began to wring her hands nervously. "Amelia died. It was so sad. Phillip lost both of you. But he never stopped looking for you. So, his grandson found you? How odd is that?"

Julia uncrossed her legs and picked up the cocktail glass tracing her fingertip around the rim. "It's ironic. Andy has Phillip's journals. I'm reading them to find a way back home."

Sloane rubbed her eyes and said, "What difference does it make now?"

"It could make all the difference. If I find my way back, Phillip and I will get married. I will be there for you, Mom, and Dad."

Shaking her head, Sloane said, "But what if you go back and change my outcome? Brooks and I may never marry. He came to me because of your disappearance."

"What are you saying? That you don't want me to go home? You expect me to live here? I can't, Sloane. I belong to the period that I was born in, not this one." Julia stood and walked to the tall window, placing her hands on the frame. She heard Sloane rustling to get off the couch but didn't turn around. Julia stared out the window and, with tears in her eyes, she asked, "Is that what you want me to do?"

Sloane shuffled slowly across the room and grabbed one of Julia's hands. "No. That was selfish of me to say. If Brooks and I are meant to be together, we will be. I want you to find your way home, Julia. I want us to grow up together. I want us to grow old together. If it's God's will, then I'll marry Brooks. If not, then I'll accept the consequences. Come home to me. Ah, Julia, why did you color your hair black? And why are your eyes blue?"

Julia chuckled and turned around to face Sloane. "Did you know the town celebrates my disappearance every year?"

Laughter bubbled out of Sloane. "Yeah, I knew it. So, that's why you changed your looks? Is Phillip's grandson here?"

"Yes, he's outside talking with Jessica. He looks so much like Phillip. Do you want to meet him?"

Sloane went over to the recliner and slowly eased herself down. "Yes, I'd love to see him again. I met him years ago when he was a boy. Does he have any plans on how he intends to help you?"

"I hope so."

CHAPTER 6

The Far Side of the Moon

Ruben chuckled. It would be good to live on Earth again. Jeans-clad and shirtless, his russet brown hair hanging to his shoulders, Ruben held the flame from his lighter to the end of his cigarette, took a puff, and placed the lighter back into his pocket. He took a longer drag, then put the cigarette in the ashtray on his platinum steel desk. His trusted and loyal dog lay at his feet.

On a mission trip to Jarulean, an outpost in the galaxy, Ruben found the alien-bred dog that resembled a mix between an English Bulldog and a Jack Russell terrier. He had a solid white coat with a dark blue spot over his right eye and killer instincts. Klock had been easy to train, and Ruben considered him as a soldier. Ruben could also understand every word Klock said when he barked, thanks to the translation chip embedded in his wrist.

Reaching down, he scratched Klock's ear. "You ready to go on a trip, fella?"

Klock's ears perked up, he barked and jumped into Ruben's lap. "Yeah, Boss!"

Aliens existed in the Universe, and the different planets' speech patterns and languages were the only way to tell them apart from the human species. The Lord Supreme created an intergalactic translation system using a gold chip inserted into the Tracker's skin. Without the chip, Ruben would've lost his hearing long ago.

Rubbing Klock's back, Ruben searched the hologram screen for the morning readings and tallies from yesterday's Spinners from his personal unit on ATTRA's space station, located on the far side of the moon.

The Alien Time Travel and Research Agency (ATTRA) worked with an intergalactic council to monitor natural time portals on Earth and its neighboring planets. They also worked on research and development into time-space exploration.

The agency used Trackers, like Ruben, to locate individuals they referred to as Spinners, who fell through the natural portals of time. A Spinner had two possible outcomes. The Time Tracker got to the Spinner before the fall and redirected them on a different path, or the Spinner fell through the time portal and either died on reentry or was recruited by ATTRA. To go back in time, the Spinner had to complete ATTRA's rigorous Time Tracker training program, which of course meant Spinners could not go back to their old life but now belonged to ATTRA.

ATTRA only recruited and trained the strongest of the Spinners to be Trackers. The other Spinner refugees were assigned various jobs in space and on Earth. Ruben had been drafted shortly after WWI as a Time Tracker.

Ruben didn't mind joining the agency. It was an adventure in the beginning. His grandfather had died before WWI, and he had no other living relatives. So, Lunar City became Ruben's home. His ability to adapt physically, mentally, and emotionally during time travel secured and elevated his position in the hierarchy of the organization. ATTRA employees no longer aged due to the pioneering efforts of the Jupiteranians, but they were still mortal.

The human's destructive life patterns with the development of the A-Bomb during WWII revved up ATTRA's recruitment process to prevent Earth's annihilation. Earth's natural resources fueled

ATTRA's projects, and as the sun increased its energy, it looked as if time travel may be the only way to save the species on the planet.

But while ATTRA had the resources to send their Trackers around one hundred years into the past, time travel into the distant past had never been achieved.

Ruben's job took him to and from Earth during different time periods spanning one hundred-years. His newest assignment was a female Spinner named Julia Boatwright caught in a natural time portal in the town of Burkett Falls, North Carolina, USA.

The Lord Supreme had hand-picked Ruben for the mission. Ruben was honored, although he wasn't sure why he'd been chosen. All he needed to do was find her and evaluate her for the Time Tracker program, right?

The Lord Supreme had mentioned something about Julia's offspring being detrimental to future exploration in time travel, but he didn't elaborate. The Lord Supreme sometimes spoke in mysterious ways, so Ruben figured he'd just dig in and do his job. He scanned the data, memorizing the details regarding Ms. Julia Boatwright.

The unit's door hissed open, and Commander Monica Adams strolled into his room, wearing a white body-hugging suit with a pair of shiny black boots.

Klock jumped down from his lap and snarled and growled at Monica. "Hate the bitch, hate the bitch."

Ruben said, "Knock it off, Klock." Klock's ears pinned next to his head, his hair on his back rose. He could tear out Monica's throat with one word.

Monica paused at the door until Ruben secured Klock into his crate. She glared at the dog. "You better zip it, Skippy, or you'll end up in cook's soup."

Monica had screwed Ruben's brains out last night trying to extract information from his most recent meeting with the Lord Supreme. She was great in bed, but the damn woman had ice in her veins.

Ruben returned to his desk and swiveled the chair around to face Monica. "There's something about you that Klock just doesn't like.

The dog is trained to kill the enemy." With a raised brow, he said, "So, there's a rumor going around you sold some Spinners on the black market to General Agriaous."

Monica placed a hand on her hip and narrowed her eyes at Ruben. "Did Charlie tell you that?"

Pointing his finger, he said, "Ah, hah! I was right. I haven't seen Charlie in a good decade, and you fell right into that one, Monica. The Lord Supreme is going to give you the ax when he finds out."

She straightened her spine. "I didn't sell anyone, and if I were you, I'd be cautious. You're not expendable." Ignoring Klock's low rumbling growl, she asked, "Are you ready to travel?"

"You don't scare me, and I'm not afraid to die. So, stop with the threats, and you know I'm always ready to travel." Ruben stubbed out the smoldering cigarette in the ashtray.

"Why do you smoke? It's a filthy habit."

He stepped over, circled his arm around Monica's waist, and pulled her off the floor. He leaned in close, and Monica parted her lips, but he released her, setting her on her feet. Beauty, brains, but cold-blooded. He decided never to sleep with her again.

Taking a step back, he said, "And why shouldn't I smoke? It isn't like the agency is going to allow one of their best Trackers to get lung cancer. Yeah, I found out. You guys altered my genome and took out any mutated genes."

Ruben picked up the gel compact holding the information of his new life. "So, I'm heading to Burkett Falls."

Monica shrugged and trailed her fingers along his desk. "I read the brief this morning. Why is this assignment so hush-hush? I'm the Commander of this unit, and I only received a four-sentence paragraph on the details."

"That's interesting." He pushed her against the wall.

Monica wet her lips and said, "The Empyreal Palace made your arrangements, and I'm not privy to the information on your new assignment. That's bullshit. So, you tell me, what's up?"

With a raised brow and sly grin, he replied, "Interesting. Really. Interesting."

The Lord Supreme had issued Ruben's new assignment. Ms. Boatwright had entered an alternate reality in a parallel universe. It was Ruben's job to find her and make sure no major paradoxes took place. He had to access her physical, mental, and emotional state and report to The Lord Supreme. His instructions had been somewhat vague, but the Lord Supreme didn't want Ruben to impose any preconceived notions that would influence Julia Boatwright's actions.

Monica trailed her hands up his arms. "Hey, Ruben, you have some pretty incredible silver-gray eyes. We have time for a quickie before your transport leaves."

"Nah, last night will do me for a while." He moved away from Monica and crossed his arms over his bare chest.

"Whatever." Monica shrugged and said, "Look, if you know what's good for you, you'll keep me in the loop. I have a quick temper, as you may remember."

Ruben laughed. "Aw, Nicky, you know I love the rough stuff."

Monica looked at the red light on her name bracelet. "Don't call me Nicky. Be serious. It's time for you to go. Safe travels, Ruben." She left the unit.

ATTRA's Gateway had an intricate teleportation suite containing three walled panels with comprehensive project software that calibrated time travel specifically designed with the Tracker's DNA. That way the Tracker arrived at the destination point intact and not as a puddle of matter mess. Before Ruben entered the program, Time Tracker trailblazers had learned the hard way. One tracker to a craft; otherwise splat on reentry. Klock was too small to have his DNA added to the sequence to mess with the equation, and so far, he'd arrived in the different time periods unharmed.

Ruben punched in the code for his new mission and approached his time machine. The Needle-Horn was an anti-matter craft powered by a positron reactor. The nuclear propulsion system combined with radiant energy made time travel possible.

Ruben pressed his remote to open the Needle-Horn's door. He checked the date on his wrist monitor with the time travel craft. They were synchronized. He locked Klock's straps, then slipped inside the pilot cabin and backed into the chute standing up, and the automatic straps secured him into the harness. Ruben tapped the screen on his wristband to initiate the sequence. Three, two, one, the next stop, the Black Mountains, then onto Burkett Falls.

***

2017 BURKETT FALLS

Ruben spent the next year developing his identity at BFU, researching Phillip Clayborn and Julia Boatwright. He made an appearance in the past to guide Phillip without sabotaging his career with the agency. Klock stayed at his side getting clearance through the Dean with the explanation Ruben had multiple allergies that could kill him. Ruben stated Klock was a trained medical dog to warn him if he was in danger. *Eh, it worked.*

In fact, aliens walked among the humans, and they carried latent viruses and bacteria which could release airborne disease with the potential to wipe out the civilization. Most aliens went through a rigid screening before being allowed access to the planet. Klock was brilliant, far superior to any breed on Earth, and his nose was sensitive to alien scents. Klock was Ruben's very own alert system.

Ruben genuinely liked Phillip, and he became close friends with his grandson, Andy. Hanging out with Andy reminded him of the days before he went off to WWI before ATTRA recruited him. Ruben knew his days were numbered on the assignment, and the agency would send him on another case. But he intended to enjoy the time with his new friend, and the quaint town of Burkett Falls.

Ruben drove along the state highway before turning onto Country Park Lane. He glanced at Klock and grinned. Klock's head stuck out the window with his tongue dangling out of his mouth. He loved Earth's atmosphere.

Ruben had been expecting Andy's call to meet Julia, aka, Kaye Bailey, when he was invited to dinner on the patio. He'd learned during his research that Kaye was Julia's middle name, and Bailey was her mother's maiden name. His pulse began to race. He was minutes from meeting Julia in the flesh.

Ruben pulled his Hummer to a stop behind Andy's new Camaro SS. He reached over and grabbed his cooler filled with a variety of domestic and imported beers. Klock jumped out and ran to the bushes and peed.

Looking more like a student than a professor, Ruben wore a black Zeppelin T-shirt untucked over tight jeans rolled up at the hem, and black Crocs.

Walking around the back of the house, Ruben unlatched the gate, and Klock ran through the backyard and jumped into Julia's lap, licking her face. *Hmmm. Klock didn't like anyone, except Charlie.*

Julia sat in one of the teak Adirondack chairs. She threw her head back, laughing while she rubbed Klock's ears. "Where did you come from, boy?"

Julia's beauty made Ruben's heart skip a beat, and he quickened his steps over to meet her. "Uh, I'm sorry. Klock never takes to anyone so quickly. Heel, Klock." Klock peeked over his shoulder then placed his head in Julia's arms.

She laughed again, and said, "Oh, he's all right. I love his coloring. I don't think I've ever seen a dog quite like him."

Andy threw up one hand in greeting while flipping burgers with the other. "Hey, Ruben. Glad, you could make it." He covered the grill, turned down the thermostat, and placed the spatula on the grill's hook. "Hey, Kaye is the friend I was telling you about working on her thesis. I thought maybe you could give her a few suggestions and point her in the right direction on time travel. She's staying with me this summer."

Ruben dipped down and placed a kiss on the back of her hand. Klock growled at him, and barked, "Back off, big boy, she's mine."

Ruben narrowed his eyes and said, "Dog, don't bite the hand that feeds you." He looked at Julia and said, "It's a pleasure to meet you, Kaye."

"It's nice to meet you too. I've heard a great deal about you from Andy. His family and mine go way back."

Ruben raised a brow and said, "Well, then, Andy's a lucky man. I brought some beers. You want imported or domestic?"

She giggled and said, "I'm not picky. You choose for me."

Ruben forgot how ladies used to allow men to make decisions for them. He smiled and said, "I want you to try Blue Moon." He sat down the cooler, pulled out a beer and grabbed an orange slice, then squeezed the juice into the bottle.

Julia wrinkled her nose and said, "Orange juice in beer?"

Ruben sat down in the Adirondack chair beside Julia and handed her the beer. "Try it. If you don't like it, I'll drink it."

Andy, Julia, and Ruben were eating dinner on the patio table when Julia began to ask him questions while Klock lay at Julia's feet.

Julia pushed her plate aside and placed her forearms on the table. "I've studied Einstein's Theory of Relativity. The groundbreaking work he and Tesla did with the Philadelphia Experiment was quite remarkable even with the naysayers. My research uncovered interviews with some of the family members of the victims from the project. From the data that I gathered, Einstein used his unified field theory. He and Tesla merged electromagnetism and gravity by placing Tesla's coils around the ship."

The more excited Julia became while she talked, the more exaggerated were her hand gestures. "They were trying to make the ship disappear from enemy radar. It's rumored the entire ship vanished into thin air. Supposedly, eyewitnesses relayed part of the crew materialized into the steel of the ship on reentry. Do you think that time travel is possible?"

Ruben listened to Julia lay out her time travel synopsis. She was accurate on most accounts. He wasn't ready to reveal who he was or the fact that she was never going home again. "Yes, I've read the reports on that. And yes, I believe time travel exists. The problem is developing reliable and documented proof. I don't think the world super powers will ever admit time travel, and if it exists, they would never release the information. The thing is, you can't change the past. It's already happened. But hypothetically, a time traveler could influence the future if they went back in time."

SPINNING TIME

Ruben pushed his chair back and crossed his leg, so his left foot rested on his right knee. "Time warps or curves may allow portals to open coupled with high force-velocity which could propel a person or thing into the future. For the longest time, space was viewed as nothingness. But space is like a fluid piece of fabric, like spandex that stretches and bends. In the space-time continuum model, you can't have one without the other."

Julia cocked her head to the side and said, "What's spandex?"

Andy reached over, pulled on the fabric of her legging and let it go. Chuckling, he said, "Your leggings are made of spandex. It's a synthetic fiber that adds elasticity."

Looking at Andy, Julia nodded and said, "Oh, I see. That makes sense. I'm beginning to understand what happened." She turned to Ruben and asked, "Do you believe in portals? Do you think that a person can travel in a portal to another decade, hypothetically speaking of course?"

Ruben caught the look of surprise on Andy's face.

Andy frowned at Julia and shook his head, but Julia didn't flinch. She stared into Ruben's eyes, and he couldn't lie to her. Ruben replied, "Yes, I do."

Julia jumped away from the table and danced a jig. "Thank the Lord!" she repeated several times, and Ruben watched her with a grin on his face. The woman didn't seem to possess a pretentious bone in her body. Her honesty and levity were quite refreshing.

After dancing for a couple of minutes, she smiled at Ruben and Andy. "I'm glad you believe in portals. I do too. Now, I have to figure out how to find them."

Seeing the tension building in Andy, Ruben stood and said, "Please excuse me, I have to visit the loo." Inside the house, Ruben crept into the sunroom to peek at them. Andy was talking a mile a minute, shaking his fist in the air and Julia listened but seemed untroubled.

Ruben returned to the patio table and sat down. Julia and Andy exchanged glances, and Andy gave her a quick nod.

Julia straightened her spine and placed one hand over the other one. She cleared her throat. "Ahem. Ruben, I want to share something with you that needs to remain between us three. I need your help, but I also need you to keep what we discuss in strict confidence. Will you agree?"

Ruben's chest tightened, and it was hard to breathe. "I know you're Julia Boatwright."

Julia's hand flew to her mouth. Her eyes widened, and she looked at Andy.

Throwing his hands up in the air, Andy said, "Don't look at me. I didn't tell him."

Julia said, "How did you know?"

Ruben placed his hand over hers. "I would've known who you were if your hair was colored purple. I've studied your disappearance." Ruben's chest relaxed just a little. He didn't rat out ATTRA. For some unfathomable reason, he couldn't lie to Julia, but he couldn't tell her the whole truth either.

Tears glazed over her eyes, and she looked away. Wiping her eyes with the heels of her hands, she turned back to Ruben. "Will you help me? I don't belong here. I want to go home."

Ruben dragged his fingers over his mouth. He wasn't sure why, but he knew this woman was unlike any he'd ever met. Her very presence pulled at something so deep inside him that he found himself wanting to help her, no matter what the rules were. "I'll do what I can to help you. But you must understand, time travel poses significant risks. Individuals can die during travel, or they may lose limbs. It could scramble your brain. One more thing, there's no theory on how time portals work but I'm pretty sure navigation is your biggest hurdle."

Julia placed her hand on her forehead. "I agree. The portal I was in felt like a tunnel spinning around me so fast while I stayed suspended in air, and then the next thing I knew Andy was dragging me out of the water of the Falls. I had no control."

Ruben said, "You need to think about your next step. You are alive, and you seem healthy. Take some time to consider the risks. If you still want my help, Andy has my contact information. Come, Klock." Klock looked at Julia and Ruben then went to his master. Ruben grabbed his cooler. "I have a meeting in the morning. Andy, thanks for dinner, and, Julia, it's been an honor to meet you tonight." Turning, he and Klock left through the backyard gate.

Inside the Hummer, Ruben's hands trembled. He narrowed his eyes at Klock. "So, you think she's pretty too?"

Klock barked, "Hot as hell, brother."

Ruben hadn't compromised the agency, but he had offered his help, and it could get him killed. Was it loss of control over a gorgeous woman? Or was he standing up for what was right despite his orders? He had to be very careful how he handled ATTRA and Julia.

Ruben liked Julia, and it wasn't her fault she fell into a naturally-occurring time portal. The Needle-Horn was designed for only one traveler. Truth be told, there was no way to take her home. To his knowledge, all the natural time portals went forward in time, not backward. "What am I supposed to do?"

"One day at a time. We'll figure it out," Klock said.

"How do you know that?"

Klock turned in a circle twice before lying in the seat. "We always do."

Ruben cranked the ignition, backed out of the driveway, and pulled onto the street. He had an idea. Phillip was an incredible physicist. Ruben would hack into ATTRA's system for the Needle-Horn's design and deliver it to Phillip. Maybe he could find a way to alter the craft for more than one person. "Do you think I'd travel down this slippery slope if Julia wasn't so damn good-looking, and a damsel in distress to boot?"

Klock barked again and rested his chin on Ruben's forearm. He shook his head and said, "Probably not."

CHAPTER 7

1950 Burkett Falls University

Phillip wrote frantically to capture every word Dr. Ruben Callaway spoke regarding the possibility of time travel. He signed up three weeks ago, after spotting a poster for The Time Travel Symposium in Madison Hall in the main wing of the science department. Dr. Callaway had worked beside the greats like Einstein and Tesla.

The tiered arc seating filled McPherson Lecture Hall to capacity with a mixture of cologne, coffee, and body odor. The wooden chairs and desks butted up against each other giving very little room to write. Phillip, being left-handed, used every inch of space with his journal and kept several sharpened pencils in his shirt pocket.

Julia had disappeared nearly two years ago, and listening to Dr. Callaway confirmed some of Phillip's suspicions about time travel. Just maybe, Julia was still alive somewhere in time.

Dr. Callaway wrote several formulas on the massive chalkboard and turned to the crowd. "I worked on an experiment in the Philadelphia Naval Yard during World War II. We used Tesla's coils to create large quantities of plasma, then placed them around the hull of the ship. Our primary objective was to design a weapon that would make ships undetectable by radar, but instead, the ship disappeared entirely." Gasps went throughout the lecture hall. He paused for effect and emphasis, Phillip guessed.

Dr. Callaway said, "Of course, you won't read about what actually happened that day. When the ship reappeared, several of the sailors working in the hull were melted to the steel." Another wave of gasps and muttered whispering filtered among the crowd.

One of the students raised his hand, and with a nod, Dr. Callaway gave him permission to address the room. "Scientists around the globe debunked the Philadelphia Experiment. Tesla believes in aliens, for god's sake." A few chuckles spread throughout the crowd.

Dr. Callaway narrowed his eyes at the student and calmly said, "They would, wouldn't they? Some scientists will negate theories which are unexplainable. However, many things on the planet and the universe are unexplainable. Einstein's Theory of Relativity gave credence to the space-time continuum. And do you honestly think that Albert Einstein would work alongside Nikola Tesla if he thought him delusional? Time Travel into the future is plausible. We prove it every day as time continues to march on. Are there any more questions?"

Another forty-five minutes of questions and answers took place before Phillip put his journal in his satchel and made for the podium to catch Dr. Callaway before he left the room. Phillip waited patiently in line for his turn.

Phillip went up to Dr. Callaway and said, "I believe time travel exists. Would you have lunch with me to discuss it further, if it's convenient of course?" Dr. Callaway's dog stood at his feet while a local newspaper photographer snapped several photos of Ruben with Phillip.

The dog growled and snapped at the photographer. Dr. Callaway said, "Do you think you have enough pictures or do you want Klock to eat the film?"

"Thanks, Dr. Callaway." The photographer turned and fled the hall.

Ruben looked back at Phillip and reached out to shake his hand. "Please call me Ruben, and your name is?"

"I'm Phillip Clayborn. It's an honor to meet you. I thought we'd go to Sissy's Café. She has the best meat and three in the county. Although, I'm not sure they'll allow your dog in the restaurant."

Ruben chuckled and muttered, "Klock goes where I go." He turned to Phillip and said, "And I hope you feel that way about me after lunch."

Phillip had a million and one questions to ask Ruben regarding time travel as they walked across BFU's campus which burst with spring. The tulip gardens were in full bloom with a variety of vibrant colors near the Washington Memorial Chapel. Birds sang happily in the towering evergreens.

Phillip and Ruben passed by elegant buildings that offered both charm and beauty, while students and professors chattered and walked to and from classes along the sidewalks.

Ruben glanced at Phillip and said, "So, Dr. Clayborn, you believe in time travel? Why?"

"My fiancée disappeared two years ago; she slipped and fell from Burkett Falls into the churning water. She just vanished." Phillip explained the events before the disappearance and after. "Her remains were never found. There's no other explanation I can fathom."

Phillip continued talking about Julia's disappearance as they approached Sissy's Café which was adjacent to the campus right off Burkett Falls Boulevard. Phillip and Ruben ran across the street and went inside. The restaurant offered its patrons a buffet and a soda fountain shop. The service was quick, and the establishment prided itself on its great food.

The café had black-and-white checkered flooring with smooth high-back black vinyl upholstered booths and stainless-steel tables. The soda fountain shop held forty or so revolving stools with black vinyl seats. A Wurlitzer Jukebox kept spinning the pop hits of the day. Cigarette smoke mingled with hamburger grease permeated the air. After going through the buffet line, Phillip noticed an empty booth and slipped into the seat. Ruben sat down in seat opposite of him.

Sissy stepped over and took one look at Klock and said, "If I get one complaint, you and the dog are out. *Capiche?*"

Ruben gave a sharp nod, and the dog ran under the table and lay next to the wall.

Phillip could barely contain himself, much less eat. Pushing his food around with his fork, he looked at Ruben. "Is it true? Does time travel really exist?"

Ruben ate heartily and gulped down his soda pop. In between bites, he said, "Yeah, time travel exists. I set up the symposium today to meet you."

Phillip's brows rose, and his eyes widened. "Me?"

Ruben wiped his mouth with a napkin and laid it on his plate. "I work for a secret organization tracking individuals who travel through natural time portals." Phillip tried to interrupt, but Ruben raised his hand. "Please, give me a minute to finish. Natural time portals open and close every day all over the world. It's my job to search out travelers to make sure the person doesn't upset the apple cart so to speak."

Phillip ran his hand through his hair and exhaled deeply. "Are you telling me that Julia traveled in one of those portals?"

Ruben extended his right arm on the back of the booth. "Yes, that's exactly what I'm telling you. Julia traveled nearly seventy years into the future Burkett Falls. She arrived intact, which is rare. The agency assigned me to her case, and I met her last night."

Phillip placed his hands on the table and leaned in. "You what? You spoke with Julia last night? Holy mackerel." He rubbed his face with his hands.

Ruben leaned toward him and whispered, "Phillip, control yourself. We don't want to attract attention. I'm here to help you. Is there somewhere we can talk in private? Perhaps an office?"

Phillip slid out of the seat and said, "She's alive. I knew she was alive. Come on, man. My house is just down the block." He practically ran out the door, and Ruben and Klock followed behind him. He whipped around and asked, "Is Julia okay? Who found her? Did she mention me?"

Ruben placed his hand on Phillip's shoulder. "It's okay, friend. She's fine physically. Phillip, there are some things I can't disclose."

Without warning, Ruben suddenly threw Phillip to the ground before sprinting into Knox Gymnasium behind Klock. It looked like he was chasing someone. Phillip raced after him to catch up. Ruben knocked what looked like a gun out of a tall redhead's hand before placing his fingers around her throat and slamming her against the lockers. "Why are you here, Charlie?" Breathing hard, Ruben glared at the woman.

Klock pawed at the woman's leg and whined.

Charlie glared back at Ruben. "I'm trying to save your ass, you moron. Stop choking me so I can talk."

Charlie struggled to get out of Ruben's grasp, but he pressed his thigh against her, holding her firmly against the lockers. She turned to Phillip and said, "I'm sorry for your loss. But Julia's never coming home again. Is she, Ruben?"

Ruben squeezed harder and said, "Phillip, pick up the gun and shoot her right between the eyes."

Phillip bent over and reached for the weapon. His hand began to shake as he pointed it at Charlie. "I can't do it. I can't shoot her."

Ruben shouted, "If you ever want to see Julia again, shoot her, now."

Everything seemed to go in slow motion right as Phillip pulled the trigger which released a black round bullet. Charlie kicked Ruben in the balls as the bullet hit her between the eyes. Instead of splattering brains across the lockers, the black bullet spread ooze across Charlie's face. She stood immobile and unblinking.

Ruben released Charlie and shouted, "Damn, woman," and took a step back holding his nuts. "Let's get her into the janitor's closet; then we'll go to your house. I don't have much time."

"What was that? Why is she frozen?"

"There are different varieties of Black Beauties. The weapon she had is designed to paralyze the victim for a short time. It scatters memories and thought patterns for about twenty-four hours, and Charlie will wake up pissed with one hell of a migraine."

Luckily, classes hadn't let out, and no one was in the hall. Phillip and Ruben picked up the beautiful redhead with steel blue eyes and propped her in the back corner of the janitor's supply room. Ruben locked the door from the inside before they left the gym.

After a short walk from campus, Phillip opened the door to his pad. A simple two-bedroom brick house with one bathroom and a small backyard. Inside, he locked the door and strode into the kitchen.

Phillip opened the cabinet over the stove and pulled out a bottle of Tennessee whiskey. Grabbing a jelly glass, Phillip poured two fingers worth and killed it. Breathing hard, he turned to Ruben. "Do you want one?"

"No. I don't drink when I time travel."

With a raised voice, Phillip shouted, "When you time travel? It's like a damn Buck Rogers movie. You need to start talking before I lose my temper but good."

Ruben didn't seem overly concerned about his threat. He leaned against the kitchen counter, gripping the lip with Klock standing against Ruben's leg. "Get your journal and sit down at the table. I have information to give you before I leave. You may ask questions that I can't answer. All I can tell you is I'm trying to save Julia's life." Ruben crossed his arms over his chest.

Phillip went into the den and grabbed his satchel before stepping back into the kitchen. He pulled out his journal, pencils, and pen. "Please tell me what's going on. I need to know. I love Julia, and the pain of missing her grows daily. If you can time travel, why can't you bring her home to me?"

"Ding, ding, ding, Klock, we have a winner." Ruben sat down in one of the kitchen chairs. He reached over for his briefcase and popped it open and pulled out a file.

He explained about ATTRA, and how the agency recruited him. "I'm giving you the plans for my craft, the Needle-Horn. No way could you even begin to build one from scratch. But I think it could be refitted to accommodate more than one person. I don't have time to get into the specifics. You'll have time later to study and work on formulas. Time travel is a dangerous business. It's a miracle Julia arrived through the portal intact. There's no way for her to go back in time without a craft. Natural time portals only propel one into the future, not into the past."

"That's bullshit."

Ruben handed him the folder and said, "The information in these classified documents places you at risk. ATTRA, with the help of some advanced technologies not of this planet, created human-made portals for Trackers to travel back and forth in time machines. My craft is designed with my DNA only. One person, get it? The Needle-Horn has the capacity of traveling within a hundred-year window. The only way for Julia to go home is a spacecraft built by ATTRA. My time machine is her only chance. If you can figure out how to alter it."

Phillip perused the first page and looked up at Ruben in dismay.

Ruben frowned and breathed in deeply and exhaled. "The human body isn't designed for time travel. Our molecular structure changes during the process and most people arrive with limbs missing or worse. My craft, the Needle-Horn, is calibrated with my DNA. You need to figure out a way to transport more than one person in my ship. It's impossible to bring Julia home otherwise. Look, I only play a physicist, I'm not one. I have learned a great deal since 1918 but not enough to refit the machine and make it safe."

Pulling out a chair, Ruben sat down. "A select group of people moves through time and space without consequences. It makes Julia a commodity. She arrived whole in body and mind, and she's on the list for ATTRA recruitment as a Tracker. The only way for her to time travel is to become a Tracker, but once you're with the agency, you never leave unless it's in a box."

Phillip flipped through a few pages of the documents until he came across what he assumed was a time machine. "Is this the craft?"

"Yes, that's my baby, the Needle-Horn. I'm not sure if you'll be able to develop the technology, but it's Julia's only chance. I come from the year 2017. You have a grandson named Andy who has followed in your footsteps. You're going to leave him dozens of journals regarding time travel. Just maybe between your work and Andy's research, we have a chance. But we're running out of time."

Phillip shook from head to toe with emotion. "I have a grandson?

How is that possible?" With downcast eyes, Phillip shook his head and took several intakes of breaths. "If Julia is in 2017 with my grandson, then she doesn't come home." He looked up at Ruben. "I will never see her again, just like Charlie said, right?"

With a sigh, Ruben said, "Time is elusive, Phillip. Never say never. We have a chance, so don't give up, man. What happens to her now depends on you."

With a look of determination, Phillip straightened his back and replied, "I'm ready to take any risks to bring Julia back to me."

Ruben pushed away from the table. "Awesome. Take comfort that Julia has Andy, Sloane, and me in the future trying to help her home. Keep the journals secret and locked someplace safe. I'm going outside for a smoke while you work."

Phillip opened his journal and began to transcribe and sketch the contents from Ruben's folder. So many questions swirled in his mind about Julia and his grandson. He didn't know if he could trust Ruben, but he was the only chance Phillip had to get Julia back.

* * *

NURSING A MAJOR HANGOVER, Phillip sat behind the desk in his school office. Meeting Ruben and finding out Julia survived the time travel portal unraveled him. Julia lived in another time and place. She might as well live on a different planet. Ruben promised to keep Julia safe and help her to find a way home.

The door opened, and a young woman in her twenties walked into his office. He threw up his hand and said, "I'm not meeting with students today. You'll need to book an appointment with the department secretary."

The attractive redhead wore her hair pulled back in a ponytail which set off her deep blue eyes and high cheekbones. She smiled and said, "Don't you remember me?"

Phillip frowned, and recognition lit his face. "Charlie? Are you here to finish the job?"

Charlie walked around the desk and leaned against the edge,

clasping her hands in front of her. "You have me all wrong. I wasn't trying to shoot you. I was aiming at Ruben." Throwing her hands up, she said, "Did Ruben give you any information about ATTRA?"

"Yes, why?"

Charlie took a deep breath and said, "Without blowing your mind, I'll only say Commander Adams wants something Julia has and is willing to kill for it. She sent me here to kill Ruben and bring Julia to her."

Phillip jumped out of his chair. "Julia's in danger?"

Charlie pressed her lips together. "You may want to sit down."

Phillip ran his fingers through his hair in frustration. "No. Tell me why you're here."

Charlie scratched the top of her head and said, "Very well. Ruben has already made you a player. Julia is pregnant with your son."

Phillip fell back against the chair and slid down. "What?"

"See, I told you to sit down. She gave me a direct order to kill Ruben and bring Julia to Monica, my commander. She's seen the Plates of Prophecy which target Julia's offspring developing a time machine that breaks the time barrier into the far distant past. That machine will give Monica, my commander, the ability to influence future events for Earth. Monica is already selling Spinners as slave labor to a General that lives in another galaxy. If Monica controls the new time machine, she has the potential of overthrowing our Sovereign, the Lord Supreme."

Phillip's mouth dropped open, and said, "For God's sake stop talking."

He opened the bottom drawer of his desk and pulled out a flask of whiskey. He poured the contents of the morning's coffee into the trash and poured the liquor into the cup. He drank several gulps. "I've studied for years about science, the fabric of time and the endless possibilities that our scientists haven't scratched the surface of yet. You're telling me the love of my life is carrying my child, and my child will create the new version of the machine that Ruben gave me the blueprints to alter?"

Crossing her arms over her chest, Charlie said, "Well, that's what I think. If Monica thought you were the one to develop the machine, she would've come for you. Instead, she thinks it's the child. Monica's alliance with General Agriaous is treason. She's using his gold to build an army. That's why I was trying to find Ruben, and then you shot me."

Phillip's eyes bugged, and he mumbled, "Sorry, I didn't want to shoot you."

"Whatever." Charlie began to pace back and forth across the room. "Look, the past can't change but the future can. I hacked into Monica's personal system in her office this morning, and a person died from my breach. I must stop Monica, and I can't do it by myself. She killed an innocent woman when she should've killed me."

She stopped and turned to Phillip. "Monica intends to travel into the past to gain information from an advanced civilization of giants that lived here before the humans. They built structures around the Earth and traveled to and from another galaxy. Monica thinks they fled Earth before the asteroid hit and wiped out most of the living organisms on the planet. She wants to know where they fled. She thinks Julia's child will create a machine to take her far enough into the past to find them. On the flip side, the Plates of Prophecy are continually changing because humans are unpredictable."

Placing her hand on Phillip's shoulder, she said, "Do you know where Ruben traveled?"

"2017, Burkett Falls. He's trying to help Julia. Charlie, I'll work day and night trying to figure out a formula to change the Needle-Horn's mainframe. But, without the machine to work on, it's impossible to know if any of the theories I devise will work."

Charlie shoved her hands into the back pockets of her brown leather pants and slowly walked to the door. She took one last glimpse at Phillip. "That's all you can do. I have to go."

"Charlie?"

Charlie held the doorknob. "Yeah?"

"Tell Julia I'll never stop loving her."

Charlie nodded and walked out the door.

Phillip poured another drink, turned up the cup, then wiped his mouth with his sleeve. He opened the folder and began to read through the documents on the Needle-Horn. "Please, God, open my eyes that I may see, open my mind that I may have clarity, and please, please keep Julia and my child safe."

Hours later, Phillip walked to the window and looked up to the night sky. The pain reverberated deep in his soul. The door opened, and he jerked around startled by the intrusion.

Amelia stood in the doorway. Her voice quivered, "Have you learned something new about Julia?"

"Amelia, I need your help. I may have found Julia. I need a research assistant. Will you help me?"

Amelia nodded and said, "I'll do anything for you, Phillip, and for Julia too."

CHAPTER 8

*P*resent Day

Monica and her team of enforcers—Azaria, Kalsan, Stormy, Johnnie, and Zane—entered the Earth's atmosphere, landing ATTRA's elite warship in the Black Mountains. After placing a shield of invisibility around the craft, the team, donned in the apparel of the day, headed for Burkett Falls. Ruben was in town, so her team operated in secrecy.

Before arriving at the house of Andy's neighbors, the Allister's, Monica used a small drone to case the neighborhood to ensure Andy, Julia, and Ruben were nowhere in sight. The retired couple lived alone and had no living children. Monica and her team walked up to the front door with a dozen roses and balloons. She chuckled. They looked like a commercial for one of those goofy TV sweepstakes of this time. She rang the doorbell, and an older lady opened the door.

With a look of surprise, Mrs. Allister said, "Oh my, what beautiful roses. May I help you?"

Smiling, Monica poured on a Southern accent. "Why, yes, Mrs. Allister. Is your husband home?"

"Yes, he's taking a nap in the recliner. Do you need him?"

Monica leaned in and said, "We need you both. Congratulations!

You've won the ATTRA sweepstakes." It took everything in Monica not to laugh out loud.

Mrs. Allister opened the door and said, "Please come in. I'll get Thaddeus."

Once inside the door, the team of enforcers acted swiftly, executing Thaddeus and Meredith Allister; then Zane proceeded to dismember the bodies and stored them in the garage freezer.

"Great work, team. We'll set up the base here. I must return to Lunar City in the morning. Zane, if you see a window of opportunity to move in and take Julia, do it and bring her to me. I want no survivors, understand?"

"You got it."

Monica looked at the others and said, "Zane's in charge. I need you to follow orders because we don't want the local authorities snooping around until we find the girl and get out of town."

Stormy rolled her eyes and said, "Not my first rodeo."

Johnnie stepped over and draped his arm around Monica's shoulders. "You can count on me." The team members knew Monica slept with Johnnie on the sly.

Monica patted his cheek and said, "Good boy. Look, I'm going to take a shower and then sleep for a couple of hours. Zane, please come up in a minute and grab my clothes. I need you to wash them for me before morning."

Monica went up the stairs, overcome with exhaustion from the day. Stripping down, she kicked the bloody clothes to the side, turned on the shower, and stepped inside, allowing the scalding water to cleanse her skin.

Monica had been plotting and planning her rise to power for decades. She ran the Tracker division on Lunar City under the authority of the Empyreal Palace. Lunar City was her base of command, but Monica wanted more, lots more. She had learned of an ancient civilization that lived on Earth one million years before the humans. A race far superior, but they fled before the enormous meteor hit, wiping out most of Earth's living organisms.

General Agriaous had implied the Lord Supreme and Prince Aelius were descendants of the ancients. Both were immortals with power to create or destroy entire galaxies, wormholes, and planetary systems including all life forms.

Monica needed the damn time machine to travel back to the distant past to research the Lord Supreme's origins. Gaining information on when and where his people fled was crucial to her plan. The Lord Supreme and Prince Aelius ruled everything in the Milky Way.

If Julia's son discovered a time machine with no past or future limitations, she could control and influence all future time events. Monica needed to travel into the future beyond the Plates of Prophecy to calculate and secure the number of warriors she needed to conquer the Empyreal Palace. She needed to know if there were others like the Lord Supreme that would come to his aid when she initiated the coup.

If her abduction plan worked, Julia would live on Lunar City with Monica. She'd take Julia under her wing and make her feel safe. Then after the baby boy was born, Julia would be eliminated. In Monica's youth, she had fantasized about a family. Julia Boatwright was going to give her one.

Monica lay on top of the covers, nude. She rarely thought of her former life. The sweet girl from long ago no longer existed. Closing her eyes, she could picture every mental image. It was the only thing she had left of her past

1902 Adamsville, Colorado

Monica Adams sat with her parents in their parlor after breakfast. Sunday services began in an hour, and Monica had no intention of attending. She feigned a headache and sighed, "Mother, would you mind checking my forehead? I'm not feeling well, and my head hurts."

Eleanor rose from the Victorian settee and went to her daughter, placing her hand on Monica's forehead. "Hmm. You don't feel warm, but if you have a headache, maybe you should lie down. Colin is coming over this afternoon to visit. I'm sure you'll want to see him."

Ugh! Colin Pinewood was a bonehead. The last thing Monica wanted to do was spend any time with the man. But she and Daniel had made plans to run away today and didn't want to raise any suspicion. Her packed bag waited for her under the bed until she could make a mad dash into the forest. "Yes, Mother. I'm sure you're right. I should lie down. Is it okay to miss church service?"

Her father, Theodore, coughed a couple of times, then chuckled. "I think I may be coming down with something too."

Eleanor placed her hands on her hips. "Teddy, you aren't sick. We'll miss the singing if we don't leave soon. It's my favorite part."

Teddy smiled and said, "Aw, Ellie, I wouldn't want you to miss that. Come along." He turned to Monica and raised a brow. "No mischief, young lady. Go straight to your room, and we'll be back around lunch to check on you."

Monica went to the stairs and turned to them and said, "I love you. I'll be right as rain when you return." She'd written letters to her father and mother explaining her elopement. Monica would write to her parents as soon as she and Daniel were married and settled.

She watched from the second-floor bedroom window as her parents and the servants walked along the path to the church at the end of the street. Reaching under the bed, Monica grabbed her bag, put on her boots, then ran down the servant's steps and out the back door. She was completely out of breath before she stopped.

Looking up, Daniel sat on a boulder next to a bubbling brook. He stood with a huge grin on his face.

And what a face—he had the greenest eyes like spring grass. Hitching up her dress, Monica ran toward him and fell face-first into a vine-covered ravine that opened into vast darkness.

Brilliant lights floated in the air when she hit hard on the ground in the year of our Lord, nineteen hundred and twenty.

Monica stared into the face of a menacing warrior wearing black clothes hugging his body and covering everything but his head. Dark wavy hair, sun-bronzed skin, and even darker eyes glared at her, and she fainted.

Monica woke in Lunar City in the private quarters of Commander Drummond Prescott. She learned later that Drummond traveled to Earth on an expedition for new recruits from the time portals.

He had found Monica, trained her personally to be a warrior, but he also trained her to be his whore.

Years of abuse at Drummond's hands had turned Monica bitter and cold. She put up walls and vowed never to let them down. Only when she felt so alone and isolated, did she think of the girl she used to be and the true love she'd lost. The mental images didn't last. Then she clung on to what she wanted more than anything else.

Her passion became power. Her desire became control.

Monica killed Drummond twenty years to the day he had made her his whore. She had cultivated others like her who were loyal and lethal. The most lethal were Zane, Stormy, and Johnnie. She began building an army, a legion of warriors under her control.

At Drummond's death, the Lord Supreme appointed Monica as an interim Commander. She kept the position and the title. She made all the right decisions. Monica knew how to pour on the charm, use her brains, and if she made a promise, she kept it. The Lord Supreme trusted and respected her.

Then in 1967, during one of Monica's space explorations with General Agriaous traveling through a wormhole in the Andromeda Galaxy, the two of them discovered an inhabitable planet Monica named, Veetreous.

Memories flooded her mind the day she'd first explored the new planet.

One day while they walked together exploring the new world, Monica talked with Agriaous. He was one of the few generals that had access to the Plates of Prophecy. He said, "It's prophesied that a major eruption from the super volcano in Yellowstone is destined in the next hundred years. An explosion so large the like has never been seen in modern civilization."

Monica gave him a sympathetic sigh as she placed her hand in the crook of his arm. He stared into her eyes and stopped walking. "The eruption will obliterate everything in its path for hundreds of miles around the surrounding area, and ash inches deep will cover North America, killing all vegetation. If we start colonizing Veetreous now, we'll have a place for the human species to survive."

Monica said, "Agriaous, I want to be Queen of this planet. Will you be my King?"

He pulled her into his arms, kissing her. "I would like nothing better."

Wrapping her arms around his neck, she said, "We mustn't tell anyone of this planet. I can start sending Spinners to help you colonize. Of course, you'll still have to make appearances at court. But when the time is right, you and I will declare our planet and our rule."

Monica partnered with General Agriaous and began to siphon tens of thousands of Spinners over the last five decades to work as slaves building the colonies on Veetreous. While Agriaous had the survival of the species at heart, Monica's goal was to become Queen and sole ruler. No free election system. The people of Veetreous would be subject to her rule. Agriaous had fallen in love with her and believed her. *What a fool!*

Lunar City's former Commander Prescott had taught Monica how to be ruthless. He'd taught Monica how to bend others to her will. Men looked at a beautiful woman and wanted sex, and she knew exactly how to use that against them.

CHAPTER 9

resent day, Burkett Falls

Over the next several days, Julia learned how to work the household appliances, and Andy continued to train her on his computer. In the evening, Andy divided Phillip's journals into two stacks. One stack of journals contained Phillip's work on time travel, and the other journals were letters to Julia. Andy worked through the time travel journals looking for any material that could help them devise a plan, any plan to get her home. Julia went through Phillip's letters and placed them in chronological order. She intended to read the letters in private.

After keying in a couple of hours' worth of complex mathematical formulas into his laptop, Andy yelled out, "Shmoly! I think I found something we can use." Julia pushed her chair away from the table and moved it closer to Andy. He pointed to a page and said, "Phillip has a blueprint for a spacecraft of sorts."

Julia reached for the folder and said, "May I look?"

"Sure thing." Andy handed Julia the document and let out a deep breath.

Julia read down the pages. With an edge of frustration in her voice, she said, "How in the world are we going to construct a time travel machine?"

"I think I can work with his plan to create a prototype of the craft he sketched, but it'll cost hundreds of millions of dollars to build one. But let's not worry about that part yet. The main thing, I have a plan with his formulas to work in my project software. It'll help me move on with developing applications, data processing, and analyzing the information. I can troubleshoot Phillip's code. I feel like he's with us, watching over us."

Andy let out another deep breath, then rubbed his hand over his mouth. "You might as well enjoy your time while you're here. Theories and formulas are great, but proving time travel, even with the craft, is a daunting task. But, hey, I love a challenge. I haven't been this excited in years. Julia Boatwright, I think you have opened my eyes to my real purpose in life."

Andy moved away from the desk and hugged her. "I'm glad you're here. You make my grandfather alive again. And together, you and I are going to accomplish something great."

Andy stepped over to the refrigerator and pulled out two bottles of water and handed one to Julia.

She said, "I'm counting on you, Andy. Every time I look at you, I see him. You're so much like Phillip, and he would be proud of you. I know I am. Do you think you could help me buy a laptop? I can type sixty-five words a minute. You can teach me how to key in data. I want to help."

"You got a deal. We'll go to Electronic Beats in the mall and pick you out one."

Julia scooped up a handful of letters and turned to Andy. "I'm tired. I think I'll read these letters in bed. Are you still going out of town tomorrow?"

Andy pushed the journals aside. "I was planning on it unless you don't want me to. I can call Denise and reschedule." Andy's friend traveled for work, and they hooked up once a month. He'd made plans before Julia arrived to take Denise to Phillip's Chalet in the mountains for the weekend. Andy had told her that it was Phillip's private retreat, learning of the property after Phillip's death.

"No. You go and have fun. I'll be okay. Besides, I have lots of reading material, and it'll give me time to hone my skills on the computer and sail with the TV remote."

Andy's hearty laugh filled the room. "It's surf, not sail. I'll be back Sunday afternoon, and remember, the cabin is only forty-five minutes away. Ruben's going to drop by around five tomorrow. He wants to do an intake form on your time travel experience. Is that okay?"

Julia leaned against the door frame. "Sure, I'm up for anything that'll help me get home faster. I'll see you in the morning?"

"You betcha. We'll eat breakfast together before I take off. Sweet dreams, Julia Bean."

Smiling, she said, "You too, little Phillip."

Walking into the bedroom, Julia closed the door, turned on the nightstand lamp, then changed into her nightgown. She jumped into the bed and grabbed Phillip's letters. She began to read about their glorious night under the stars.

*　*　*

1948 Stargazing

Out in the open field, Phillip set up the telescope under the moonlight. Dreams were made on nights like tonight. The warm, gentle breeze created a faint rustle of leaves from the trees. A heavy scent of fresh cut hay mingled with honeysuckle filled the air while crickets sang their sweet summer song.

Julia dipped under Phillip's arm to look in the telescope's viewfinder.

Leaning over her, Phillip caught a sweet whiff of Julia's perfume and closed his eyes. Phillip burned for Julia and noticed her every movement from the slight tilt of her face, her upturned grin, and even the way she talked with her hands.

Julia said, "I see the moon. It's incredible." She raised her head and looked over her left shoulder. "Want to see?"

"Julia?"

Tilting the angle of her face, Julia's eyes connected with his gaze. "Yeah?"

"Did you read about an incident last year in Roswell, New Mexico?"

She squinted at him as if she were trying to figure out a mystery. "Hm-hmm, the people from the area thought a weather balloon was a flying saucer."

Phillip rubbed his hands up and down her arms and took a deep breath. "A friend of mine from the Air Force worked the crash site. He overheard a man whispering to the local sheriff that he found a flying saucer. The man found materials made from chemical elements not found in our periodic table. He hid them on his farm. That was June 14, 1947, and on June 20, 1947, the first rocket program was initiated. Whether the two events are related is merely conjecture, but my friend contacted me yesterday and invited me to Cape Canaveral for a possible job." He paused and searched her eyes. "I want to take you with me."

Julia's eyes widened, and her mouth fell open. With a shaky voice, she replied, "You want to take me with you?"

Phillip reached into his pant pocket with one hand and took a ring out of a black box. With his other hand, Phillip caressed the curve of her cheek. "The touch of your lovely face, the flowery scent of your silky hair, and the promise of a kiss from your sweet, full lips makes my heart burn brighter than all of the stars shining above us. I want you in my arms every morning and every night." He leaned in and kissed her and whispered against her lips, "I love you, Julia. Will you marry me?"

"Yes, Phillip, yes, yes and yes." Julia's face flushed with warmth.

Phillip twirled them in a circle again and again. "You've made me the happiest man on the planet. My heart is near bursting out of my chest."

He gently lowered Julia onto the quilt and reached over to brush the hair away from her face and then slipped the ring on her finger.

Leaning down, Phillip tilted his face to the right and kissed her slowly and sweetly to savor the blissful moment.

Breathlessly, Julia said, "I love you, Phillip."

Phillip held her face in his hands, kissing her and ever so lightly brushed his lips across Julia's cheek up to her ear. "I love you too."

Blood thundered through his veins as he traced his fingers along the outer part of her thigh. Breathing hard, Julia closed her eyes and arched her back in response.

"Oh, my sweet angel. You're so sweet. So, soft and sweet." Phillip placed tender kisses down the column of her neck.

Julia's chest heaved up and down from breathing so hard. Her voice hoarse, she said, "Phillip?"

"Yes, my love?"

"Make love to me."

He chuckled. "I thought that's what I was doing."

She took another deep breath and said, "I'm serious. I want you to make love to me. You're mine, Phillip Clayborn, all mine."

Julia wet her lips and moaned.

It was too much. "I want to touch you, Julia." He ran his hand between her jean-clad thighs.

Julia reached her arms around him. "I want you to touch me."

Phillip kissed her gently and muttered against her lips. "You don't have to be scared. Anytime you want to stop, just say the word."

Julia's wide-eyed innocence nearly undid him. She stood up and unzipped her pants and let them fall to the ground.

Phillip's stomach fluttered. He stepped in front of her and slowly unbuttoned her shirt, pausing in between to lean down and place kisses across the top of her breasts. Pushing the fabric off Julia's shoulders, he let the shirt fall to the ground next to her jeans, leaving her standing in matching white lacy bra and panties.

His heart pounded as he kissed the top of her shoulders while rubbing his hands lightly up and down her arms.

Julia spun around and pressed her back next to the brick wall of his chest. Her head fell back against him, and he draped his arm around her waist. He reached up with his free hand, pulling the pins from her hair and shaking loose the soft curling strands to flow over her shoulders and down her back.

Turning to face him again, Julia stared at him with heavy lidded eyes and unclasped her bra. Her nipples hardened in the cool night air.

Phillip bent over and placed one in his mouth. He sucked and pulled on it before circling her nipple with his tongue. He knelt on the ground and rolled down her panties, sliding his fingers inside her warmth, and she released a loud moan of desire.

She twisted her fingers into his hair and moved restlessly under his ministrations.

Phillip picked her up again, and she circled her arms around his shoulders burying her face in the slight depression between his shoulder and neck. He laid her with care on the quilt, and Julia stared at him, barely blinking with her lips parted. She was so beautiful lying in the moonlight, so damn beautiful that he could've stared at her all night.

Phillip kissed her mouth slowly, savoring the feel of her full sweet lips, and then nuzzled into her neck before nibbling and tugging on her earlobe. He moved to kiss her shoulders while gently splaying his fingers across her chest, down her flat abdominals, and over her hips.

Phillip said, "Roll onto your stomach."

"What?" she asked anxiously.

He nuzzled her neck and muttered, "Trust me?"

"Yes, I believe you. Phillip?" She looked at him nervously.

"Yes, my love?"

"I don't know what I'm doing so I sure hope you do." She giggled and rolled onto her stomach.

Phillip massaged her shoulders, the blades between her back, and placed kisses along the curve of her spine as her fingers gripped and twisted the quilt.

His hands roamed over her firm buttocks, and he traced his fingertips close to her valley of desire. He leaned in and slowly placed feather light kisses along her inner thigh to the back of her knee.

Julia turned abruptly and kicked him in the head. She quickly cupped his face with her hands. "Oh, I'm sorry, I'm so sorry. Did I hurt you?"

Phillip reached to the back of his head and rubbed his scalp. "Just my feelings. I was trying to be romantic."

"You were, or you are very romantic. But I have a terrible tickle bone, and I couldn't stand it. Forgive me, please? And don't stop. I just got tickled."

Julia lay back on the quilt as he propped himself over her. "Oh, I'm not stopping. I want to see how much I can tickle you, sunny side up. I want to kiss you here." Phillip firmly cupped her privates, and she closed her eyes.

Julia's cheeks reddened in the moonlight. "People do that?"

He threw his head back and laughed, then leaned close to her face. "People do that, and they love it. May I?"

Julia let out a deep breath. "You may. Just don't be surprised if I wiggle like a worm in hot ashes."

Phillip moved between her legs, trailing kisses on her inner thighs. His intricate strokes aimed at her pleasure points. He deliberately took extra time caressing Julia, touching her face, looking in her eyes between each erogenous zone he targeted. His fingers stretched and trailed over every inch of her delicious body while kissing and tugging on her most tender areas. Her sweet face flushed while her hands clenched and released the quilt. Julia finally lost all inhibitions, yelling out with unbridled passion.

He moved back up across her body and breathed her in. "I love you, Julia. Let's elope, tonight. We'll drive all night to Las Vegas."

"Oh, Phillip, I've dreamed of my wedding day since I was a little girl. Besides, I want our families and friends with us." Julia circled her arms around his neck and kissed him, making him crazy with the want of her.

Phillip kissed her again and released his grip on her thighs. He stood and removed his clothing. "It will be as you wish. Did you like what I did?"

Julia smiled and threw her arm over her forehead. "Oh, my goodness, I loved it." She giggled and then she propped herself up on her elbows. Her eyes widened at the sight of his naked body. "Good grief, Phillip. Is it going to hurt much?"

He knelt beside her and held her hand. "I'll never hurt you. Like I said, you tell me the word, and I'll stop. But I'm pretty sure you're ready." Julia gushed with desire, and he would enter her as gently as possible.

He said, "There may be a moment of discomfort, but I promise things will get much better."

Julia released a sigh. "I know. I read all about doing it for the first time. I'm not scared anymore, Phillip. Make love to me. What can I do to make it better?"

"Wrap your legs around my waist." Julia did as he instructed, and he began to move inside her, slowly and shallowly back and forth stretching her to accommodate his width until he pushed past the barrier between them.

"Oh, Phillip." Julia held him tightly as Phillip moved back and forth with a gentle rhythm.

Soon Julia began to move with him, and his strokes became bolder as she released moans of ecstasy. The building of their lovemaking was intense and incredible. More than he could've ever dreamed possible. Making love to Julia was the most exciting and memorable moment of his life. "Julia. I love you."

Phillip rolled onto his back, out of breath, and Julia slid on top of him.

She bent over, placing kisses on his face, neck and upper chest. "Can we do it again with me on top?"

Phillip grinned and brushed his fingers along her jawline. "You're my little vixen. Give me a minute, darling. We can do it all night long if that's what you want."

Julia leaned down and kissed him passionately. "Time doesn't exist when I'm with you."

* * *

Present Day, Burkett Falls

Julia read Phillip's letter several times before eventually crying herself to sleep. She loved him with every fiber of her being. An invisible cord stretching across decades of time tethering her heart to his. An unbreakable tie.

Their love story transcended time.

She just knew he could feel it too. As Julia dozed somewhere between dreams, she saw Phillip in his bed, her eyes focused on him in the dim light. He saw her too, and simultaneously, they reached for each other, the tips of their fingers touched, before Phillip shimmered away.

* * *

THE NEXT MORNING, she dragged herself into the kitchen to the smell of Applewood bacon, scrambled eggs, and fresh coffee.

Andy handed her a cup and said, "Rough night?"

"Some of my dreams were the sweetest, but the others were nightmares. Breakfast smells good. What time are you leaving this morning?" She sipped on coffee, holding the cup with both hands as she sat on one of the kitchen bar stools.

Andy loaded a plate with food and placed it before her on the kitchen bar counter. "Denise should be here any minute. I want you to meet her. She's going to love you." He moved to the stove to grab another plate and joined Julia at the bar.

"What does Denise do for a living?" Julia nibbled on a piece of bacon.

"She's an accountant for a large firm and travels in the Southeast." He ate several bites of bacon and eggs before washing it down with orange juice.

"Are you in love with Denise?"

"Ah, I guess I could fall in love with her. She is so sweet and kind. We like the same things, but I'm taking this one slow. Let's just say, for now, Denise is a friend with benefits." He waggled his brows. "I fell head over heels for the one who will remain nameless, and my heart couldn't take another devastating disappointment." After eating the last piece of bacon, Andy pushed the plate away.

"You can't make Denise pay for someone else's mistakes. It's not fair to her or you. Give love another chance, because you never know when you'll get another one." She finished the rest of her breakfast, then helped Andy with the dishes.

He shoulder-bumped Julia and said, "Hey, I have a surprise for you. Follow me."

Julia followed Andy out the back door to a detached garage. Opening a side door, he hit a button on the wall, and the garage door opened. A vehicle covered with a tarp sat inside. Andy looked at Julia and gave her a wide grin, then removed the cover.

Julia gasped, and her hand flew to her mouth. "Oh, Andy, it's my car. You have my car. I can't believe it."

Andy leaned against the garage work counter. "Phillip bought it at the Boatwright Estate sale. He had it remodeled and left a note on the importance of regular car maintenance. So, I take her out for a spin about every other week. Now, I'm giving her back to you. It's yours. At least while you're here."

He reached into his back pocket and pulled out a small card. "I also made you a fake driver's license. It's a good one. I don't think you'd have any problems with the local police, but you might with the state cops. So, try and follow the speed limits, and with any luck, you won't need it. Just in case you do get pulled over, the registration and insurance information is in the glove box. You have to show all three if you do get pulled over."

Andy handed her the fake license, and she turned it over in her hands. He said, "I printed off the driving directions to Sloane's, the mall, and the grocery store, and left them in my office. That way you can start getting a good feel for living here."

Reaching into his jacket, Andy pulled out a phone and gave it to Julia. "And I bought you a prepaid mobile phone and programmed my contact information, in case you need me while I'm away. I also left my numbers on sticky notes in my office. I want you to be happy here, Julia. I want you to think of my house as your home.

"Oh, you've made my day. I was so depressed this morning that I didn't want to get out of bed. Thanks, Andy, you're the best." She reached up on tiptoes and kissed his cheek.

A red sports car pulled into the driveway, and a long-legged blonde stepped out. Denise smiled broadly, showing two dimples on each cheek, and she had freckles sprinkled across her nose. She wore black sunglasses, jeans, and a long sleeve red flannel shirt. "Hey, honey. I love the ride. That's very retro."

Denise stepped over and extended a handshake to Julia. "Hi, I'm Denise, and you must be Kaye. I've heard a lot of great things about you."

Julia said, "Nice to meet you. It looks like you're going to have great weather for your trip."

Andy draped an arm around Denise's shoulders. "Yup, looks like it. You ready to roll, juicy fruit?"

Denise circled her arm around his waist. "Ready." She giggled, then turned to Julia and said, "Why don't you come with us?"

Julia shook her head. "No, no, no. You two have fun. I have a lot on my to-do list this weekend. Number one is to take this baby for a spin."

Minutes later, Julia waved at Andy and Denise as they backed out of the driveway. She was alone for the first time since she'd slipped down the rabbit hole. She wouldn't dwell on the loneliness that filled her soul. She went inside with a plan to take a shower and then she'd drive to see Sloane.

*　*　*

DRIVING the convertible along the familiar scenic back roads, passing miles of lush mountain meadows with sweeping curves and whitewater rapids, grounded Julia and gave her a sense of peace.

Regardless of her seventy-year jump into the future, in her mind, it'd only been one week since she and Phillip made love. Only one week since Phillip proposed marriage.

It seemed like a lifetime ago.

Julia had memorized directions from Andy's print-out. Only one more street and she'd arrive at Sloane's place of residence. It was hard to wrap her brain around the fact that her vibrant and vivacious sister was eighty-seven, but at least she was still feisty.

Delores worked in a small office behind the glass at the retirement home and remembered Julia. She opened the sliding glass window at the check-in counter and smiled. "Ms. Davis is looking forward to seeing you this morning, Ms. Bailey." Delores handed Julia the key fob and beeped her through the security door.

Sloane sat outside on the patio reading the paper and glanced up to watch a foursome tee off from the ninth hole when Julia arrived.

Julia leaned over and kissed Sloane's cheek. "Wanna play a round?"

Placing the paper on the table, Sloane chuckled. "The spirit is willing, but the flesh is weak. Hey, you want a cup of coffee or tea?"

"Coffee, but I'll get it." Julia walked over to the baker's rack next to the brick wall and poured a cup from the coffee service. Sitting down in the seat opposite Sloane, she said, "Andy gave me the keys to my convertible this morning. Did you know Phillip restored it? It drives like a dream."

Sloane cast Julia a look with bright eyes and nodded in agreement. "Phillip was a good man. Have you made any progress on finding a way back home?"

Julia stirred the coffee with a swivel stick. "Andy's helpful, and we found blueprints for a spaceship in one of Phillip's journals, but it would cost millions to build. Oh, I did meet a colleague of Andy's from the University. Ruben Callaway is working on some time travel theories. To be honest, I don't think I'm going anywhere anytime soon. I think I'm stuck here for the foreseeable future."

"You can move in here with me. We can spend whatever time I have left together." Sloane held Julia's hand.

Tears welled in Julia's eyes, and she blinked them away. "I'm not supposed to be here visiting my baby sister in a home for the aging. It's not right. I'm not meant to be living in 2017."

Sloane let out a deep breath and leaned back in her chair. "Life is never what we think it's supposed to be. Remember what we learned in church? It's God's will, not ours. Try to embrace the opportunity, and maybe you'll find purpose here in this life."

Julia closed her eyes and said a silent prayer asking for guidance and patience. "How did you get so smart?"

"I pay attention." Sloane giggled, and for an instant, Julia heard the girl Sloane used to be.

With a grin, Julia asked, "Want to go shopping with me at the mall? Ride in my convertible like the old days?"

Sloane's face lit up like a Christmas tree. "Do you think my mobile scooter would fit in the trunk?"

"There's only one way to find out."

Julia and Sloane spent the day shopping with a break for lunch, and during the afternoon they had Manis and pedis. Sloane was spry for her age, and the motorized scooter had Julia practically sprinting most of the day.

In one of the boutiques, Julia tried on a summer dress, the color of lilac irises. The store clerk walked up and said, "That color looks spectacular with your hair."

Julia turned and smiled. "Thank you."

The store clerk's eyes widened, and she gasped. "OMG! You look just like Julia Boatwright."

Sloane giggled under her breath, and her shoulders moved up and down. "She gets that all the time. Kaye's a distant relative."

With a wide grin which made her jaws ache, Julia replied, "Thank you again for the compliment. I'll take it."

Sloane bought Julia tons of outfits, shoes, and matching accessories. She wouldn't take no for an answer. "Look at it as your inheritance."

Pulling back into Sunnyside Meadows, Sloane tilted her head toward Julia and with a quiver in her voice, she said, "You've given me a great gift today. If I go to meet my Maker tonight, just know I love you. You were the best big sister growing up. I've never forgotten, and today, you reminded me how much I had missed you."

Tears flowed down their cheeks as Julia reached across the car and hugged Sloane. "I've missed you too."

* * *

ENTERING Phillip's house without Andy gave Julia a disconcerting feeling. Photos of his son and grandson peppered the walls, telling a story of Phillip's life without her, while his letters cried out for Julia's return.

Julia paused and stared at a larger photo of him that hung in the main living area. Phillip had been handsome as a young man, but with age, he seasoned into a fine wine that she longed to taste.

Shaking out of her reverie, Julia took her shopping bags and ambled down the hallway. Ruben would arrive soon to ask questions for his time travel study, and she needed to get dressed. She swiftly showered and readied herself for the evening.

Sloane had helped Julia pick out a long sleeve denim shirt that snapped up the front and hit low on the hips, and for a bit of fun, Julia added a gleaming silver concha belt. She mixed it up with a Southwestern skirt that had multi-colors of dark purple, blues, and orange in an A-line hitting at her ankles. She'd also bought a pair of dangling turquoise earrings.

When Julia had tried the outfit on in the store, Sloane's eyes smiled with wrinkles creasing in the corners. "You remind me of the desert at sunset. Brooks used to take me to Arizona in the winter months."

Sloane's eyes seemed to unfix as she drifted off into a daydream. "We'd play golf and then go partying at night. I wish you could've seen how incredible Brooks was to me." Based on Sloane's testimony, Brooks had turned out to be a good husband, and Julia was glad that Sloane had a long and happy marriage.

Glancing at the alarm clock on the nightstand, Julia slipped on bedazzled sandals and walked into the kitchen to open a bottle of wine. Just as she pulled the cork out, the front doorbell rang. Her sandals made a clip-clack sound on the tile floor in the foyer as she stepped over and opened the door.

A slow grin grew wide across Ruben's face, and his dog, Klock, sat next to him wagging his little stub of a tail. Ruben whistled, then fanned his fingers out and moved them back and forth. "You acclimate well to your new surroundings." He looked down at Klock and said, "Stay." Julia could've sworn the dog nodded. Klock sat next to the front door in what appeared to be a guard position scanning the front yard.

"Hi, Ruben, come on in. I just opened a bottle of merlot. Would you like a glass?" Julia ignored the heated look Ruben gave her. She noticed a black leather notebook tucked under his arm.

"I'm not much of a wine drinker. Do you have a beer?"

He followed her into the kitchen and placed his notebook on the table. Julia opened the fridge and pulled out a Samuel Adams and held it out to him. "Is this okay?"

Ruben nodded. "Sure."

Julia picked up her wine goblet, went to the table, pulled out a chair and sat down. "So, Andy says you have some questions for me?"

Sitting the beer on the table, Ruben joined her. He opened the notebook and took out a pen. "Most professors use online apps for their forms, but I'm old school. So, you've been here for how long?"

"Seven days, four hours, and twenty-seven minutes give or take a few seconds." She sipped wine and looked at him over the rim of her glass while tapping the heel of her sandal on the floor.

Laying the pen next to the notebook, he asked, "Do I make you nervous?"

"Not really. I suppose I'm curious and a little anxious about how you can help me. Andy and I found a folder with blueprints to a spaceship or what looks like a spaceship to me. But, he said it would cost millions to make, so that's not going to happen on my budget." With a raised brow, she said, "Unless you have access to a boatload of cash."

Ruben pushed back slightly from the table, placing his forearms on the armrest of the kitchen chair. "Hmm. A spaceship you say? That's quite a find. We'll table the spaceship talk until Andy gets back."

Ruben rubbed his neck, and his gaze darted to Julia. "Hey, I spoke with a friend of mine from NASA about their astronaut training program. He emailed me an exercise plan to help you get physically fit and start a nutritional regime, with an organic diet. We need to limit your sugars and increase your protein. It's amazing to me you don't have any side effects. If we find a way to send you back, you need to be in the best shape of your life."

"Exercise? You mean like jumping jacks? And don't I look fit? I hate diets." She crossed her leg over her knee and caught Ruben staring at her ankles.

He chuckled. "You look fit, but I'm more concerned about your heart and other major organs. And no, I don't mean jumping jacks. We'll start slow, nothing too drastic."

Julia felt her cheeks redden under his intense stare and she looked away.

Ruben leaned in and said, "I thought we could go on a short run tomorrow so I can assess your physical stamina."

"Running? I guess I could try, but don't expect too much. Sloane was the athlete in our family. I was a cheerleader."

"Cheerleaders are athletes," he replied.

"Not in the 1940s. And besides, I don't have any exercise clothes, and I only have one pair of tennis shoes." She scratched her left eyebrow. *Exercise.* Wouldn't Sloane have a field day with that scenario? She snapped, "So that's it? Exercise? Diet? For goodness sakes, I thought you'd have more ideas."

"Hey, look, I'm only here to help. You don't have to bite my effing head off." He gulped beer.

Julia leaned in and linked her fingers together. "I don't mean to snap at you but I'm angry, and I'm sad. I don't want to live here. I want to go home, and by the looks of things, I could be here a very long time. Heck, Sloane wants me to move in with her at Sunnyside."

Ruben closed his notebook and stood. "Let's go to dinner. You need some downtime, and I can ask questions later. Are you hungry?"

She allowed her anger and frustrations to dissipate. "I'm starving. I could eat a horse."

He laughed. "Well, I don't know of any places serving horses, but I know of a great place that serves steak."

Julia grabbed her clutch purse, locked the door then stopped short and pointed. "What kind of vehicle is that?"

"This is a Hummer. You like it?" Klock ran to the door next to Julia.

She chuckled. "It looks like a tank mated with a Jeep. It's different. Is it a truck?"

"Oh, it's a big truck." Laughter rolled out of Ruben's chest. He went around to the passenger side and offered her a hand to step inside; then Klock jumped in and sat on the floorboard next to her feet. The interior had more gadgets than Andy's Camaro.

Julia stared at Ruben, taking in his physical attributes. He had wavy shoulder-length dark russet hair, silver-gray eyes, and a strong jawline. She could tell by the cut of his jacket he was physically fit. Broad shoulders and a narrow waist, but Ruben had legs the size of tree trunks.

He wore a tan sports coat with a light purple button-down shirt revealing the underlining muscles of his chest, and a pair of jeans with loafers and no socks. Ruben was more than attractive.

Fastening his seatbelt, Ruben turned to Julia and said, "Buckle up, buttercup."

Once again, Julia felt the familiar tug at her heartstrings. Big Joe affectionately called her buttercup or tulip on any given day. "So, where are you taking me?"

Driving along the hustle and bustle streets of downtown Burkett Falls, Ruben seemed at ease. He looked at her before turning his attention back to the road. "Chesney's. They have the best steaks in town. Louis's secret is garlic butter, and he makes this blue cheese cream sauce that's drizzled over the top. Oh, man, it's mouthwatering, girl."

And just like that, Julia and Ruben hit it off talking about food. Maybe it was because food was a universal language and everyone had to eat.

Chesney's name lit up in fuchsia neon in big bright letters over the restaurant, with a martini glass in white neon and the olive in green.

Ruben cracked the windows and partially opened the sunroof. "Klock, you must stay. Push the red button if you need me." The dog barked and Julia thought he answered, "Yup" as they exited the Hummer.

The restaurant's exteriors were in natural pine. Wrought-iron tables scattered on the patio under a black covered awning, and soft jazz music played with a backdrop of people talking and laughing in hushed tones.

Chesney's interior resembled a speakeasy of the 1920s. It had a grand bar full of people out for a good time. They followed the maître d down the stairs into a decadence befitting a scene out of *The Great Gatsby*. The jazz music was soft and sad as Ruben reached for her hand at the bottom step.

He leaned down and said, "Chesney's booked Mamie for the weekend. She croons songs from the 30s and 40s. I thought you'd like it."

"Burkett Falls has stepped up in the world."

Dark mahogany walls, walnut hardwood floors, and thick red velvet drapes covered unseen windows, creating a warm ambiance. Opulent sconces spaced out around the room dimly lit the restaurant. To the right of the dining tables was a small dance floor and stage with a Persian rug covering the area, and a beautiful older woman sang a Billie Holiday tune at the microphone.

The well-heeled crowd of Burkett Falls' finest filled most of the tables. Ruben somehow managed to find a table close to the stage nestled in a secluded corner—until Julia noticed Ruben slipping the maître d' a wad of cash. She smiled at his effort.

"Will you permit me to order for you?" Ruben asked.

"Yes, but to start off, I'd like a martini, please." Julia felt a little underdressed compared to the other women in the restaurant, but Ruben didn't seem to care.

The first bite of the Kansas City strip melted in her mouth. She nodded to Ruben and said, "True to your word, Ruben. Best steak I think I've ever eaten."

Taking a sip of beer, Ruben leaned over and said, "You tell the cook. He's on his way over here."

The chef gave Ruben a slight bow and spoke English with a thick French accent. "Monsieur, Ruben. We're so happy to have you this evening. Is the steak to your satisfaction?"

Ruben touched his finger to his lips and kissed them with a loud smack. "*Oui*, Louis. May I introduce my friend, Kaye? She's visiting a relative in town. I had to treat her to the best restaurant in the city."

Chef Louis smiled, turned and slightly bowed to Julia. "Mademoiselle, you're a true vision of loveliness. Are you enjoying your dinner?"

Julia imitated Ruben and said, "*Oui*, Monsieur Louis."

"Oh. La, la, la, Ruben, you have a heartbreaker? No?"

Ruben nodded and said, "*Oui*." The three of them laughed.

"Please, let me know if I may be of further service this evening." Chef Louis disappeared back into the kitchen.

Julia wiped the corner of her mouth with a white linen napkin, then put it on the plate before pushing it to the side of the table. "How do you know the chef?"

"Andy brought me to dinner here last year, and I fell in love with the food. I eat here at least once or twice a week. So, I'm on a first-name basis with Louis."

The waiter cleared the table and brought out another martini and a glass of beer. Mamie began to sing, At *Last*. Ruben stood and offered his hand to Julia. "May I have this dance?"

Julia demurely looked down for a second and gave him her hand. Ruben ushered her onto the dance floor, placing one hand on her low back and the other held her hand. After a moment, Julia lost herself in song and memories. She closed her eyes and placed her cheek against his left pectoral, resting her face near Ruben's neck.

Bittersweet memories flooded Julia's mind of the magical night with Phillip under the stars at the Old Dyer's Farm, the night she'd given him her innocence. Tears dampened her cheek as the song ended.

Julia took a step back, looked up in the soft light, and her vision blurred, seeing Phillip instead of Ruben.

Ruben leaned in to kiss her, but Julia broke from his embrace. "I'm sorry, Ruben. I didn't mean to lead you on. I got lost for a moment. You seem like a very nice man, but I'm in love with Phillip."

Shaking his head, Ruben said, "No, I'm sorry. I got carried away with the music and your beauty. It won't happen again. Please forgive me." He reached into the pocket of his jacket and pulled out a handkerchief and dabbed her tears away.

"There's no need to apologize. The song brought back memories that are still so fresh in my mind. Thank you for the evening, but I'm ready to go home."

They sat in silence as Ruben paid the bill. After leaving the restaurant, neither of them spoke on the ride to Phillip's house while Klock slept soundly in the backseat.

In the driveway, Ruben turned to Julia and took her hand in his. "I'm sorry I ruined the evening. I should've maintained my distance. But I'm glad we danced. I'll walk you to the door."

"That's not necessary."

"I promised Andy I would watch out for you. Would you mind if Klock stayed with you? He's a great guard dog."

Julia turned in the seat to look at Klock, and he seemed to be smiling. "I'd love for Klock to spend the night."

Ruben walked with Julia and Klock to the door. Once they went inside, he made a security check around the house before he felt comfortable enough to leave Julia. Klock would contact him if he sensed anything amiss.

CHAPTER 10

Sighing deeply, Julia kicked off her sandals. "Let's go to Phillip's room. I feel close to him around his things."

Klock and Julia padded down the hallway into the spare room that held Phillip's things. Flipping on the light switch, Julia looked around, then flung open the closet door. Like a mad woman, she began taking out his clothes and inhaling the scent of his jackets and coats as if she could make Phillip miraculously appear.

Klock cocked his head to the side and whined.

"I'm okay. I just miss Phillip so much."

An old leather trunk sat at the end of the bed. Kneeling on the floor, Julia opened the trunk and dug down under the loose papers. Klock circled twice and sat next to her on the floor.

Julia pulled out an old shoebox and opened the lid to dozens and dozens of photos of her and Phillip together. Photos he'd taken of her and pictures others had taken before she had met Phillip. High school photos in her cheerleading uniform. Pictures of her with her sorority sisters. Some were with Sloane. Julia's heart broke again.

Reaching back into the trunk, she pulled out a newspaper clipping and screamed. She stared at the image, not believing her eyes. The caption read, "Dr. Callaway's Time-Space Continuum Symposium.

Sold Out Crowd." The date read October 5, 1950. Phillip and Ruben stood next to the lecture podium, and the icing on the cake was Klock. He was at Ruben's feet, snarling.

"Klock!" she shouted, and he jumped off the floor barking. For some reason, Julia showed the dog the photo. He let out another whine and looked at her with the saddest eyes. He nudged her leg. "This is you, isn't it? You and Ruben knew Phillip. Ruben lied to me. He lied to Andy."

"That lying son of a bitch," Julia shouted. Reading the first sentence of the article made her see red. *Protégé of Nikola Tesla, Dr. Callaway claims time travel exists.*

She stormed into the kitchen and laid the newspaper clipping in the center of the table. Staring at the image of Phillip and Ruben, she wondered—who in the hell was Ruben Callaway?

"Klock, your master has some explaining to do. I wish you could talk. Sometimes it seems as if you and Ruben are carrying on a conversation." She went into the bedroom and Klock jumped on the bed while she changed into her gown.

Julia slipped in between the sheets. Klock inched closer and placed his head on her arm. He whined again, and she rubbed his ears. "I'm not mad at you. I'm mad at Ruben. Now go to sleep." Klock closed his eyes.

There was something special about Klock. Having the dog near her made it easier for her to breathe, and she fell into a deep sleep.

* * *

CHARLIE SAT in the dark waiting for Ruben to arrive at his house. She arrived in the twenty-first century in just enough time to follow Ruben to a house on Country Park Lane. Ruben had been oblivious to her tail. He was getting sloppy. Charlie had to warn him about Monica's plans. Minutes after entering the home, Ruben and Klock left with Ms. Julia Boatwright. Charlie shook her head, sitting behind the wheel of her car parked across the street. "Ruben, Ruben, what are you doing, my man?"

She tailed Ruben to Chesney's, then proceeded to watch him make a total fool out of himself with the black-haired beauty. Charlie left after the kiss fiasco and went back to Ruben's crib, picked the lock, and sat in the dark.

The roar of Ruben's Hummer pulled into the driveway, and the clickety-clackety sound of the automatic garage door opened, then closed seconds later. Ruben stomped through the side door of the kitchen. Slamming the cabinets, opening and closing doors until he pulled out a fifth of Patrón, he opened the liquor and took a drink from the bottle.

Charlie chuckled and said, "Damn, Ruben, you got it bad, man."

Startled, Ruben spewed the tequila across the brick tiled floor and wiped his mouth with his sleeve. "For space sakes, what the hell are you doing in my house sitting in the dark?"

Ruben crossed the room in two strides, placing his hands on either side of the armrest, towering over Charlie.

Charlie wore a pair of brown leather pants with a dark gold spandex top and a pair of brown biker boots. Her red hair spiked on the top, and the sides slicked back behind her ears. A silver cross hung around her neck.

Charlie shoved Ruben away and stood, tilting her chin in defiance. "You're getting sloppy, old man. I followed you tonight, and you were completely clueless. I crossed a parallel universe and traveled over a couple of time eras to find you. Just to save your sorry ass and what do I find? You're trying to make a move on your assignment. At least, she seemed to have the wisdom to shut you down."

Charlie punched Ruben in the gut, and he doubled over with a groan. "That's for having Phillip shoot me with a Black Beauty."

Ruben slowly sank into the chair Charlie had vacated. "What do you want?"

Charlie propped her boot on the side table and leaned in with her forearm on her knee. "I tried to tell you in 1950 with Phillip, but you stuffed me in a janitor's closet. Monica wants Julia for a specific reason, numbnuts. And it isn't good."

"For space sakes, why?"

Charlie pulled the footstool next to Ruben and sat down. "Did you know Julia's pregnant? The Plates of Prophecy states her son will break the barrier to time travel with no limitations. And not like ATTRA's time machines, either. I'm talking tens of thousands of years into the past or the future."

She placed her hands on his knees. "Ruben, a recruit died because of me. I had spotted on the deck of the Gateway a warship full of Spinners heading to the freaking Andromeda Galaxy. Monica was on a scheduled mission and not due back for a couple of days. So, I crept into her office and hacked her system to see what she was up to."

Shaking her head, Charlie began pacing about the room. "Once I got in, I found out so much it'd turn your hair white. Monica and General Agriaous are colonizing a planet called Veetreous. She's building an army, and if the Plates of Prophecy are correct, the machine Julia's son is going to build will give Monica knowledge to control and influence time events to suit her every wish. She's plotting a coup to take over the Empyreal Palace. All she needs is the machine to manipulate the outcome. Do you think the Lord Supreme knows?"

"Take a breath and get a drink. You're hyperventilating."

Running her hands through her hair, Charlie said, "Monica has files on the Lord Supreme and Prince Aelius. I suppose Agriaous helped her gain access to the Plates of Prophecy, which are predicting a major volcanic explosion in Yellowstone Park."

She walked into the kitchen, picked up the tequila and took a couple of gulps. Charlie released a sigh and rubbed the heels of her hands into her eyes. She turned to Ruben. "Life on Earth is going to change in a big way. From what I read, everything living will die. Monica's been sending the Spinners to that planet for fifty years to train warriors and work as slaves. What in the hell are we going to do?"

Ruben cocked his head to the side and said, "Julia's pregnant?"

Charlie shouted, "Good god, man. I give you information that can change the history of our planet, and all you can say is 'Julia's pregnant.' Snap out of it! Where's Ruben? What alien has abducted the best damn Time Tracker I know because he sure as shit isn't in this room?"

Ruben shook his head and stood to face Charlie. "Don't get your panties in a twist. It makes sense now. That's why the Lord Supreme sent me? Am I supposed to protect Julia and her unborn son from that deranged woman? Wonder why the Lord Supreme didn't give me those specifics."

Ruben pulled on his neck and groaned. "Look, the Lord Supreme and Prince Aelius are immortals. They control the Milky Way Galaxy, so I'm confident they're monitoring Monica's actions. They must've permitted Monica to colonize the planet to allow progenation of the species. But I'll plan a trip to the Empyreal Palace as soon as I know Julia's safe. At least while Julia is pregnant, Monica won't harm her. She wouldn't jeopardize the boy."

Then he looked up and added, "For the record, I'm sorry I made Phillip shoot you with a Black Beauty." Ruben smiled, and Charlie melted. "You're working for me now. I'll call my liaison with the Lord Supreme to officially change your orders. We can't allow Monica to hurt Julia or take the baby. Will you help me?"

Rolling her eyes, Charlie replied, "You do know Monica is trying to kill you? I was ordered to kill you, goofus. Are you willing to die for Julia? And if I go to work for you, then I'm as good as dead too."

Frowning, Ruben said, "There are worse things in life than dying. Sacrificing oneself to preserve the Lord Supreme's Universe is worth dying for, is it not?"

Taking a deep breath, she sighed. "And how are you going to convince Ms. Boatwright to play along with your plans?"

"I'm going to tell Julia the truth and stop by the pharmacy and pick up about a dozen pregnancy tests."

"Ruben? Where's Klock?"

Ruben draped an arm around Charlie. "He's with Julia. Oh, the back of the Hummer is full of tools and weapons from our more advanced savvy neighbors. If I were a betting man, Monica will probably send maybe four to six enforcers. Too many would alert the

ATTRA militia on Earth that's under Prince Aelius's command. Do you have any weapons?"

Ducking out of his arm, Charlie placed one hand on her hip. "I never leave home without them. I want to kick Monica's ass because if I don't, she'll put my head on a spike in Lunar Square. She's lost her mind."

Ruben lifted Charlie's chin with the tip of his forefinger. "I won't let anyone hurt you, Charlie. Plus, we'll be waiting for Monica." He kissed her forehead.

Charlie would die for Ruben. He was the only person in the Universe that mattered to Charlie.

One day, maybe he'd realize that.

* * *

Julia sat in one of the Adirondack chairs on the patio, holding a cup of coffee in her hands with Klock at her feet. The caffeine had her nerves on edge. She was still furious from the newspaper clipping she'd found last night about Ruben, that had kept her awake most the night.

Julia placed the newspaper clipping in a manila folder and put it on the patio table, securing it with a decorative stone so it wouldn't fly away in the breeze.

The backyard fence opened, and Ruben rounded the corner. He carried a pharmacy bag in his hand. "Hi, gorgeous!"

Julia snarled and narrowed her eyes at Ruben. She went over to the table, picked up the folder and shoved it into his hands. "You're a lying sneaking bastard. I want to know who the hell you are, and what you want with Phillip and me."

Ruben's eyes widened as he opened the folder. Taking the newspaper in his hand, he looked at Julia. "You have every right to be mad at me. But let's go inside to talk about the newspaper in private. Give me ten minutes. If you aren't satisfied with my explanation, I'll leave, and you'll never see me again."

Ruben's answer infuriated her more. "Oh, I bet you have a doozy of an explanation. I can't wait to hear it." Julia spun around and went inside the sunroom, plopping on the sofa with her hands in her lap, back straight, chin lifted.

Ruben sat on the other side of the couch and swallowed hard while Klock settled on the floor. "I'm a Time Tracker. I work for ATTRA. Which means Alien Time Travel and Research Agency. Our galaxy is ruled by the Lord Supreme, who issued an order for me to find you once you traveled through the portal. I know the basics about you and Phillip. I studied you, researched you, and found you. You are of great importance. I traveled to 1950 to give Phillip the blueprints to the Needle-Horn, my time travel craft."

Rubbing his hands on his thighs, Ruben shook his head. "It's the reason you and Andy have Phillip's folders. My ship is designed for one traveler, and it's custom fit to my DNA. You can't time travel without joining the ATTRA program, and if you joined the program, you would never see any of your family again."

He watched Julia's face turn paper white. "Unfortunately, Phillip didn't find a way to alter the craft's design. The Plates of Prophecy state your son will create a time travel machine with no limitations."

Twisting around to face him, Julia opened and closed her mouth, then anxiously asked, "I can't go home? Why am I important? What son?"

With a look of exasperation, he said, "Ten minutes, please, Julia."

She crossed her arms over her stomach. "My heart is nearly bursting through my chest. This is more than I can bear."

Hands extended, Ruben said, "People like you and me are known as Spinners. I was a Spinner too. I fell into a natural time portal in 1918. ATTRA recruited me into the Time Tracker program. The entire ATTRA organization is made up of Spinners, like us. The Lord Supreme assigned me to protect you and your baby."

Julia shook her head and blinked several times. "What baby? And you were a Spinner too?"

"Yes, I was a Spinner." Ruben handed the bag over to Julia, and she opened it, and he said, "The bag is full of pregnancy tests."

Pregnancy tests?

Ruben nodded and placed his arm on the back of the couch. "Another Tracker, her name is Charlie, followed me to the twenty-first century. She waited for me last night and informed me that our time travel Commander, Monica Adams, wants you, but more specifically, she wants your baby. Up until now, scientists and physicists proved time travel happens in the future, and ATTRA can only manipulate a hundred years into the past. Your son's discovery may prove disastrous in the wrong hands."

Julia shook her head and stood up. "My son? You're talking as if you know him already when he hasn't even been born yet." She walked mindlessly about the room then she glared at Ruben. "Phillip's notes mention he doesn't trust ATTRA, and neither did my father. Why should I trust you?"

The *rat-tat-tat* of mini sonic booms echoed in the air as bullets hit the sunroom windows shattering glass, spraying shards across the room. Klock ran to the door barking and snarling. Ruben yelled, "Get down, Julia! Don't move." He reached from the back of his pants and pulled out what appeared to be a small handgun.

The high-pitched sound still reverberated in Julia's ears as Ruben and Klock dashed out the back door. She didn't know what to do. She froze in fear, plastered to the tile floor.

Suddenly, Julia thought about the possibility that she was pregnant and carrying Phillip's son. No longer afraid for herself, she crouched low to the ground and crawled her way into the hallway next to Andy's office and went into the half bath. At least, she had walls between her and the bullets.

The door swung open, and a tall red-haired woman in leather stood with one hand on the doorknob, staring down at her. "Julia, I'm Charlie. I work with Ruben. Come with me into the inner part of the house. Ruben's tracking down the shooters. It won't take long."

Julia didn't budge. "How do I know that you're not the shooter?"

The woman chuckled and said, "Because you'd be dead. Please. I promise I'm not going to hurt you."

A couple of minutes later, Ruben stuck his head in the bathroom and Klock pushed passed Ruben and ran his head into Julia's hand.

Ruben said, "The coast is clear. Two shooters, both are dead. They were Monica's enforcers. It's time to flip scripts, Julia."

Julia trembled at the realization Ruben had just shot two people trying to kill them.

Ruben crouched down and slowly approached Julia. In a low and even tone, he whispered, "I'll lay my life down for you. Do you believe me?" Julia nodded but remained silent. He said, "They were shooting at me, not you. You're no longer safe here."

Julia released Klock. She stood and stepped out of the half bath, looking both ways before she went back into the sunroom. "We have to call the police. Look at the windows."

Ruben reached over and held Julia's hand. "I'm sorry, but we don't have time to call the police. I have Andy's cell number, but I need the Chalet's."

Exhaling deeply, Julia walked into Andy's office and pulled the post-it off the bulletin board. "Here's Andy's numbers. I'll not lie, I'm frightened to death, but I don't want to place Andy in harm's way. Call him and tell him what happened, but can't we find somewhere else to stay?"

"Give me a minute." Ruben took out his device and went outside. A few moments later he walked back in. "Grab some clothes. We're going on a trip."

"I suppose I don't have a choice." Julia left Ruben and Charlie in the sunroom. She should call Sloane but was afraid it might place her in danger too. Opening different closets, Julia found a couple of suitcases. She put in clothes and a few other essentials. Then she ran into Phillip's room, and Andy took the journals with him so, she grabbed her letters. *Oh, Phillip can it be true? Can I be carrying your child?*

Julia strode into the kitchen where Ruben, Charlie, and Klock waited for her. She said, "Give me one of those pregnancy tests. I'm not going anywhere until I find out if I'm carrying Phillip's child."

Charlie handed Julia the brown paper bag. "The instructions are on the back, but it's relatively straightforward. Pee on the stick. You'll know pretty quick if you're pregnant."

Julia went into the main bathroom and pulled the test out of the packaging. She read the instructions while sitting on the pot. Minutes later, the test read positive. Julia's heart began to soar. If she had to live in this century, at least she'd have a part of Phillip with her.

Wiping the tears from her cheeks, Julia felt stronger and had an inner love for the life growing inside her womb. Straightening her back, she went into the bedroom, grabbed the suitcases and walked into the kitchen. Smiling despite the danger, she said, "I'm pregnant. Is it okay to call Sloane?"

Ruben placed his hands on his hips and breathed deeply. "I'm sorry. But Monica may have operatives watching Sloane's residence, and the phones might be bugged. By the way, give me your phone."

Julia placed the suitcases on the floor, reached into her purse and handed him the phone Andy had bought her.

Ruben opened the back and pulled out something, then smashed the thing under his heel. He looked at her and said, "It's a computer card that tracks everything you do. We're going off the grid. I've instructed Andy to drive out of town and do the same with his SIM cards. No devices, no Wi-Fi, no computers, unless Charlie and I inspect them first. We'll issue new cards and phones that aren't traceable." Julia nodded.

Charlie scratched her bicep absentmindedly. "Hey, Ruben, even if she wanted to, Julia can't time travel while she's pregnant. It'll risk their lives. Well, we know Monica's enforcers are watching this place. So, what's the plan?"

Ruben rubbed his jaw and then latched onto Charlie's elbow. "I've made the call for your reassignment. Go to your condo and get your toys. Just give me a quick sec to write down the directions. You can meet us there in a couple of hours."

Charlie shrugged out of his hand. "No need. I went to the condo last night after you went to sleep. I'll follow you and keep an eye out for any tails."

With a sharp nod to Charlie, Ruben turned to Julia. "We're going to Phillip's Chalet in the mountains. After we arrive, Charlie, Klock, and I will make sure the location is secure. I'll throw a Cloak Shield around the Chalet. We'll place Security Breach Beams around the property's perimeters. I also have my monitoring equipment case in the Hummer. It's not foolproof, but it's all I have for now."

Turning back to Charlie, he said, "Keep up, baby sister. I'm going to push the Hummer to the limits. I'll take several back roads before heading to the interstate. If I lose you, just make sure you don't have any tails before you arrive at the Chalet." Charlie gave Ruben a nod of agreement.

Cloak shields? Security Breach Beams? Monitoring equipment? What was Ruben talking about? Julia said, "But, but..."

Ruben shook his head from side to side. "No buts. We'll make other arrangements if the need arises. Okay?" He looked at his watch and said, "Sixteen hundred hours, Charlie." She nodded again.

Julia placed her hand over her stomach, then looked up at Ruben. "I guess I'm as ready as I'll ever be. Ruben, Charlie, thank you for helping me."

Pregnant. Oh God, please protect my child. Please, show me the way.

CHAPTER 11

After securing her seatbelt, Julia twisted around to look at Ruben, and Klock sat between them. She said, "Where are the records of my son's birth? How do you know he's the one that develops the new time travel theory? Maybe it was someone completely different, and your records are wrong?"

Looking in his left rearview mirror, Ruben accelerated the speed and pulled onto the interstate. He gripped the steering wheel as he weaved in and out of traffic. "I need to concentrate on driving."

Steering the Hummer into the slow lane of traffic, Ruben pressed his lips together in apparent frustration. "Julia, I've told you most of what I know, but I'll tell you again. I'm a Tracker for ATTRA. Often my assignments are given with minimal instructions because a Tracker may unknowingly influence a decision that could trigger a paradox. I have basic information about you and Phillip, but Charlie is the one who told me about your son."

"Is she a Tracker too?"

"Yes, up until last night, Charlie worked directly with Monica, but went rogue and broke rank because she hacked into Monica's computer. Charlie found files that implicate Monica in high treason. Monica also issued an order to kill me so that she can capture you."

Resting his arm on the console, Ruben said, "I don't know the how or when of your son's discovery; only that Monica wants his machine. Charlie thinks if Monica has your son, she'll control her destiny. Only certain individuals have access to the Plates of Prophecy. General Agriaous is one of those people, and he's partnered with Monica." He gave her a one-shoulder shrug. "Prophecy is merely a prediction; it's not infallible."

Julia looked out the window, nervously biting her fingernails. They were climbing elevation, and her ears started popping. "Who is the Lord Supreme? Is he God?"

Ruben chuckled. "That is a fifty-billion-dollar question. I've met him. He looks like a person, but he's immortal. I suppose he's God in that respect. He creates and his son, Prince Aelius, created everything in our Galaxy. Julia, I won't allow Monica to hurt you or the baby. That's my job."

Julia's voice quivered, and with broken words, she said, "So you can't take me home in your time machine? My place is with Phillip. I miss my mom, and I don't like seeing my baby sister using a walker. I don't belong here."

Ruben shut his eyes for a moment, then stared into Julia's dark green eyes. "The Needle-Horn is calibrated for one person, me, and my genome is tied into the mainframe's control system because of matter changing during time travel. Most accidental Spinners don't survive the time portals. Your son is supposed to change that."

"Well, I guess my chances to go home are slim if I have to wait for my son to develop a time machine."

Ruben drew in a ragged breath and exhaled before running his fingers through his hair. "You're living in an alternate reality in a parallel universe. Every decision you make changes future events in your life."

"Alternate realities and parallel universes, ugh. I'm getting a splitting headache." She reached down into her purse and pulled out a bottle of aspirin.

Ruben took the bottle from her and placed it inside the console. "Aspirin isn't good for the baby."

"Okay, okay."

* * *

Surrounded by tall cedar trees and firs, Phillip's timber-framed Chalet nestled on the side of a mountain adjacent to the Pisgah National Forest. The ridge ran north and south and offered incredible views from nearly every angle.

Andy gripped the ornate wooden railing of the large covered front porch framed in red cedar with wide planked floors. Rustic wood-hewn furniture sat on braided rugs with red and white striped cushions. He'd been pacing the floors since Ruben's call.

Denise panicked, packed her things, and before peeling out of the driveway, she said, "I like you, Andy, and we have lots of fun together. But your friends are sketchy at best, and I'm not ready to dive into the skeletons of our closets. Call me when you work things out, and we'll see whether to revisit this relationship."

An hour later, Andy spotted Ruben's Hummer coming up the driveway. Ruben and Julia exited the vehicle, then Klock burst through the open door in midair and ran off into the woods.

Andy yelled out, "I've been worried sick about y'all. I did as you requested and removed all the SIM cards from my devices and disconnected the wireless server. But Denise wouldn't relinquish her phone. She asked me if I was involved in something illegal, for chrissakes. So, she left. I guess I lost another one." Andy jogged down the steps and helped Ruben with their suitcases, eyeing the weapons in the back of the Hummer. *Hmm, that isn't a good sign.*

Andy nudged against Julia's arm. "Are you okay? I shouldn't have left you."

Julia started to reply when Ruben placed a hand on Andy's right shoulder. "Charlie's pulling in behind us. Take Julia inside while we secure the property."

With an arched brow, Andy said, "Who is Charlie?" Charlie pulled into the driveway and got out of the car. Andy's stomach did a cartwheel. She was the most gorgeous creature he'd ever seen.

She waved and said, "Hi, Andy. I'm Charlie."

Ruben frowned and glared at Andy. "Look, it may take a while to put safeguards in place. Maybe you and Julia could prepare some food?"

Andy nodded. "I have steaks marinating and baked potatoes in the oven unless, of course, if anyone has specific dietary restrictions." He looked at Julia and said, "I'm placing you in the master bedroom on the main floor. It used to be Phillip's room." He turned back to Charlie. "I'll put you in the room across from mine on the second floor."

Tilting her head to the side, Charlie chuckled and replied, "Sure thing, hot stuff."

Ruben grumbled, "We have a job to do, Charlie. Pay attention, please."

Andy and Julia walked up the steps and into the main floor of the house. Sunshine streamed generously through all the windows and glass doors.

Julia's mouth opened as she took in the interiors. "Andy, this place is great." She traced her fingers along the soft caramel leather couch sitting on a ten-by-ten colorful Oriental rug. A small fire blazed in the large stone fireplace.

"It's Phillip's place. I never knew it existed until meeting with the lawyer after his death. He left a note, detailing the reasons he kept the place to himself. Phillip wrote that he built the place for you. He felt close to you here."

Julia's brows creased as she turned to Andy. "Me?"

He shrugged. "Yeah, weird, huh?"

Holding the suitcases, Andy gestured with his head toward the hallway. "Come on, let's put your stuff in the master bedroom."

He led them down the hallway to the last door on the left. The cozy room was decorated in browns and russet colors and had an awe-inspiring view of the mountains, a natural pine king-size bed with matching side tables, and a dresser.

Julia bypassed the bed and walked straight to an oil painting that looked to be about eighteen by thirty-six inches. Her breath caught. "It's me at the Dyer's farm." The painting had Julia lying on Phillip's old quilt looking up at the stars in the middle of the pasture. She traced her fingers over the painting and turned to Andy. With tears threatening to spill, Julia blinked them away and said, "It's the night Phillip ask me to marry him."

Andy placed the suitcase on top of the bed and unlocked the latches. "I wondered who you were the first time I saw the painting."

Julia placed her hand on Andy's forearm. "Please sit down, Andy. I must tell you something. Ruben asked me not to, but I think you have a right to know regardless of the consequences."

Andy sat on the bed, placing his hands on his knees. "Oh, man, you look fit to be tied."

Julia sat down beside him and reached for his hands. She took a deep breath, looked straight into his eyes, and said, "I'm pregnant. I'm going to have Phillip's son."

Andy dipped his chin into his neck and leaned away from Julia. "You what? How do you know it's a son?"

Ruben stuck his head in the bedroom and narrowed his eyes at Julia. "You just couldn't help yourself, could you? Come on out into the den, and I'll explain."

Andy and Julia went into the main room with Ruben. "Charlie's finishing up the Security Breach Beams, and Klock's running the property perimeters for threats. I placed what we call a Cloak Shield around the house from ATTRA's bag of tricks. It'll be almost impossible for Monica to find the place."

Andy paced about the floor. "Are you sure? Most of the locals know me, and they knew Phillip too. He built the Chalet during the sixties."

Ruben sat on a stool and swiveled back and forth while his right arm rested on the bar counter. "Monica isn't going to blow her cover by approaching the locals. We have eight months, seven days, six hours and oh, five minutes or so to keep the shield in place."

Andy's pulse thrummed so fast he began to feel lightheaded. "What are you keeping from me?"

Ruben proceeded to tell Andy about his mission regarding Phillip and Julia, detailing the information about the time machine, and Monica's plot to overthrow the Empyreal Palace.

Charlie walked in with Klock as Ruben wrapped his explanation. Klock trotted over to the fireplace and made three circles before crashing on the rug.

Charlie leaned on the bar counter next to Ruben. "The rest of the story, about Julia having a son, came from me. I worked directly under Monica's authority until last night. She assigned me to kill Ruben and capture Julia."

Andy sat in a love seat opposite of Julia. His eyes darted to each of them while his right knee bounced up and down nervously. "May I address the elephant in the room?"

Everyone turned to Andy, and he extended his finger toward Julia. "What if I'm Julia's grandson? What if Monica is looking for me? My father sold insurance, for crying out loud. He and my mother died in a small airplane crash returning from a convention in the Caymans when I was a baby."

Ruben placed his hand on Charlie's forearm. "Go and look in the back of the Hummer and bring in my medical bag." He turned back to Andy. "I have a DNA kit in my vehicle. If you're Julia's grandson, then we're treading in some perilous paradoxical territory."

Julia went over to Andy, scrutinizing his face. "You know, I never thought you looked a thing like Amelia."

Charlie brought in the bag and said, "Where's the nearest bathroom with the largest counter?"

"In the master bedroom, down the hall on the left, first door on the left," replied Andy.

"Well, there's no time like the present. Julia, Andy, after you."

Inside the master bathroom, Charlie began to lay out the instruments from the kit along with the needles to draw blood. "Who's first?"

Julia said, "Me." She pushed up the three-quarter-length sleeve of her sweater and laid her arm on the bathroom counter.

Wearing vinyl gloves, Charlie took a rubber strap and tied it at Julia's bicep. "Give me a couple of fist pumps so I can find which of your veins is best." Julia did as Charlie instructed, and minutes later, her blood was in a vial for testing.

Charlie turned to Andy and smiled. "It's your turn, Andrew."

Andy stepped over to the counter and rolled up his sleeve. Charlie repeated the procedure. While she took his blood, Andy inhaled Charlie's sweet scent of citrus mixed with jasmine. He stared into Charlie's crystal blue eyes, and then his gaze dropped to her full pink lips, and a surprising knot of heat tightened his groin.

Charlie finished by placing a cotton ball over the puncture and looked up into Andy's eyes. "Press hard for a minute or two. I should have the results soon. Did you mention steaks? I haven't eaten in nearly twenty-four hours."

Andy nodded and asked, "Rare, medium rare, or well-done?"

"Not rare. Anything is better than what's served on the moon. Now, scoot."

Julia and Andy looked at each other and mouthed, "The moon?" then stepped out of the bathroom and made their way back to the kitchen.

Julia giggled. "Andy, I believe you're a little sweet on Charlie."

"For space sakes." Ruben stalked into the kitchen and began opening and closing cabinet doors. "Hey, Andy, where are the plates?"

Julia looked at Andy and silently mouthed, "Ah, I think Ruben's sweet on Charlie too."

Steaks warmed on the stove's griddle, baked potatoes roasted in the oven, and Julia made a tossed salad with Caesar dressing, chopped tomatoes, onion, peppers with bacon bits, and anchovies.

Andy looked over Julia's shoulder and wrinkled his nose. "Anchovies?"

Julia moved around Andy and placed the huge salad bowl with the condiments on the counter. "I know, right? I guess I have my first food craving."

Ruben pierced the steaks with a fork and placed them on a platter. "As soon as Charlie comes out, we'll eat."

Minutes later, Charlie stepped into the kitchen and said, "Well, I finished. Yum, the steaks smell fantastic. My mouth's watering and my belly's growling."

Andy stepped over to Charlie and placed his hands on her shoulders. "So, Charlie, don't keep us hanging here. What did you find out?"

"Congratulations, it's a boy. Andy meet your grandmother, Julia Boatwright." Charlie pulled away and stepped over to the counter and popped a cherry tomato in her mouth.

Julia went to her knees, but Ruben grabbed her before she hit the floor. He said, "It's okay. Everything is going to be fine."

"My head's spinning. I think I'm going to be sick. Help me to the bathroom." Ruben placed her arm around his shoulder, and his arm circled her waist as they made their way to the bathroom. He sat Julia in the little chair next to the Jacuzzi tub, but she jumped up, pulled up the toilet seat, and puked.

Andy couldn't process the information fast enough. Julia was his freaking grandmother. He stepped into the bathroom just as Ruben ran cold water into a washcloth, squeezed out the excess, and placed it on the back of Julia's neck.

A shaken Julia stared at him. "You look so much like Phillip."

"You want something to drink? Anything?"

"How is it possible that you're my grandson? How did Amelia come into the picture? I don't understand."

Ruben stood just inside the bathroom entrance. "I'm going to visit the Lord Supreme. We need reinforcements. Freaking A, we have three generations to protect."

Julia closed her eyes and sighed. "I must've died. That can be the only explanation."

Charlie walked over and sat on the bathroom countertop. "Not the only explanation. You're living in an alternate reality within a parallel universe. Ruben's the smartest Tracker I know. He'll find the answers for you and Andy."

Julia swayed a bit when she stood, but Andy held onto her. "I can't think about it right now. All I can think about is my baby." She touched her stomach and glanced at Andy. "Your father," she added and faltered again. "I-I need to eat some crackers to settle my stomach. There's no way I can have morning sickness this soon. I think it's my nerves. Sorry, but I don't think I can eat steak." She pushed away and walked slowly back to the kitchen.

They ate in silence. Everyone seemed too afraid to talk about the coming events with the arrival of Julia's child. Halfway through dinner, Julia excused herself early and went to bed.

Cleaning up after dinner, Andy looked at Ruben and Charlie and said, "I think I'm the one who develops the time travel formula."

CHAPTER 12

*R*uben walked to the rail of the front porch and tilted his head to the sky. The Milky Way seemed so close to the mountains, and a ring of mist floated around the higher elevations. The captivating stars and constellations were what Ruben missed most about Lunar City. Leaning against the railing, he looked at Andy and Charlie. "I'll leave for the Empyreal Palace in the morning. I have to find out what happens to Julia."

Andy stepped over to the railing. "Whoa, brother. You need to give me a day or two to tie up loose ends with my house and the university. I made a phone call from the local store to a friend of mine that works for the Sheriff's Department. Several neighbors heard the gunshots. He's checked on the house and boarded the windows for me, but I'm stopping by the station to fill out paperwork. I'll put in for a leave with BFU. Then I'll stay with Julia until she gives birth to my father. That's still kinda freaking me out."

Ruben looked at Charlie, then turned to Andy. "Take Charlie with you. Monica probably has your house staked out. Charlie is an excellent Tracker— and lethal. That's why Monica asked Charlie to kill me."

Charlie leaned forward and placed her hands on her thighs. "Andy, why do you think you're the one that develops the theory?"

Andy sat in the rocking chair while Ruben joined Charlie on the loveseat.

Andy said, "Julia and I went through Phillip's journals. One of the journals has a blueprint of a ship with several formulas that I started sequencing into my laptop. Most of the equations didn't work out, but one of the methods has promise. I labeled it, *Spinning Time*."

Andy rocked back and forth with a steady rhythm. "To my knowledge, my father never worked on any time travel projects, but Phillip spent his life trying to find a way to Julia. I have every theory he worked on stored on my laptop. I scanned most of the relative data including the sketches of the spaceship from Phillip's journals."

Ruben leaned in and said, "Do you have any copies at home or the university?"

"I brought the only copies with me, and they're in Phillip's study upstairs."

Charlie exhaled and said, "Have you said anything to anyone about the project?"

Andy turned to Charlie and glared. "I'm not an idiot. I haven't talked to anyone about Julia or the journals except the two of you."

Ruben draped his left arm on the back of the loveseat. "The ship in Phillip's journal is my Needle-Horn. The Plates of Prophecy state you find a way to travel without sequencing DNA, and it allows for transport of more than one person. The new ship's capacity of time travel holds no bounds."

Turning to Andy, Charlie said, "My ship, The Bus, is identical to Ruben's so, you have two different ships available to work your theories."

"The Bus?" Andy chuckled.

"Columbus, get it? The greatest navigator of all time."

"Good one, Charlie."

Placing his hand over his mouth, Ruben seemed buried in thought. "Go back to Burkett Falls tonight. First thing in the morning, secure the house, then put in for leave with BFU. I had already requested leave last week. I'll put out feelers for our replacements. Leave no forwarding address, no mobiles, and no emails, nothing that can be tracked by the dark net. I'll contact my liaison and send someone I trust to protect Sloane."

Andy offered Charlie his hand and said, "Let's go. You gotta drive because my date left me stranded."

Charlie took Andy's hand and stood. "Hey, give me ten minutes to change clothes. Then, we'll roll."

Ruben first clasped Andy's shoulder, then Charlie's. "Drive to Mount Rieve College and park Charlie's car in one of the busiest parking lots. Then borrow one. You can report it later."

Ruben stepped away and leaned against the porch rail crossing his arms over his chest. "I brought in several untraceable devices you can use to make calls or if you need to log onto the internet. Here's my digits, nine–two-six, three-seven-one, six-two-one-zero. But call only if you're in dire straits. No one has my contact information except the Lord Supreme and Prince Aelius. When you get back to the Chalet, I'll travel to the Empyreal Palace."

Thirty minutes later, Ruben watched Andy and Charlie drive away, then went back inside to check on Julia. She slept in the master bedroom curled in a fetal position with her arms around a pillow.

In the main room, Ruben slipped off his boots and pulled the quilt off the back of the couch. Klock jumped into his arms and nestled his chin on Ruben's chest. "You're a good dog." Ruben closed his eyes as his thoughts ran the gamut of disaster. As he drifted off into a restless sleep, the idea that Julia would die on his watch was unbearable.

* * *

"WAKE UP, JULIA."

Julia stretched and yawned. Her voice drowsy with sleep, she asked, "What time is it?"

His deep laughter struck a familiar chord and Julia bolted upright in the bed. Rubbing the heel of her hands into her eyes, she blinked unbelievingly. "Are you a dream? Is this a dream? Or are you here with me, Phillip?"

Phillip reached for Julia's hand and pulled her from the bed. He placed his arm around her waist and whispered into her ear, "If this is a dream then I pray that you never wake up." He cradled her face in his hands, leaned in, and softly brushed his lips across her mouth. "You taste good. So perfect. So beautiful, you're just as I remembered."

Julia sighed and slipped her arms around Phillip's neck. "I've missed you so much."

Phillip twirled her in a circle before placing her feet back on the floor. "Come with me."

Julia ran with Phillip up the winding staircase to the third-floor landing of the Chalet. He pushed the double glass doors open, and she followed him onto a wooden deck with sweeping views of the mountains. "I built this Chalet for you. Every room, every cabinet, every stick of furniture placed in the Chalet is for you, my darling."

Julia leaned against Phillip's shoulder and looked up into his beautiful eyes, and before she could utter a word, he kissed her. The energy between the lovers grew, building with a whoosh of release. She had longed for his sweet kiss since the day she left.

Breaking slightly away, Phillip stared down at her with a lazy grin. "I quit teaching and began to write. At first, the writing was therapeutic. But then it became the only way for me to be near you, alone and away from the world. I began to research dreams because I kept having dreams of you and I found articles on lucid dreams." He grinned broadly and rubbed his hands together. "Oh, and I built you a room with a recording studio, and you're going to love it."

Phillip held her hand as they rushed down the stairs to the second-floor landing. It seemed like ages ago since Julia had been with Phillip. But in an instant, the time melted away, and it was like she had never left him.

Swiftly walking down, a narrow hallway and around a corner nook, Phillip pushed open a door. "Your very own soundproof recording studio. With a wireless server, you can broadcast to anyone, anywhere in the world. I didn't forget. You dreamed of having your own radio show."

Julia circled her arms around Phillip's waist, and tears freely flowed down her cheeks. "It's wonderful, Phillip. I can't believe it."

Phillip kissed Julia's forehead and brushed the tears away with the back of his hand. "Believe it, love. Let's step outside on the front porch. The views are just as spectacular as the one from the top floor."

Outside, Julia said, "I love it here. I never want this to end. I never want you and me to end."

Phillip tucked a wispy strand of Julia's hair behind her ear. "I like the short hair, but I'm not quite sure about the black. I want my platinum blonde back."

She giggled. "If you look at the roots, you'll see the blonde growing. I promise not to color it again. I did it because Andy suggested it."

"He's a good boy, isn't he?"

Julia nuzzled her face into his neck. Looking up into Phillip's eyes, she said, "He's the best. He reminds me so much of you."

Phillip caressed her cheek with his hand. "We don't have to leave here. When you dream, think of me, and we'll be together. Do you believe me? This is real, Julia. I found a way for us to be together. I found a way to travel through time beyond life or death using lucid dreams. Physical laws don't apply here."

She reached up and kissed him softly on the lips. "I hope this dream lasts forever. Oh, Phillip, I'm pregnant. I'm going to have your son."

Tears filled Phillip's eyes, he dropped to his knees and placed his cheek next to Julia's abdomen as he slipped his arm around her waist. "You've made me the happiest man in the world, Julia. I love you."

* * *

"Julia, what are you doing on the porch in the middle of the night?" Ruben asked.

Ruben gently placed his hand on Julia's shoulder, and she swept her arms up and around his neck, kissing him with so much passion and desire his mind went blank.

D. F. JONES

Nudging her face into the crook of his neck, she whispered, "I love you, Phillip. I love you so much it hurts."

Ruben swallowed hard, holding her tightly in his arms. His heart broke for Julia. She was sleepwalking. Scooping Julia into his arms, Ruben kicked the door ajar, stepping inside.

He laid her on the bed, tucking the covers around Julia. He leaned down and kissed her forehead.

Phillip Clayborn was a damn lucky man.

* * *

CHARLIE DROVE the back roads to Mount Rieve College while Andy punched in his playlist and clicked until he found Rufus Wainwright's version of *Across the Universe*. *Damn, I can't get her off my mind.* Andy hoped she couldn't read his thoughts.

Charlie parked the Dodge Charger SRT Hellcat in a nearly full parking lot.

The car matched her personality—sexy, sleek, and needed to be driven fast. Andy shook his head with a double take when Charlie cut her big baby blues at him. He had tried pushing the sexy images out of his mind so she wouldn't pick up on his vibe. He swallowed hard again.

She turned to Andy and said, "We have to steal a car."

Stealing a car? Crap. He was turning into a criminal.

"Andy, I like you. I do. But you need to stop looking at me with those incredible bedroom eyes."

"I'll try, but you're oh so sexy, and I'm so into you." Andy returned her smoldering gaze, and she never looked away.

Placing her hand on his forearm sent desire pooling in the pit of his stomach. She looked at his lips. Smiling, she said, "Pretty boy, it's been a long time since I've had sex. I'm afraid that I'd hurt you."

Andy smirked. "I think I could handle some hurt."

Charlie released her hand and threw her head back in laughter. "You're funny. But we have a job to do."

Andy brushed away the lock of hair that fell into his eyes. With a raised brow, he teased, "Okay, Ms. Charlie. But when we get to my house, I make no promises."

They exited the car, and Charlie opened the trunk and pulled out a small case and a license plate. She scanned the parking lot and spotted a royal blue Ford Shelby GT350. In no time, smoke rose as Charlie left blisters on the asphalt. The look of unadulterated joy spread across her face as the car jolted from zero to sixty in about three and a half seconds. Hugging the curves spiked his adrenaline. God, he loved this woman.

Charlie backed off the gas once she made Sugar Hill Road.

He turned to Charlie and said, "How did you become a Tracker?"

One hand rested on the steering wheel, and her forearm leaned on the console. She briefly turned to him and then back to the road. "I went to Woodstock in '69 with a group from Berkeley. I was the consummate hippie back in those days. I studied hard, but on my downtime, I partied hard. It was the coolest scene. Everyone was stoned, but the festival was about peace, love, sex, and rock and roll. Some dude gave me a hit of acid, and I tripped. I ended up in 1989, and Ruben found me."

Shaking her head, Charlie exhaled deeply. "I fell for Ruben in a big way. I would've done anything he asked me back then and guess I still would. But Ruben isn't into me. Oh, so that you know, ATTRA injects their citizens with a serum that makes physical aging stop. We can die, but we don't age."

Twenty minutes later, Charlie turned left onto Country Park Lane. She took another left onto Rucker Road and parked. "I need to case your place before I pull into the garage. Don't move."

Charlie straightened her spine and reached into her backpack pulling out several weapons, placing one in her hand, one in her boot, and another one in the back of her pants. "Breathe, Andy. I'll be back soon." Charlie stealthily disappeared into the inky night.

Andy was physically fit. Lean, muscular from strength training, and he ran five miles every other day. But he'd never been in a fight in his life. He kept glancing at the car clock. Time seemed to pass interminably slow. After an hour, his heart began to pound, his pulse raced, and his pits started sweating. *Where in the hell is Charlie?*

Andy opened the door and slid out of the car seat, when someone grabbed him from behind, placing him in a choke until his knees buckled.

Charlie whispered, "I told you to stay put, idiot." He felt her warm breath against his cheeks. "I've checked inside and out, but that doesn't mean we're in the clear. Go on and pull into the garage. I'll backtrack two blocks and enter from the patio. Okay?"

Andy tilted his head back. "I will if you let me go. Damn, woman, you're strong. You scared the shit out of me." Shaking like a leaf, Andy started the car and drove down Country Park Lane, pulled into his driveway, and parked in the garage. He grabbed his duffel bag and went inside.

Terry, his friend at the Sheriff's Department, had boarded up the shot-out windows in the sunroom and cleaned up the mess. Andy stepped into the kitchen and pulled out a Samuel Adams, opened it, and drained the bottle. His nerves settled down some, and he took another deep breath.

The doorbell rang.

"What the hell?" Andy thought Charlie was supposed to be invisible. He walked through the house and flung the front door open. He stared in shock. "Laney? What are you doing here? It's late. What's wrong with you?" Laney, his ex-fiancée, had broken his heart into a million pieces six months ago, but damn she still looked good.

Laney stood on the front porch in a skimpy outfit, her long blonde hair falling over her shoulders, and biting her bottom lip. "I'm sorry, Andy. Is it a bad time?"

Bad time? Hell yeah, in more ways than one. "Yeah, it's a bad time. What do you want?"

Laney pushed by him, and he grabbed her upper arm. "I don't believe I invited you into my house."

Tears welled in her eyes, and her lips quivered. "I need you, Andy." She fell into his arms, and he looked around for Charlie.

"I'll give you five minutes then you're outta here. Understood?"

Laney nodded and went into the kitchen. "Are you alone? Is someone here?"

Andy glared at Laney and placed his hands on his hips. "You lost that privilege when you had sex with one of my students in my laundry room. You told me you loved me. You were my fiancée, for crying out loud, and you brought a student into my house and fucked him. Do you know how messed up you are?"

Laney ran her fingers up his chest. "I was scared, and I made bad decisions, but that doesn't mean that I didn't love you. So, I hear some woman has been living with you. What's her name? Do you love her?" He knocked her hand away from his face.

"Last time, Laney. What do you want?" Andy stepped away from her and leaned against the kitchen counter, his arms crossed over his chest.

"I want you back. I miss you, and I need you, Andy." She leaned toward his chest, and he threw his hands up.

Andy grabbed Laney by the elbow and escorted her to the front door. "You should've thought about that before you brought another man into my home. I'm so over you. I don't want you. Don't ever come back here again."

"Please, Andy. Let me explain," she begged.

"Not on your life. Knock on someone else's door with your bullshit. I've already got a plate full of it here." He slammed the door on Laney and pressed his back against the frame.

Charlie must've seen Laney. Where did she go? Suddenly, exhausted from the last twenty-four hours, Andy walked back to his bedroom and flopped on the bed. He was asleep in seconds.

* * *

CHARLIE STOOD in the shadows watching Monica talk with Andy. She nearly drew her weapon, but Andy recognized Monica. *What the hell?* She crept along the landscape and through the bushes to peek inside the kitchen window. Andy yelled at Monica, and she was acting like some besotted teenager.

Pulse racing, Charlie watched and waited until Andy threw Monica out the front door. Then she followed Monica across the street. Out of earshot, Charlie couldn't tell who Monica called, but it wasn't good if Monica knew Andy.

Charlie waited outside for another hour before she felt comfortable enough to go inside. She slipped through the patio and used the house key Andy had given her. The quiet was deafening. She tip-toed down the hallway, peeking into each room until she saw Andy sprawled across a king-sized bed.

It was against ATTRA protocols, but Charlie climbed on top of Andy. Her hands ran up his chest, and suddenly he grabbed her wrists and flipped her on her back. She chuckled and said, "It's Charlie."

Andy's eyes seem to adjust, and he let out a breath. He released her hands. "Dammit, Charlie. My ex showed up at the front door. I thought the deranged bitch broke in." He leaned against the headboard.

Charlie straddled him again and brushed the hair away from his face. "We have a problem, Houston."

Andy grabbed her hips and scooted her closer. "What's that?"

"Your ex is my ex-boss."

Andy flung Charlie off him and stood. "What? What are you saying? Laney's your boss? Like, who exactly?"

"Laney, huh?" Charlie backed against the headboard and drew her right knee to her chest. "That woman, my dear, is none other than Commander Monica Adams. How long have you known her?"

Andy plopped onto the bed, and his face fell into his hands. He rubbed his face vigorously before he collapsed on his back and turned to Charlie. "This is craziness. I met her last year at a faculty party. We dated for six months, and I fell in love with her. I asked Laney to marry me. She was sweet yet strong, sad but happy. Then one day, I came home early from school and caught her screwing some dude in my laundry room. I was livid and broke our engagement. She left, and I never heard from her again until tonight."

Charlie crawled over to him and draped her arm across his chest, resting her head on his shoulder. "Boy, is she one cold-hearted, calculating bitch. She wants Julia. Monica also knows you're Phillip's grandson. But she doesn't know that you're Julia's grandson or that you're the one with the time machine formula. Or you'd be living in Lunar City with Monica's thumb stuck up your ass."

"Ew, that's a gruesome image."

Twisting his hair into her fingers, Charlie said, "After we close the house, and you place your leave at the university, we need to make you disappear with no trace. Or she'll find all of us. While you're at the university, I'll start eliminating any paper trails. By the time I'm through with you, it'll be like you were never born."

Andy grabbed her by the nape of her neck and kissed her hard. He chuckled. "But first, I need you to hurt me."

Charlie straddled him. "Gladly."

With a husky and slightly breathless voice, Andy said, "Hug me, kiss me, love me all night long." Threading his fingers through Charlie's short red hair, Andy pulled her down, kissing her and delving his tongue into her warm hot mouth. He teased and tugged at her full pink pouty lips.

Escalating sexual tension unleashed as Charlie tore at his clothes. He yanked down her tight ass pants, and then she straddled him again.

Wild and fierce, Charlie grabbed his hands and pushed them over his head. She licked his lips with slow and sensual strokes making his adrenaline kick in, and lightning unfurled in his belly. Charlie's sweet hotness pressed against the length of him.

She pulled her black spandex top over her head and revealed she wore no bra. Her perfect peach-size breasts were firm and ripe for the sucking. He reached up to place an elongated nipple in his mouth, and she shoved him back on the bed, shaking her head no.

"I'm going to take you hard and fast. Then I'm going to love you painstakingly slow and deliberate until there's nothing left of you."

Moaning, he said, "Use me up, baby."

"Oh, I'm going to, baby."

Charlie made good on her word. Suddenly, they were all over the bed. He knocked off a lamp, and it broke against the wall. He laughed and rolled her onto her back before she took control of him again.

Switching multiple positions as Charlie played Kama Sutra cards, in the bed, the chair, and against the wall until they collapsed onto the floor exhausted, breathless, and sweating.

Charlie slipped back on top of Andy and leaned next to his ear. She whispered, "Don't get comfortable." Andy sighed and moaned as Charlie went into the bathroom and the silhouette of her perfect naked body reflected in the light.

He threw his forearm over his head. Laney, or well, Monica had shredded him emotionally. But Charlie would destroy the remnants of his remaining manhood. *Why am I into dominant women?*

Images of sweet Denise crossed his mind. They were so compatible in many ways. But the magnitude of his sexual experience with Charlie went off the Richter scale. He was glad Denise was out of town for another month. She never made demands of him, and by the time she came around, maybe Charlie would be gone.

He sucked in a breath as Charlie strode back into the bedroom. She exuded confidence and raw sex appeal. With a grin, Andy said, "Hey, I think I'm crazy about you."

Reaching down for his hand, Charlie pulled Andy to his feet. With a wry smile, she said, "Yeah, well, just don't fall in love with me. I'm going, to be honest with you, Andy. I'm in love with Ruben and always have been. He just doesn't romantically see me. If you understand that, we'll do it again."

She stepped slightly back, and Andy licked his lips. "Oh, yeah, I get it, baby. You bet your sweet ass we're doing it again, and you can use me anytime you want to make Ruben jealous."

Leaning down, Charlie placed feather-light kisses across his chest, then sucked his nipples hard while trailing her fingers down his biceps. Andy moaned, "Oh baby, yeah, you can use me anytime you want."

Charlie moved around to his back and trailed her tongue down his spine to his buttocks, then moved back to the front and dropped to her knees.

No doubt, Charlie would leave him for Ruben.

No doubt, she'd leave him scarred for life.

* * *

Monica stared out of Andy's neighbor's master bedroom window with her arms tight around her chest. Her fingernails bit into her skin. Her team set up residence watching and waiting for Andy to return home after the debacle of losing Azaria and Kalsan. What a freaking mess. Julia had been alone all night and her team, living next door, had been oblivious. They blamed it on the damn dog, Klock.

To her surprise, Charlie returned with Andy and cased the place, which meant she'd turned traitor and was working for Ruben. The shadows cast on Andy's bedroom window left nothing to the imagination and revealed that Charlie was screwing Andy too.

Zane walked into the room without turning on the lights. "Why are you torturing yourself? Just say the word, and I'll exterminate the bugs."

Turning, Monica placed a hand on Zane's shoulder. "Not too fast, Zane. Let's meet with the others." The plush baby blue carpet cushioned the soles of her tired feet as she walked into the small dining room. Stormy and Johnnie stood at the antique walnut table peering at a map of the Black Mountains.

Monica said, "By god, in the morning, we're going to follow them. Charlie is slippery as a snake, so she'll try to lose us. They'll lead us to wherever Ruben has Julia in hiding."

Standing between Johnnie and Stormy, Monica pointed at their location on the map. "I'd use the drones again, but that'd trigger satellites. We're going old school on this surveillance operation. I've given Zane untraceable devices we'll use while we track. He's also placing a GPS tracking device on the vehicle once the lovers go to sleep."

Monica dragged her fingers through her long blonde hair. "I want Julia's location by the end of tomorrow. Then Zane and I will head back to Lunar City. Johnnie and Stormy will set up residence in whatever town they're hiding in."

Stormy's black eyes narrowed, and her thin lips curled around her teeth. "Twelve-hour shifts until Ms. Boatwright delivers? That's a long eight months. What's in it for me?"

Raising a brow, Monica laughed sarcastically. "For one thing, you get to stay alive, Stormy." She giggled and shrugged. "I'm only kidding. What do you want? How may I be of service to you?" Monica kept Stormy as an enforcer because of her killer instincts, but she had the mentality of an insane person. That made Stormy a high-risk property. Monica wouldn't think twice about killing Stormy if she got out of hand.

Stormy jutted her chin and squared her shoulders. "I want Ruben's job when he's assassinated. I want his digs too."

Zane raised his voice in a high-pitched shrill, "Hey, that's my job, bitch. My digs."

Monica ran her hands down Johnnie's muscled biceps. She shook her head and shouted, "Finish the damn job. Then we'll see whose left standing before I issue new room assignments." She grabbed Johnnie's big hand and said, "I need you to rub my shoulders. I'm getting a headache."

"Sure thing, Boss." Johnnie was the jock type, all brawn with little brains, but he was one hell of a lover and followed her directions without falter. He'd been the reason that Andy broke their engagement. Too bad. Monica would've already had the girl if it hadn't been for the big brute.

Johnnie scooped Monica up in his arms, and she giggled. Draping an arm around his thick neck, she said to the others, "Get some rest. Tomorrow is going to be a long day."

Stormy yelled out, "What if the baby boy isn't the one we seek?"

Glancing back, Monica glared at Stormy and said, "Oh, he's the one, and Stormy, I like your assertiveness, but the next time you talk back to me, I'll kill you. Understood?"

Stormy lifted her chin and replied, "Understood."

Zane laughed and pushed Stormy, which led to a scuffle as Monica left the room.

The next eight months were going to be long. Monica didn't want to trigger suspicions too soon. The Lord Supreme knew of her ambitions. He liked that about Monica, but she doubted he'd like her plotting to take over the Empyreal Palace.

CHAPTER 13

Julia rolled over in bed. She lay on her back looking up at the ceiling. Streams of sunlight poured through the windows. Smiling, she wondered if Phillip was real. Was it all a dream? She sat up and swung her bare legs over the edge of the bed and locked eyes with Ruben. The desire in his eyes struck deep, and she glanced away. "Did you sleep in here last night?" The thought of him watching her sleep made her cheeks darken in color.

"No. I was sleeping on the couch when I heard the front door open. You were sleepwalking last night."

Placing her hands on her knees, she said, "I never sleepwalk. You're joking, right?"

"Nope, I found you on the front porch."

Abruptly, she stood. "Oh, Ruben, I dreamed about Phillip. It was so real. He was here in this house and took me for a tour. I have to see if it's real." She took off running, taking the stairs two at a time until she reached the door on the second floor.

On the verge of hyperventilating, Julia opened the door, and there it was—the recording studio. "Ruben, it's here." She yelled, but Ruben stood behind her. "Phillip built this studio for me."

Ruben leaned against the door frame and chuckled. "What else did Phillip say?"

Julia placed her hand on the back of the chair to help her balance. She felt dizzy, and Ruben swooped in and picked her up before she hit the floor.

Ruben said, "Are you okay?"

"Just a little dizzy."

Ruben carried her into one of the bedrooms on the second floor and sat her down on the bed. He pulled a straight-back chair close to the bed and sat down. "Do you want a glass of water?"

"No. I just need to sit for a second."

"So, tell me about your dream."

Julia went through the dream step by step. "I didn't know about the recording studio. We were on the front porch. I told him about the baby."

"Do you feel like walking downstairs? I'll make breakfast, and we'll talk about your dream. You hungry?"

Julia sighed, and said, "I'm starving."

He chuckled. "Me too. Craving anything special?"

"Hmm. Sausage and gravy and chocolate milk."

* * *

RUBEN AND JULIA walked down the stairs, and she asked, "Have you heard of lucid dreams? Phillip said that we were in a lucid dream where physical laws didn't apply."

"I have heard of lucid dreams. From what I recall, the person in the dream is aware they're dreaming, and Phillip is correct in that physical laws don't apply. The person in the dream remembers every detail after waking."

Julia blinked several times. "I had all of those. So, maybe our souls reunited on another plane. If I can live in an alternate reality within a parallel universe, then why shouldn't I be able to exist on an astral plane?"

Dropping his head, Ruben rubbed his face and then looked up.

"This is way above my paygrade. Who am I to say it didn't happen? I have to confess something."

Tilting her head, Julia said, "What?"

"When I found you on the porch you thought I was Phillip. You kissed me. Sorry, I kinda kissed you back."

She laughed. "I am so embarrassed. I suppose you thought I was nuts."

"It was the middle of the night. People do weird things in the night. Let's make breakfast."

Julia said, "Thanks for not discounting what happened. Just hearing myself, I'm skeptical, but it felt real."

"Then look at it as a divine gift."

In the foyer, she smiled and said, "Do you mind if I leave you to make breakfast while I take a shower and change clothes?"

"Not at all. I love cooking."

The main living area had graduated vaulted ceilings with lots of glass windows and doors, and to the right of the room was the kitchen with red cedar and a gray stone bar which separated the two areas.

Rummaging in the stainless fridge, Ruben looked up at Klock's barking. "Open the door, Ruben."

Ruben went to the back deck and opened the door. "Did you find anything?"

Klock wagged his stub of a tail. "Nope. No breaches that I could find. Whatcha cooking? I'm hungry, man."

"Sausage, or would you prefer bacon?"

Another bark came from Klock. "Both. Wake me when breakfast is ready. I'm going to catch a quick nap." Ruben watched Klock trot next to the fireplace and crash out on the rug.

After retrieving the desired items from the fridge, Ruben started cooking. He loved Earth's cool kitchen gadgets most likely developed from Alien technology.

Without using the Wi-Fi, Ruben punched his saved playlist and used Bluetooth to sync to his boom blaster and got into the slow rhythm of Brownstone's, "If You Love Me," while he cooked. He wondered when Charlie and Andy would get to the Chalet.

Sometimes, Ruben got lonely. Not the physical kind of lonely, but what wouldn't he give to love or be in love with someone so much that the love transcended time? Ruben thought about Charlie. She was the only female friend he'd ever had. She never took his crap.

He thought of his grandfather. The one part of his former life he missed. Ruben's grandfather had taught him the worth of a man was his word. Honesty. Integrity. Compassion. Ruben tried to keep those traits. He wondered what his grandfather would make of time travel.

He punched in Michael Jackson's, "Billie Jean" and started dancing while he finished breakfast.

Julia's laughter made him turn around. She giggled, "You can dance, Ruben."

Ruben did a Michael Jackson spin and moonwalked. "Best thing about Earth is the music and arts."

Julia clapped, and Klock woke up barking. "What? What's going on?"

"Breakfast is ready." He set a plate down on the bar for Julia, then placed another plate on the floor for Klock before grabbing a plate for himself. "How's the chocolate milk?"

Julia sipped, and with a slight milk mustache, she replied, "Yummy." He chuckled and joined Julia at the bar.

After finishing his food, stillness washed over him. He prayed he wouldn't let Julia, Phillip, Andy, or Charlie down. They were all counting on him.

Julia must've sensed a change in him. She reached over and kissed his cheek. "Thank you for breakfast. Thank you for helping me. Let's just enjoy the rest of the day because tomorrow will worry about itself."

The skin on the back of his neck tightened and his voice broke. "Phillip's a lucky man."

She tilted her head and said, "Did you know that Charlie's in love with you?"

Klock barked again. "He's blind as a bat."

Ruben shook his head and laughed. "Be serious, for space sakes. I highly doubt it." He paused and stared out into daydream land. "I remember the first time I saw Charlie. She fell through a time portal from a rock concert in 1969 and fell forward into the year of 1989. Charlie was so young, completely dazed from acid, and wearing a fringy psychedelic tunic with a pair of hip-hugger jeans. She had long, straight red hair down to her butt. Charlie held up two fingers and said, 'Peace, man.' I trained Charlie for ten years, and then Monica placed Charlie on her tracking team a while back, and we lost touch until I received your assignment."

Julia began to help him clean the kitchen. "Charlie is the same age as I am."

Ruben cocked his head to the side and raised his right brow. "Forever twenty-one." He washed the skillet and placed it back into the cabinet.

Wiping down the counter, Julia looked up at Ruben. "Maybe you should take another look at Charlie."

He draped his arm around Julia's neck. "Aren't you the little matchmaker?"

She wiggled out of his arms and turned around to face him. "I never try to match-make. I see Andy is forming a crush on her. But the way she looks at you is the way I look at Phillip."

"Hmm, I've never thought of Charlie that way." He looked down and said, "And I wished you hadn't put that thought in my head because I'm never going to be able to erase it. Grab your tennis shoes. Let's go for a walk. Remember, we have to keep you physically fit."

Klock barked, "Me too, me too."

Ruben placed the hand towel on the counter next to the sink. "Why don't we all go for a walk?"

Julia frowned and asked, "Are you talking to Klock? It's like you two can communicate."

Ruben and Klock both laughed, and Klock rolled onto his back with his legs kicking in the air. Ruben said, "I understand Klock, and he understands me." He showed Julia the back of his wrist. "See that little scar? It's an Alien language translation chip. Klock is an alien, and he talks."

Julia bent over coughing. "You're not kidding, are you?"

"Nope."

* * *

SPRING SEMESTER HAD ENDED at BFU, and only a skeleton staff remained for the summer classes. Charlie dropped Andy off in front of the Science Building, and the warm breeze blew his hair off his face as he jogged up the steps and through the double doors.

After climbing the stairs to the third floor, Andy took a left and made his way to the department office midway down the hall. The science department office manager sat behind her desk clicking away at her keyboard.

Ms. Rogers took off her glasses. With a grin, she said, "Hello, Andy. I received a phone call from Dr. Callaway about your leave of absence. I can't believe both of you are going on leave. Here's the form I need you to complete, please date and sign it. I've arranged for graduate students to take over your classes until your return. I'm going to miss your cheery disposition."

Andy picked up the form and perused it. "Ms. Rogers, you are too kind. A year will go by in no time flat." He leaned over and signed and dated the form. Andy couldn't remember the last time he missed work, and he'd never requested leave. "Please redirect all my calls and emails to the central science department. I won't have much access to either while I'm away."

Ms. Rogers raised a brow and leaned in. With a look of concern, she asked, "Where are you going?"

Andy handed her the form then squeezed her hand. "Now, Beatrice. I have personal and professional issues that have arisen, and I can't divulge the information. I'm sure everything will turn out all right." He didn't know if he was trying to convince Beatrice or himself. "The department is left in accomplished hands. Goodbye, Bea."

"Goodbye, Dr. Clayborn."

Taking a deep breath, Andy turned and left the office with a single-minded purpose of meeting Charlie in the parking lot. He started down the stairs when he noticed a female student rummaging through her backpack on the second-floor landing. As he stepped around the girl, the hair on his arms rose. The student grabbed his ankle, causing him to fall face-first on the painted concrete floor.

In an instant, the female had Andy on his back with a knife at his throat. Pale face, black hair, darker eyes stared down at him. With a rough voice, she said, "Where is Julia Boatwright? Don't fuck with me or I'll gut you like a fish."

A male student on the third floor leaned over the railing and yelled, "Hey, I just called the police."

It was enough of a distraction for her to look over her shoulder when Andy's fight or flight instinct kicked in. Andy grabbed the woman and flung her down the steps toward the first floor. The male student rushed to his aid and helped Andy to his feet. Andy said, "Thanks, man, thought I was a goner for a second."

The male student pointed to his throat. "You're bleeding."

Andy felt rivulets of blood trickling down into his shirt. He placed his hand on the stairway rail and looked over to see if the woman was dead. She was gone. "She's history. What's your name? Will you walk with me back to my office?"

"My name's Kenny. I've taken several of your classes and admired your work, Dr. Clayborn. I'll help you any way I can."

Andy opened the door to the office, and Beatrice's hand went to her mouth. "Oh, Andy, what happened?"

"Bea, please hand me the first aid kit, and Kenny will tell you what happened while I go to the restroom and clean up this blood."

Bea's hand trembled opening the cabinet door. She tore into a bandage and pressed it against Andy's neck.

Andy said, "I'm okay, Bea. Really. The student probably got an F on the final."

Bea's voice broke. "That's not funny."

Shaking his head, Andy went out the door and across the hall into the men's room. Placing the kit on the bathroom counter, Andy turned on the water and splashed his face and throat, then squirted antiseptic on the wound. His attacker barely grazed the skin. Dabbing the skin, Andy used a little antibiotic ointment on the cut, then rolled gauze around his neck three times, securing it with medical tape.

He looked like a deranged priest from a horror movie.

Andy needed to get to Charlie fast. Leaving the men's room, he ran into the Campus Police.

"Dr. Clayborn, we were in the building when Ms. Rogers radioed in that you were assaulted. We need to get your statement and description of the suspect."

Andy closed his eyes for a second, then opened them. With an exhale, he said, "I have to make this quick. I'm heading out of town, and I'm late as it is. I appreciate your hard work, but I'm not pressing charges. One of our students, Kenny, called the police, and he's with Ms. Rogers in the office. I'm sure he can give you a full description of what happened. All I remember is a girl on the steps going through her backpack, then tripping me and placing a knife at my throat. The rest is hazy."

The interrogating officer held an iPad and quickly typed on the screen. "Did you recognize the student? Do you need to go to the hospital?"

Andy dragged his fingers through his hair in frustration. "I didn't recognize the student, and she only grazed the skin. Look, I'm taking a leave of absence and was heading out the door when someone attacked me. I'm late as it is and must go. Please talk to Kenny, and report any findings to the department. Good day, officers."

Scratching a brow, the officer said, "Oh, I see, sorry to have detained you, but we have to follow through with our line of questioning. If you're not pressing charges, then our hands are tied. Just the same, I'll keep in touch with the science department."

With a sharp nod, Andy turned, ran down the steps and out of the building. He looked left and right. There was no sign of the girl. His heart pounded loudly, and his ears began to ring when he heard a couple of honks.

Charlie sat in a silver and black Grand Cherokee Jeep. She'd stolen another vehicle. He jumped in. Anxiety pulled the skin tight across her face when she shouted, "Phillip Andrew." Andy looked up startled. She touched his neck. "Who did this to you?"

He gave her a sideways grin. "Aw, you care about me."

Charlie punched him in the arm. "Dammit, I'm not joking. Who hurt you?"

"She had ashen skin, shoulder-length black hair, black lips, very dark eyes, and piercings everywhere."

"That bitch. I'll rip out Stormy's freaking innards and feed them to Klock."

Several students stopped and gawked at them as Charlie flew through the ten-miles-an-hour speed zone. Looking in the rearview mirror, she said, "There's a black Escalade following two cars back."

Charlie lowered her voice and said, "Hold on tight, lover boy."

Andy braced himself against the dashboard with one hand while the other hand reached for the overhead grip.

Rarely did Andy ever break the law, but since he'd met Julia, Ruben, and Charlie the infractions kept piling up. Julia had turned his sane and very predictable world into a made for TV science fiction series.

Charlie sped through the campus streets. "Change of plans, sweetheart." She pulled behind the school cafeteria and parked the Jeep next to the dumpsters. "Get out now and try to keep up."

Running down the sidewalk, Charlie dashed into the library before Andy caught up. She turned to him and said, "I'll explain later, but right now, you have to trust me. We're going to slip through several buildings until I can find a place for us to hide out for a while."

Andy didn't ask any questions.

Three buildings and multiple stairways later, Charlie found an old cloakroom on the top floor of the English department. "Climb the bookshelves. It looks like there's a ledge next to the transom window. It'll give us cover, and the window will give us access to find Monica and her cohorts."

With a tilt of his head, Andy said, "You first."

She let out a sigh and hugged him. "I'm so sorry, Andy. You could've died."

"I didn't. Now, scoot."

The shelves were nailed securely into the wall frame. Charlie climbed to the top shelf and looked down. "It's okay. The shelves are sturdy, climb on up, and we'll wait until it gets dark before we leave."

Andy made his way up to the ledge and crawled to the back corner. Dust floated in the air and made him sneeze. "So, what's the plan?" He leaned against the wall and drew one knee to his chest, draping his forearm over it.

"Monica's team has probably found the Jeep. So, she's probably logged onto the internet and found the police report on the stolen vehicle. She'll think we've taken another car which is what I intend to do once it gets dark. That'll give us time to slip out of here."

Andy hit the back of his head against the wall. "I've become a criminal. Breaking and entering with Julia, stealing cars, and some psycho slit my throat."

"Believe me, if Stormy had wanted you dead, you wouldn't be here. You'd be on a slab in the morgue."

"And that's supposed to make me feel better?"

Turning her head, Charlie pressed her forefinger to her lips and pointed at the door. Johnnie came into the room, moving clothing and knocking over chairs. Charlie had her weapon drawn.

Andy's heart skipped a few beats while they waited. Charlie's back straightened, and her jawline tightened. It was the first time he'd seen what looked like rage in Charlie's face.

After a few tense minutes, Johnnie left the room, and a few moments after that, Charlie let out a breath. "Good. We have a shot at making the Chalet undetected. Let me look at your field dressing."

He chuckled. "This reminds me of a scene in the first *Terminator* when Sarah Connor is concerned for Kyle Reese."

With a one-shoulder shrug, Charlie looked in Andy's eyes and said nonchalantly, "I've never seen the movie." Carefully, she unrolled the gauze around his neck.

Brows raised, eyes widening, Andy exclaimed, "You've never seen

The Terminator? Well, young lady, we have eight months to watch it, and I have a shelf full of other DVDs."

"I can't wait. Hmm, you did a pretty good job. I don't think you need the bandage, though. The bleeding has stopped. I guess I went a little crazy when I thought Stormy could've killed you. She's going to pay for hurting you."

Andy draped an arm over Charlie's shoulders, and she leaned into his embrace. Slowly, her breathing returned to normal.

"I like having a badass girlfriend."

She grinned, then kissed Andy chastely on the lips. "I've never had a boyfriend before."

Holding Charlie tight, he felt the tension release out of her shoulders. He chuckled again and teased her. "Lucky girl, you have me."

Andy straightened his back and took his arm away from Charlie. Thoughts of time travel, portals, and the formula ran through his mind when suddenly he had a breakthrough, his ah-ha moment, the freaking Doc Brown from the *Back to the Future's* flux capacitor moment.

Except, Andy didn't need a flux capacitor. "I need paper and something to write with fast."

He climbed down the bookshelves and peeked into the classroom. Andy looked inside the instructor's desk drawer and found a legal pad and several pens. Feverishly, Andy wrote down the remaining sequence to the formula. If his theory proved correct and the method completed on his laptop, then with the help of his new time travel friends, Andy would create a prototype simulator during his stay at the Chalet.

Charlie stepped up behind him, and he grinned. "By George, I think I have it. I've cracked the formula, Charlie."

She hugged him then leaned her head on his shoulder. "That's wonderful. The Plates of Prophecy had the discovery right but the wrong son. How long do you think it'll take?"

Extending his fingers, and shaking his head, he said, "You can't ask a physicist how long. It adds too much pressure, but if the sequencing works, I should be able to work on your ship or Ruben's this fall.

Maybe, before the baby is born we'll take her for a *spin*." He laughed and said, "Get it? My theory is called, Spinning Time."

"Oh, I get it, genius. It's dusk. Just another thirty minutes or so and we'll get out of here."

"We probably need to stop by the grocery store and stock up on non-perishables before heading back. Maybe in Mount Rieve."

Her fingers intertwined with Andy's. "Let's go steal a car."

CHAPTER 14

Monica clenched her fingers into fists and gritted her teeth. "You're impotent and worthless. We've lost them." She let out an agonizing cry. "Do you understand I have to go back to the command center? If I stay gone too much longer, the Lord Supreme will come a-calling."

Monica paced the empty classroom on the campus where her elite team lost Andy and Charlie. "Zane, you'll have to stay behind. Conduct another search around campus and then methodically go from town to town until we find someone, somewhere, who'll recognize one of them. They'll have to buy supplies. Check grocery stores and pharmacies. We have a little over eight months to find Ms. Boatwright. We will find her. There is no other option. Are we cool?"

Zane stood, wringing his hands, nervously, chattering. "Yes, uh-huh, we will find them. We will find them."

"Shut the hell up, Zane. You're acting like a freak-a-zoid, again. Did you bring your meds? If not, I'll send some via a courier. Keep your devices linked to my secure site. We'll communicate on a need-only basis. I'm leaving, so please, don't disappoint me again."

Stormy picked under her fingernails using a trailing point knife. "I could've killed Phillip's grandson, but you said no."

Impatient with the lot of them, Monica calmly stated, "Stormy, darling, we need Phillip's grandson. He's what I call leverage."

Johnnie came over and circled his arm around Monica's waist. "Baby, I'll find them for you. I vow to you. I'll find them." He leaned in to kiss her and Monica shrugged out of his grasp.

"Johnnie, not now, I have a headache." The old catch phrase still worked. The moron was gorgeous. He just didn't have a lot upstairs. As if talking to a toddler, she said, "Maybe when I return, if you make good on your promise, you can spend the whole night with me." She patted his cheek. "I'll touch base soon."

Monica left campus and drove into the mountains where she'd left the ATTRA warship. She pressed on the wristband, and the Cloak Shield released, and she entered the time machine, synchronized her time pattern, then clicked on the system controls. Once she arrived at the docking station in the Gateway, she exited the time machine and caught one of the hover crafts powered by Lunar City's automated road system.

Monica never tired of the incredible aerial view from the free-flowing architectural design with a myriad of circular and vertical buildings that shimmered and gleamed. In between each building were perfect proportionate green spaces created by the nuclear energy of the sun through retractable solar panel windows that went undetected by Earth's satellites. The panel tinting adjusted to the light conditions within Lunar City.

Further away from the building lay large areas of green space filled with organic vegetation providing food for the population. Ice caps on the dark side of the moon provided clean and usable water in the pipelines.

Yes, Monica thought, Lunar City ran at optimum efficiency both day and night. The natural time portals on Earth gave the city the necessary workforce to continue its existence. In exchange, Lunar City inhabitants had every conceivable luxury with incomes to match.

Zane, Stormy, and even Johnnie weren't the sharpest tools in the shed, but they were loyal and lethal. It was a shame Azaria and Kalsan were killed. Monica would find new specialists that would deactivate any protective shields or Security Breach Beams once they located Julia's whereabouts.

Monica wished Ruben was still on her team. The youth of yesteryear was oh-so-hot, strong as an ox, and in bed, well, let's just say, she'd met no other male or female with his lovemaking skills.

Monica had known before Ruben left on the Lord's Supreme's mission she had lost him. Exactly like when she decided to kill Commander Drummond Prescott.

Monica arrived at her penthouse suite; the automatic doors opened when the sensor scanned her retina. She went straight to her bedroom, stripped, and fell onto the bed. Some days were so hard she didn't want to get up much less work. Today had been one of them. Monica was so close to realizing her dreams. Exhausted, she drifted into a restless sleep.

CHAPTER 15

The stars twinkled in the velvety night sky as Julia walked over to the rail of the front porch. There was no sign of Andy or Charlie. Ruben sat in one of the rockers rubbing Klock's back, and she said, "Something must've happened."

Ruben lowered Klock to the wooden plank floor. "Go recheck the perimeters. If you see any sign of Charlie and Andy, come back to me."

Klock barked, trotting down the stairs. "Yes sir, Boss." Klock disappeared into the dense forest.

Ruben stepped over to Julia and leaned against the railing, gripping the overlay. "I agree, but I have every confidence in Charlie. She'll get them back here safe."

"What if they don't come back? What happens then?"

"Don't be so pessimistic. I'm not ready to throw in the towel. Let's give Andy and Charlie some more time before we fall into panic mode. Besides, it's not good for you or the baby."

She ran her fingers through her hair. "You're right. So much has happened that I'm not very optimistic now."

Klock came running back, his tongue hanging out, barking in

between deep breaths. "They're here. Andy and Charlie are here and driving a stolen car. We'll need to ditch the evidence."

Ruben ran down the steps. "I don't see them."

Julia yelled, "What's Klock saying? Hey, look, down the driveway. I see lights. They're in the woods."

A sleek black car drove up the road leading to the Chalet. "How does Klock know it's them?"

"Remember, Klock isn't like Earth dogs. He's an alien and sees through the darkness. You saw them, didn't you, Klock?"

Klock looked up at Ruben and barked again. "Yup. It's them."

Julia walked down the steps to Ruben, and he held her hand. "Everything is going to be okay."

The car pulled to a stop, and Andy and Charlie exited through the doors. Julia yelped, "Oh my God. What happened, Andy?" Horrified at seeing the blood covering Andy's shirt, she also noticed the gash in his neck. Hugging him, she exclaimed, "Oh, Andy, I wish I'd never traveled through time."

After Julia released him, Andy looked at Charlie then Ruben. "Stormy attacked me, but Charlie saved us. She's incredible. Hey, we bought groceries too. A little help, please?"

Charlie popped the trunk, and each person loaded up with the groceries in one trip. Inside the kitchen, Julia and Ruben began to store the non-perishables in the large walk-in pantry.

Julia asked, "Who is Stormy?"

Ruben stacked cans of tuna and salmon on the top shelf. "She's one of Monica's enforcers. She lives to torture and kill. Stormy loves the chase."

Inside the main room, Andy took off his shirt and yelled out, "Hey, I also found out that Monica is my ex-fiancée."

Julia stuck her head around the corner. "You have got to be kidding?"

"Charlie can fill y'all in. I'm washing off this dried blood. It's itching me to death." He grabbed a beer out of the fridge, then went up the steps, taking them two at a time.

Charlie sat on the bar stool swiveling back and forth. "Is there any whiskey in the house? I need a stiff drink."

Julia went to the wet bar and raised a bottle. "Is Gentleman Jack, all right?"

Charlie nodded. "Yes, ma'am." She looked at Ruben and straightened her spine.

Ruben joined her at the bar placing his hand over hers. "What happened?"

Charlie went through the details, not leaving out one morsel of information. "Stormy attacked Andy in the Science department. We lost them on campus and didn't leave BFU until dark. Ruben, I wouldn't have come back here unless I was sure. I wouldn't put Julia or Andy in any danger."

Ruben looked frazzled, shaking his head, stalking around the room like a bull. "I have to add more safeguards. Charlie, you did well." He went out the door and down the steps.

Julia handed Charlie the whiskey shot, and she drank it in one gulp.

"Thank you for saving my grandson's life. Words aren't enough, but I thank you just the same. Are you hungry? I kept plates of spaghetti warm in the oven for you and Andy."

Charlie walked to the fireplace and extended her fingers over the flames. "Man, it gets chilly at night in the mountains. Oh, I'll wait on Andy to eat."

Julia went over to Charlie and brushed the hair away from Charlie's face. "You have a love bite on your neck."

Charlie let out a laugh. "Busted. I slept with your grandson." She raised her brow and laughed again. "And I'll probably keep on sleeping with him too."

"I can tell you're in love with Ruben. It's written all over your face when he's in the room. He loves you too. He just doesn't know it yet. So, be kind to Andy and please don't hurt him."

Charlie rolled her eyes, then walked to the bar for another drink. "Yeah, right, Ruben loves me, and I'm the Pope. I like Andy very much, and I told him how I felt about Ruben."

Andy jogged down the stairs, each step shaking the photos on the stairwell wall. He dipped Charlie in a dramatic gesture, then kissed her on the lips. After a long second, he broke away but still held Charlie in a dip. "Hey, sweetness, I left you plenty of hot water if you want to take a shower."

Charlie giggled, and circled her arms around Andy's neck. "Let me see." He raised them to a standing position, and Charlie tilted his chin and inspected his wound. "I think you'll live." He pulled her off the ground, kissing her again when Ruben walked in and slammed the door.

Andy slowly released Charlie, and she said, "I'm taking a shower. Wait for me, and we'll eat dinner together." She kissed him again, then turned to Ruben and smiled before running up the stairs.

Julia watched the interaction with much interest. She'd been right, Ruben was jealous of Andy.

Andy was completely oblivious to the undercurrent and grabbed another beer from the fridge. "Anyone else want one?"

Ruben snarled and said, "Sure, but get Julia a ginger ale."

Julia smiled and sat on the couch. She hadn't watched so much drama unfold since the first semester of college when she pledged her sorority.

Andy tossed the beer to Ruben and plopped down next to Julia on the couch with his feet on the square pinewood coffee table.

Ruben smacked Andy's feet off the table and sat down. He tilted Andy's chin. At first, Ruben had a look of concern, then his nostrils flared.

Julia leaned over and looked at Andy's neck. She giggled and said, "You have a love bite on your neck."

"Yeah, so what?" Andy shrugged and took a pull from his beer. Ruben turned and stormed out of the house again. Andy said, "What's his problem?"

She stretched out on the couch and placed her feet in Andy's lap. "I believe Ruben's just figured out he has feelings for Charlie that aren't brotherly if you know what I mean."

"The hell you say. Ruben and Charlie? She loves him too, damn it. I think I'm falling in love with Charlie, and I'm not letting her go without a fight."

Charlie came down the stairs in a pair of pink silk pajamas. Andy's eyes widened, and he guzzled the rest of his beer. "Day-yum, girl. You look good."

Ruben came back inside and laughed sarcastically. "Really, Charlie? Pink? You look like a teenager."

Charlie's cheeks reddened. "I bought a few items at the superstore. Pink was all they had in my size, asshole." She pushed Ruben out of her way and held her hand out to Andy. "Eat dinner with me, Boo." Charlie accentuated the word Boo.

Julia laughed so hard her sides ached. "Oh, y'all are killing me.

Ruben grunted and sat down in the recliner, kicking up the footrest. Crossing his arms over his chest, he pouted. "Keeping you and your baby safe is all that matters."

Julia picked up a pillow and threw it in Ruben's face. "Nothing matters except the baby and me. That's a bunch of malarkey. I told you that you had feelings for Charlie. You just didn't believe it until you saw their hickeys."

Ruben threw the pillow back. He leaned in and whispered, "Their hickeys? Let's get something straight. I care about Charlie, but I'm not in love with her. You seem to forget, you and Andy are living in an alternate reality. When Charlie and I see this scenario through, Charlie won't have Andy. Don't you get it? She'll only have me. I can't risk Charlie's emotional ties to someone who's not in her future."

"Don't bite my head off because you can't or won't allow yourself to have feelings for Charlie."

Andy and Charlie stepped into the main room smiling at each other, and he said, "We have some great news."

Ruben rolled his eyes. "Oh, joy. Pray tell, what is it?"

"I completed the formula for Spinning Time. All I'm working the algorithm into my program, then run it into the animation software. It may take a few months to work out any kinks, but I think we should have a working prototype by this fall."

Julia jumped from the couch and threw her arms into the air. "Woohoo! I'm going home."

Andy said, "Not so fast. Once I work on either Ruben's or Charlie's ship, I'll need to take the craft for a test spin. We'll pick a place and time period, and if my calculations work maybe just maybe we'll have a craft ready by the time, my dad is born."

Ruben kicked the footstep down and reached over and gave Andy a big bear hug, pulling him off the sofa. "Damn, Andy. That's the best news I've had since I started this mission. We're not out of danger, and I can assure you, Monica has her team methodically checking the State of North Carolina to find us. I'll leave in the morning for the Empyreal Palace to see what happens with Julia and make a request for additional soldiers."

Julia hugged each of them and said, "I'm so tired I can't keep my head up. I'm going to bed."

Charlie said, "Oh, I bought prenatal vitamins. You can start them in the morning. The first trimester, you're going to want to sleep a lot."

Ruben grabbed Julia's hand. "I'll walk you to bed because I won't see you for a few days."

Inside the master bedroom, Ruben held both of Julia's hands. "I see the excitement in your eyes, but we have a long way to go before we know if Andy's machine works. Just rest while I'm away, and Charlie can reach me from The Bus in an emergency."

Releasing her hands, Ruben took a step away. "I'll leave Klock to watch out for you, plus, he's kind of gotten attached to you. Oh, and for the record, I like your hair growing out." He rustled the hair on top of Julia's head. "You sorta look like Looney Tunes, Penelope Pussycat with the white stripe down the middle."

"Who?"

"It's a cartoon character. Never mind. I'll leave you to rest." He kissed her forehead, and Julia wrapped her arms around Ruben's waist, leaning her head next to his chest.

Looking up into Ruben's eyes, she smiled. "You're like the big brother I never had. I love you, Ruben."

"Aw, now, you're going to make me say something silly. So, just know I love you and Andy, and yes, I love Charlie too."

"See, I knew you were a good guy. Be safe, my friend." Ruben left, closing the door behind him.

For the first time since she arrived here, Julia had hope. Placing her hand on her belly, she said, "Hey, little boy. Your mama and daddy love you. We're trying hard to find a way to be together again."

It was unbelievable the love she felt for the life inside her. She and Phillip had conceived their child in love, and Julia wouldn't allow anyone or anything to hurt her baby or Andy. Andy was the sweetest and kindest man she'd met since Phillip. He'd told Julia a little about his mother, Jensi. Phillip, Jr. and Jensi had a wonderful child, a reflection of their love. Julia had no clue why she didn't raise her son. Then fate had taken Andy's parents. Julia wanted her family together.

She thought about time. What was time? Time with loved ones and time with friends. A time to work and a time to play. A time to live and a time to die. Time is what held everything together, and time kept people apart. "Phillip, I'm coming home. I promise I am coming home."

***

After sleeping for a few hours, Ruben dressed and left the guest bedroom, walking softly down the hallway. In the main living area, Charlie waited for him. The look in her eyes made his chest tighten. "Charlie, what are you doing up?"

She rose from the couch and shoved her hands into her back pockets. Giving Ruben a one shoulder shrug, she said, "I thought I'd walk you to the edge of the property. How far away is the Needle-Horn?"

"Oh, about five miles northeast. Any coffee?"

"Yeah. I just made a fresh pot."

Ruben draped an arm over Charlie's shoulders, pressing his head next to hers. "Hey, Charlie, are you in love with Andy?"

With a mock elbow to the ribs, she replied, "Maybe. But you know it doesn't matter. A year from now I'll never see him again. Why, are you jealous?"

He hip-bumped her and said, "Maybe."

He poured a cup of black coffee in a stainless to-go mug. "I love Andy and Julia. They're different. I mean, they're so full of love, and it shines right through their faces. I guess I'm drawn to their light. In a world full of darkness, there's still light, Charlie."

On the front porch, Klock barked, "Can I go with you, Boss?"

Ruben knelt to the floor and picked up Klock, rubbing his ears and kissing the tip of his nose. "Not this time, my furry friend. I need you here watching out for everyone."

Klock licked his face and barked, "I won't let you down, Boss. I promise."

"Charlie's going to walk with me to the edge of the property; then she's coming back. Take care of yourself, hound." Ruben placed Klock on the floor, and he assumed guard position at the front door.

Ruben and Charlie walked in silence through the forest. Even though Ruben and Charlie clashed on occasion, he respected her. He'd never allowed his feelings to develop into love. Damn, Julia, now he could think of nothing else as she walked close to him.

Charlie's sweet scent of lemon and jasmine filled the air he breathed. Maybe, when the mission was over, he would ask Charlie on a date. The thought made him chuckle.

"What's so funny?"

Ruben gave her a boyish grin. "Oh, something Julia said. She told me you were in love with me."

Charlie's face reddened, and she playfully shoved him. "And what's so funny about that?"

"Well, you have an odd way of showing it. Sleeping with Andy."

"That's the pot calling the kettle black. Shall I name the laundry list of females you've slept with, including Monica?"

"Point taken. Maybe we could grab a drink at Moonbeams when this mission is complete." Moonbeams was a bar and nightclub for Trackers in Lunar City. Most Trackers met there after an extended mission and got wasted.

Ruben stopped walking and turned Charlie to face him. They locked eyes, searching each other. Then his gaze dropped to her lips. On an impulse, Ruben leaned in to kiss Charlie but instead pressed his face next to her soft cheek, and she leaned into his caress. He could feel her heart beating rapidly.

They held each other for a long minute; then Charlie stepped back and waggled her index finger. "Moonbeams? Ruben Callaway, are you asking me on a date?"

"A drink. Don't get your head in the clouds, for space sakes."

Ruben and Charlie had worked on many different time planes, alternate realities, and parallel universes. And most of the time, they'd made it out on the other side unscathed.

This time was different. This time someone could die.

At the edge of the property line, he hugged Charlie again. "Hey, don't take any unnecessary risks while I'm away."

Charlie reached up and kissed him sweetly on the lips, then said, "See ya around, spaceboy."

Ruben waited until Charlie disappeared. Then he took off on a slow jog which transformed into a run. Ruben needed to think clearly. If his calculations were accurate, he'd return in ten days tops. He hated leaving, but Julia not raising her son nagged at his brain. He couldn't bear the thought she'd die on his watch.

It took a little over an hour before Ruben made it to the Needle-Horn's coordinates. He flipped his wristband and entered the sequence releasing the Cloak Shield. "Ah, Needle-Horn, just the way I left you."

First, Ruben pressed his thumbprint on the identity pad, then he leaned into the eye scanner, and the door hissed open. He checked the equipment and watched it hum to life. Ruben strapped into his harness and rapidly punched in the code for the Empyreal Palace. Within seconds, the Needle-Horn disappeared from Earth's atmosphere and entered the realm of the Lord Supreme.

CHAPTER 16

The Needle-Horn locked into the palace portal system with electromagnetic force. Exiting the craft's chamber, Ruben met a dozen or so of the Empyreal Palace Guards. The guards mimicked the terrain of the palace grounds like chameleons, with what looked like giant butterfly wings on their backs.

The guards reacted quickly, with deadly force, to any potential threat directed toward the Lord Supreme and his Royal Court. Ruben wondered if he would see Monica as the behemoth that needed squelching.

The guards escorted Ruben to the jewel-encrusted palace door where Ruben handed over his credentials to the Sergeant-at-Arms, who dematerialized into thin air. No one in the Galaxy knew the exact location of the palace. The sequence of the palace coordinates changed frequently, and only a select few individuals were invited to appear in His Majesty's presence.

The realm had one sun and three moons which appeared in a triangular pattern in the azure sky. Rolling hills lush with vegetation gradually increased in elevation to the castle, sparkling with zillions of diamonds. Revelation River flowing with crystal clear water, curved along the hills circling the castle.

The Sergeant-at-Arms returned and handed Ruben his credentials, opening the gate doors. "This is Jailyn. She'll take you to the cleansing chamber and wait until you're properly attired to escort you into the palace."

Ruben nodded and replied, "Thank you for your assistance."

Jailyn ushered Ruben into the cleansing chamber, where he had to strip down and give his clothes to one of the servants. He stepped into the sanctification showers, and the cool cleansing water washed over him from every angle of the stall. After ten minutes the doors opened, and two servants approached Ruben to help him dress in the Royal Robes.

One servant administered fragrant oils while the other towel dried any residue left on his skin and hair. They groomed him impeccably to meet the Lord Supreme. Ruben donned a scarlet, blue, and purple robe made of the finest linen and tied it with a golden braided belt. He slipped on golden silk slippers.

Leaving the dressing area, Ruben met the Empyreal Guard, Jailyn, and she escorted him to the Royal Rotunda's War Room to meet with the Lord Supreme. The interior of the castle bustled with activity. Along the walk, males and females worked throughout the palace in various capacities wearing similar garments to Ruben's, the insignia of the Royal Crest embroidered over their hearts.

The beings living within the walls of the palace weren't human, exactly. A separate species with varying skin tones, hair, and eye color running the gamut of the color chart, they appeared similar to humans, and each worked in a seemingly perpetual state of euphoria.

The times Ruben had visited the Empyreal Palace, not one altercation had ever broken out. The guard stopped in front of an enormous marbled compound. The double white doors silently slid open for Ruben.

Inside the darkened area of the rotunda, thousands of large screens sat on glass desks in a tiered platform on multiple levels with workers feverishly pecking away on the keyboards. Variations of blues, whites, and silver illuminated the war room. An extensive digital map sat on a table in the middle of the room with the Lord

Supreme and Prince Aelius pointing and discussing a developing situation in hushed tones. Each wore an ankle-length shimmering white robe with three-quarter length sleeves; their forearms adorned with wide bracelets made of onyx and gold filigree.

Ruben was announced to the Lord Supreme and Prince Aelius, and he bowed low to the floor.

"Rise, my old friend," said the Lord Supreme. "Follow Aelius and me into my chamber where we may talk in private."

Walking through a side door, Ruben followed the Lord Supreme and Prince Aelius into a room with floor-to-ceiling mahogany paneling. Dark wood built-in shelves held ancient scrolls, and leather-bound books were on either side of the accented fireplace with ornate detailing. Ruben looked up to the cathedral ceiling and the wall of windows with a magnificent view of the kingdom.

The Lord Supreme sat in a high-back leather chair while Prince Aelius and Ruben sat on the dark maroon leather couch in front of the fireplace. "We've been expecting you. Before you start, allow me to explain a little about my people."

Ruben had been waiting decades to ask questions.

The Lord Supreme rested his elbow on the armrest of his chair. He extended the other hand toward Ruben. "The Universe has billions of galaxies. The Milky Way and other galaxies are under my domain. There is nothing or no one that can outsmart or outmaneuver us. Prince Aelius and I have allowed General Agriaous to colonize Veetreous. He's a good general, but Monica manipulated him. Prince Aelius has called on war transports to seize control of the planet after the birth of Julia's child."

Placing the palms of his hand on his thighs, Ruben asked, "Why is the birth so important? What happens to Julia?"

Prince Aelius turned to Ruben and said, "Julia and her child are important, but it is Andrew's discovery that influences future outcomes in history. His Spinning Time formula will change time travel. The discovery is too important for mere mortals to control. The machine exists."

Prince Aelius stepped over to the bookshelf and withdrew a large leather-bound book. He flipped several pages and laid the book on the solid onyx table in front of the couch. "Andy travels with Charlie to visit Leonardo da Vinci."

Ruben's body shook. The images in the ancient book were paintings of Andy and Charlie created by Da Vinci.

Prince Aelius said, "They'll visit Da Vinci when he was a young peasant. Andy presents Leonardo with images of the inventions Da Vinci will create in the future. Andy didn't change history; he perpetuated it. We have a list of historical events influenced by Andy's machine."

"If the time machine works, does this mean Julia goes home?"

The Lord Supreme released an exhale. "Ruben, I am going to try and break this down as simple as I can without you going into an existential meltdown. My people are what your present-day scientists regard as a Type III civilization. Our species is super-intelligent. That is why the Empyreal Palace is a utopian society."

He began to walk around the room, talking. "As I stated earlier, there are billions and billions of galaxies. Our kind, for a simple narrative, became bored, and we sought new planetary systems, but more specifically, planets where life could thrive. We wanted to create a new species in our image and watch it evolve. Earth and humankind are still children. We allow humanity to develop naturally like a protected park. That's why I brought in the moon to observe and intervene when the need arises. You and the other Spinners are the Rangers, so to speak."

Prince Aelius said, "Humankind has made great strides. People used to think the world was flat. Andy's time machine opens the possibility that humans can accelerate to the next level of intelligence."

Prince Aelius crossed his arms over his chest. "Our species use one hundred percent of our energy. That's why we don't have the "kill" instincts, like murder, or the need to kill for material things as a more primitive civilization does. But let me be clear, we are fierce warriors. We trained our Empyreal Armies to fight and destroy any opponent that threatens our survival or our subjects."

The Lord Supreme interjected, "The human body uses almost every aspect of the brain, but only uses twenty percent of its energy. Through Andy's discovery, we have the hope humankind will reach its full potential using all their energy, which will lead to a utopian society like our kingdom. But there's also a chance the discovery could wipe out civilization on Earth."

Ruben suddenly felt like he was Charlton Heston in the *Planet of the Apes*.

The Lord Supreme said, "It is a lot to take in. Would you like a drink?"

Ruben exhaled and said, "No, sir. Julia is the grandmother of a genius, and you want to protect her, to protect Andy, and ensure the development of a super human. It's the next step in the evolutionary process. That's why you're allowing the colonization of Veetreous. If Earth doesn't work out, you have a backup plan."

Prince Aelius placed his hand on Ruben's shoulder. "You only have to watch Earth's twenty-four-hour news networks to see how precarious the state of humankind is. Some civilizations make it to the next step while others do not."

Ruben said, "I will do everything in my power to protect Julia and her family. There are wonderful people on Earth, but I've seen the bad ones. Monica is one of them."

The Lord Supreme walked over to the fireplace and stared into the flames. "The Plates of Prophecy were a gift from my father before people existed. General Agriaous will pay for his breach. The Plates are merely a tool. People are unpredictable, and every choice, every decision can change an outcome of the future. I will not disclose Julia's future even though that's the reason you made the journey."

Prince Aelius returned the book to the shelf and turned to Ruben. "I will send two of my Empyreal Guards to help you."

Ruben bowed low before the Lord Supreme who placed his hand on Ruben's head. "It is humans like you who give me hope. You are a good man. Ruben, Julia's destiny will be as it should be. Do not worry."

Prince Aelius placed his hand on Ruben's shoulder. "It is time."

Walking into the military barracks, Prince Aelius said, "The time is drawing near when I will test the inhabitants of Earth and hold those accountable for trying to destroy the sacred planet."

Inside the barracks, rows of the military stood before the Prince. He turned to Ruben and said with an air of authority. "I have been aware of Monica and her plans. My sources say she is also working with King Anthobethia from Cancri. Our armies are more numerous than the stars in the sky. Their plan will not succeed."

The Empyreal Guards stood at attention as Prince Aelius approached them. He said, "These are my most seasoned warriors."

Ruben walked each row inspecting the soldiers, as was the custom. After he had returned to the front row, Ruben looked up to Prince Aelius and said, "I choose Azreal and Chayliel."

Prince Aelius turned to the guards and exclaimed in a loud voice, "Azreal and Chayliel, you will accompany the court's favored Tracker, Ruben. You have my authority to use your power against those who seek to harm Julia Boatwright and her family. What say you?"

In unison, Azreal and Chayliel stepped forward and replied, "As you wish, Prince Aelius."

Ruben knew the two warriors would help him stop Monica and her enforcers. "Thank you, Your Highness." Ruben paused and took a deep breath, then exhaled and said, "May I request one more favor?"

"Yes, my faithful and devoted servant."

Ruben's chest moved up and down as he stared into the Prince's eyes of burnished fire. "May I have permission to return Julia to her true reality?"

Prince Aelius placed his hand on Ruben's shoulder. "Follow your orders, and when the time presents itself, you'll receive the answers you seek."

Ruben bowed low. "I will not disappoint you. I'll fight and follow you, my Prince, unto my death."

"Rise, Ruben. You are blessed, my son."

CHAPTER 17

1950 Burkett Falls

"Looks like the rain is over." Phillip pushed the theater door open for Amelia.

"Brrr, and it left a nip in the air too." Amelia put on her hat and buttoned her coat, then placed her hand in the crook of Phillip's arm.

The local downtown businesses had decorated for Halloween with goblins, witches, and jack-o'-lanterns. The town carousel twinkled with lights, and squeals of children's laughter made Phillip smile. He placed his hand over Amelia's as they approached various vendors selling candied apples, roasted pecans, and caramel corn. "Want a candied apple?" he asked.

"Oh, no. I had plenty of popcorn and coke at the movies."

As they rounded the corner, Phillip heard someone yell out his name. He turned left and right then spotted Sam and Ethel.

Sam said, "I told Ethel that was you. How are you, son?"

Ethel nodded and said, "Amelia, you look well."

Phillip's spine stiffened, and he took a step away from Amelia. "Oh, I'm fine. Amelia and I went to see *All About Eve*. What are y'all up to?"

Ethel giggled. "Sam and I ride the carousel every Friday night during the season."

Sam wrapped his arm around Ethel's waist and kissed her forehead. "I proposed to Ethel on a carousel near the beach. It brings back memories. We won't keep you two. Come see us sometime." Sam touched the brim of his trilby hat.

Ethel squeezed Amelia's hand and said, "It's good seeing the both of you."

Phillip and Amelia walked in silence to his car, and he opened the passenger door.

Touching the side of his face, Amelia said, "Are you okay? You have that look again."

"What look is that?

Taking a deep breath, she said, "The haunted look, but I'm not surprised. You get it anytime we see people related to Julia whether they're friends or family." She slid in the seat, and he closed the door.

Phillip felt the familiar tugging at his heart as he opened the driver's side door and got in.

Phillip didn't start the car, and Amelia didn't say a word. "Amelia, why do you put up with me? I'm not sure I'll ever get over her. I am trying to move on, but I'll understand if you need to…"

"Don't say it. Not again. Phillip, I don't expect you to forget Julia." She turned in the seat and curled her finger, gesturing for him to move closer.

"What?"

"Come here. I want to whisper something in your ear."

Tilting his head to the side, he gave her a grin and scooted next to Amelia. She leaned in next to his ear and whispered, "Taste my kiss. I'm here. Give me a chance. It's okay to feel again, to love and laugh again. We have something good."

Amelia leaned slightly away and cupped Phillip's face with her hands. "Look at me with your eyes, open your mind and your heart to me, Phillip. Allow me to love you." She kissed him softly and tenderly.

Part of Phillip needed to let go of Julia, and part of him never would. "I will try, Amelia."

"That's all I ask. Want to spend the night with me?"

He nodded yes, and she kissed him again.

*　*　*

Turning into the Boatwright Plantation made Phillip's heart drop to his stomach. He drove past the house onto the dirt road that led to Burkett Falls. Phillip needed to tell Julia something.

Phillip's heart hammered inside his chest pulling up to the beach. Julia was there. She sat on a rock next to the cliffs of the Falls. Her long blonde hair was tied at the nape of her neck and cascading over her shoulders. In slow motion, she turned and waved.

It was Sloane.

Pulse racing, Phillip walked through the tall grasses onto the sandy beach and climbed the rocks to join her. "You damn near gave me a heart attack. You look so much like your sister. When did you dye your hair?"

Sloane gave him a half smile and said, "Oh, I changed my hair color in New York before I moved back home. I miss her, Phillip. I don't think I'll ever get over missing her."

Phillip placed his arm around Sloane's shoulders, their heads touching together in shared grief. He let out a sigh and began to tell Sloane about Ruben, about Julia's time traveler.

"I've worked on dozens and dozens of formulas, and I've hit a dead end. I've spent so many hours trying to figure it all out. I can't do it anymore. I came here today to let her go. I'm asking Amelia to marry me."

Sloane's sorrowful eyes threatened to spill tears, but she blinked them away. "How can it be possible that Julia's living somewhere in the future? And for argument's sake, what if Julia does come home and you're married? I'm not trying to talk you out of it. I'm just curious."

"I've thought about it, prayed about it. If I marry Amelia, and then Julia makes it home, I'll stay with Amelia. I won't break a wedding vow. I'm still in love with your sister and always will be, but Amelia loves me, and I love her. It may not be with the passion or the intensity of the love I feel for Julia, but it's still love. You never love two people the same way."

Shaking her head, Sloane said, "It's time for truths. I married Brooks. I came here today to tell Julia. This spot always makes me feel closer to her. I wish you and Amelia all the happiness in the world."

Phillip placed the palms of his hands on the boulder to prop his upper body. "Truths. Here are some truths. It still feels as though I'm betraying Julia. I feel like I'm cheating on her."

"You've gotta get over that before you marry Amelia. You're not cheating. If Julia could come home, she would've been here already. It's time for both of us to move on."

Phillip looked up at the Falls then down into the churning waters of the dark blue pools. "I dove off the Falls more than a dozen times to find Julia. Ruben said the time portals open at different places and times around the world, and there's no way to navigate back. I asked him to bring her home, but he said it was impossible. That's why he gave me the blueprints to his ship. I've tried. I have stacks of journals with formulas and possible outcomes. I can't complete the sequence."

"Phillip, it's time to stop. Life continues and time keeps marching on. We can only pray that wherever Julia is that she'll find happiness."

"A colleague of mine has some property for sale in the mountains. I think I may buy it. Build a place for me to think and write. A place where I can…"

"Be with Julia? And I'm not judging you, Phillip. Come up to the house. I know it'll brighten Dad's day. Oh, Mom isn't well and rarely leaves her room anymore." Sloane stood and reached for his hand. "Ethel is cooking her famous pot roast with red potatoes."

Phillip grabbed her hand, pulling himself off the ground. "I'd love to eat dinner with you. Maybe your mom will talk to me today."

"You might be the gander to get Bunny's goose in gear." They both laughed and made their way to the big house.

Phillip parked next to the barn, which brought back vivid memories of Julia on the night of her twenty-first birthday. They had fallen so deeply in love, and then she was gone. He closed his eyes and placed his forehead on the steering wheel as tears ran down his cheeks. Was he making the right decision with Amelia? Would Julia find her way back home?

CHAPTER 18

*P*resent Day

As a theoretical physicist, Andy stared at his thirty-seven-inch monitor and watched a formula take shape with the physics virtual animation software. But this formula was special. While his project rendered, he thought about all the UFO TV shows, YouTube videos, and articles debunked by mainstream media. He thought about the individuals who reported UFOs. People laughed at them and thought they were crazy.

There was one story about a disappearing lake swirling into the ground like a giant flushing toilet that gave Andy the idea the time portals could work like a wormhole he could manipulate into his theory, Spinning Time. If a portal were indeed a wormhole, using its supergravity, he could, in fact, create enough velocity causing space and time to bend, circling back in a loop.

Things in the past that already happened couldn't be modified—or could they? He was pumped with adrenaline as the sequencing neared the end. Based on information from Ruben and Charlie, Andy theorized Julia lived in an alternate or parallel universe, which meant she didn't alter the past but created a different future.

The rendering stopped.

Andy jumped out of the chair and yelled out, "Hot damn, I did it."

Julia stepped inside his third-floor office with its A-frame vaulted ceiling and exposed wood beams. The pine furniture and Southwestern rugs brightened the room. She said, "What's going on in here?"

Andy swooped Julia up in his arms and swung her around in circles. "I did it. The program works." He kissed her cheek and grinned. "Want to see my time machine? I need to test it, but in theory, the formula works, Grannie."

Julia rolled her eyes. "Please stop calling me Grannie. It's getting on my last nerve." Julia was five months pregnant, and her energy level seemed to skyrocket on certain days. Her parenting book suggested it was the nesting phase, which made her clean everything twice.

He chuckled and placed his hand on her growing belly. "I'm sorry."

She leaned over Andy's desk chair and stared at the computer screen. Julia's eyes widened, and she exclaimed, "Can't say I understand the numbers under the animation, but...wow. It's amazing, Andrew. *You're brilliant.*"

He placed a hand on her shoulder. "Aw, no one's called me that since I was a little boy. But I agree, the machine is incredible, and in theory, it should work." Andy pressed his forehead to hers. "It's your ticket home, Julia Bean."

Julia cried and said, "Oh, Andy. I'm so full of pride, and Phillip is smiling from heaven. When will you test one of the crafts?"

Andy dropped into the chair and began clicking on the keyboard to save his program onto the external hard drive. "Today hopefully. I thought maybe Charlie could take us to her ship on our daily run. We'll pack a blanket and bring a picnic. I love the mountains in the fall with the russet reds and vibrant golds."

Julia leaned against his desk, resting her hands on her baby belly. "I love the idea."

Footfalls pounded up the stairwell, and Charlie ran into the room. "I've been waiting on you guys for thirty minutes to run through our drills unless you'd rather walk."

Julia looked at Charlie and said, "Hiking sounds great, and I'm going to pack a picnic lunch."

Charlie went over and placed her hands-on Andy's shoulders. "Is that it?"

He tilted his head to meet Charlie's blue eyes. "Uh huh. Think we could go to The Bus? No time like the present to test Spinning Time while it's fresh in my mind."

Charlie leaned in and kissed Andy on the lips. "Aw, honey, that's wonderful. The Bus is a good five miles away, and he does resemble the Needle-Horn. How far into the past do you think The Bus can go?"

Andy chuckled and said, "The Bus is a he?"

"Of course."

Phillip pressed his lips together in thought for a second. "In theory, once I've made the adjustments, The Bus could travel anywhere, anytime. If the time portals emulate a wormhole, there would be no limits. Once a date and time are entered in the program, the craft would arrive at its destination in milliseconds. Want to test her—oh, I mean *him* out?"

"Today?"

"Sure. Pick any time in history. Who would you want to meet or where would you want to go?"

Charlie placed her hand on her hip and said, "I want to meet Leonardo da Vinci."

Andy rapidly typed on his keyboard and pulled up info on Leo and printed out several pages of Da Vinci's inventions. "We shouldn't leave Julia."

Klock trotted into the room, barking, "Do I look like chopped liver? I'll stay with Julia."

Charlie laughed and said, "Klock says that he'll stay with Julia. What do you need from me?"

"I have a kit I use to work on my electronics. Do you have tools on The Bus?"

Charlie nodded. "Yes. How long do you think we'll be gone? Ruben would kill us if something happened to Julia. He and the Empyreal

Guards went to Asheville for additional supplies. They won't return until late afternoon."

Julia waved her hand and said, "Pish, posh. I have Klock, and we haven't seen any sign of Monica's enforcers."

Charlie sat on Andy's lap and said, "Are you sure it will work? The ship is calibrated to my DNA. What if we both end up as matter mash on the floor?"

"You're the one who told me about the Plates of Prophecy. If it works with us, we can do several expeditions, up to the delivery of the baby. That'll give me time to work out any kinks."

Charlie leaned in and kissed him. "I trust you, Phillip Andrew."

* * *

ANDY AND CHARLIE pulled on their backpacks, and then their merry band of hikers set off into the Pisgah National Forest. Their feet crunched the dried leaves of fall. The blue skies of October held no clouds as they walked along the trails.

Julia said, "Hey, stop just a sec. I have a cramp."

Andy swiftly turned and went to Julia while his face drained of color. "Are you okay?" He pulled a bottle of water out.

"Don't panic. Remember, I have a life inside of me, and he's kicking the daylights out of me. Wanna feel?"

Andy went on one knee and placed his hand on Julia's belly. His eyes went wide with surprise, and he looked over his shoulder and said, "Charlie, you gotta feel this."

Charlie stepped over and placed her hand over Julia's stomach. "Yup, he likes walking too. You want to sit for a minute?"

"No, the muscle cramp is gone, but I do have to pee. Andy, excuse us. Charlie, help me in case I squat and can't get up."

Laughing, Charlie said, "Just don't pee on my hiking boots, and you have a deal."

Minutes later, they were hiking a trail deep into the forest, the firs and evergreens so thick their boughs blocked most of the sun, and only streaks of light glimmered through them.

Klock ran off into the woods and came back barking, "We're here, Charlie. Just over there in the small clearing."

Charlie pulled up her sleeve and tapped on her watch releasing the Cloak Shield.

The ship appeared, and Andy's and Julia's mouths dropped open, and she said, "Wow, this makes it real. I didn't realize it would be so big. Can I look inside?"

Andy turned to Julia while slipping off his backpack and held the strap in his hand. "Not until I make adjustments. I don't want to take any risks with your or the baby's life. Charlie, will you let me in? Let me check out the system controls. Then you and Julia can set up camp. It's a gorgeous day."

The scent of firs and evergreens reminded him of Christmas. Charlie placed her thumb on the side of the ship and leaned her eye into the craft. The door slid open. Staring at the time machine, Andy felt he'd found his life's purpose.

Looking over her shoulder, Charlie waved and said, "Come on in and meet The Bus."

Andy's face lit up as he stepped inside the ship. "Charlie, I knew you were the girl of my dreams."

Andy placed his backpack on the steel table next to the door. He'd studied the interior of the ship intensely on his computer over the last five months. Stepping over to the frame that held the ship's electronic systems, Andy clicked the levers and removed the cover. He looked at Charlie and smiled. "It's okay. Leave me and stay with Julia. I'll come get you when he's ready."

Charlie leaned in a kissed his cheek. "Take care of my boy."

Most of Andy's life, he could look at a problem and visualize the mechanics like a movie playing in his brain. He calmed his racing pulse and took a deep breath, zoning in on the mechanical system of the ship, and began to work.

* * *

CHARLIE STEPPED out of the ship and walked over to Julia, who sat on the ground rubbing Klock's back. "For better or for worse, he's working on my ship. I'm scared and excited. Just a tinge of doubt lingers that if he screws up, I'm stuck here too."

Julia started giggling at first and then she started rolling with laughter making her belly jiggle like Santa doing a ho-ho-ho. "Welcome to the party, pal."

Rolling her eyes, Charlie sat on the ground and pulled out the picnic sandwiches, drinks, apples, cheese, and grapes with bottles of water. Charlie insisted everyone drink water most of the time. Water was the key to life, and there was no need muddying it up with a bunch of chemicals.

Klock inched over and said, "Pop some cheese in my mouth, beautiful."

Charlie threw her head back laughing. "Klock, you're such a flirt."

Klock barked, "I wouldn't have to flirt if you'd adopt a bitch. I'm thinking a blonde cocker spaniel."

Laughing, Charlie tossed him chunks of cheese one by one, and he jumped in the air to catch each piece in his mouth. "You're incorrigible, hound."

Julia adjusted her position on the quilt. "What's he saying?"

"Nothing of importance," replied Charlie.

He whined, "I need to get drunk."

Charlie chuckled. "Oh, I remember the last night you got lit at Moonbeams, you hit the karaoke with Bella Notte."

Klock wheezed with laughter. "Well, in drunk years, I'm eighty-nine."

Charlie pulled a small bowl out of her back pack and poured Klock water.

Julia waddled back on the old quilt she had insisted on bringing. Leaning on her side, Julia pushed the backpack under her head. "I have no idea what y'all are talking about, but I'm a little tired. You may have to help me get up later."

"Hey, before you fall asleep, I want to check your pulse." Charlie held Julia's pulse and counted as the seconds ticked on her multifaceted watch. "You're good. Just drink plenty of water today."

"Ugh, I will, but when we get home, I'm making sweet tea with sugar in the raw."

A couple of hours ticked away before Andy stuck his head out, giving them two thumbs up. He bounded out of the ship like a kid in a candy store. "Hand me a sandwich. Then let's take The Bus for a spin."

Julia said, "Are you sure it's safe?"

"Nope, but there's only one way to find out. Charlie, I've set the coordinates to Vinci, Italy of 1465. With any luck, will find Leo. Don't fret, Julia. I'll set the return coordinates to two minutes after we leave the first time. It'll be like we never left if my theory proves true. Just in case, say a few prayers. It can't hurt." Andy gobbled up his sandwich and chugged a bottle of water.

"Charlie, after you. I want you to navigate the maiden voyage. But the next place we check out, it's my turn." Andy dropped to his knees and hugged Julia. "It's the only way to see if my theory works. If it does, when the baby is born, you can go home."

Julia wiped the tears from her face. "I'm scared—no, I'm terrified that you and Charlie are risking your lives for me."

He chuckled again and said, "Not just you. For my grandfather, my dad, and me too. This trip affects all of us."

Charlie said, "I've been time traveling since the seventies. It's old hat for me. Come on, Andy, let's ride with the wind."

"Let's *spin* with the wind."

Andy and Charlie stepped into the craft and secured themselves into their harnesses. Sitting in the pilot seat, Charlie winked at Andy and clicked on the system controls.

The Bus hummed to life. *History in the making.*

Within a minute, the time machine stopped. Andy and Charlie exchanged looks, and she pressed the button on her watch to release the door. Stepping out into the rolling hills of Vinci, Andy promptly threw up.

Charlie rubbed his back. "It happens the first time. Next time it won't be so bad."

Andy rose and took a deep breath. They had made it. They'd done it! Dozens of haystacks sprawled across an open meadow. The countryside looked like a painting. "Where to first?'

"Let's hope they don't try and kill us." Charlie placed a weapon in her boot and one in the back of her pants and handed one to Andy. "It won't kill anyone. The bullets are called Black Beauties, meant to stun or paralyze, depending on the grade of the bullet. Only the strongest Black Beauties kill, and I don't have any of those. We may need time to escape hostiles."

"Oh, boy. I didn't think of that. I was so excited about meeting Da Vinci I didn't think people would want to harm us."

"The town is to the left. Do you know any Italian?"

"Enough, do you?"

"Yes, I speak many languages."

Andy pulled on his backpack with the images of Da Vinci's inventions. They walked across the meadow, and he was in awe. His Spinning Time Machine freaking worked like a charm.

At the end of the meadow, a teenage boy leaned against a haystack staring up at the sky. He startled and stood quickly when Andy and Charlie approached. Speaking in his native tongue, the young peasant said, "Who are you?"

Andy replied in Italian, "We are looking for Señor Leonardo da Vinci."

The boy's eyes widened, and he looked at Charlie and Andy. "I'm Leonardo da Vinci, at your service. Are you English?"

"Sort of."

In Italian, Charlie began to explain to Leonardo about their mission. Leonardo's eyes widened with surprise.

Andy reached into his pack and pulled out the copies of Da Vinci's work. "You are going to be famous, and not just while you're living. History will remember your name for all time."

Leonardo looked at the drawings and said, "Sir, may I keep these drawings?"

Charlie replied, "Keep them long enough to memorize the details, then destroy them. You don't want to be tried as a witch. It's been an honor to meet you, but we must return to our time."

Leonardo bowed, and with a smile, he said, "The pleasure has been mine."

Andy shook his hand, and Leonardo frowned at the gesture. "Wow, Leonardo, this is the highlight of my life, man."

Charlie placed her hand on Andy and said, "Julia's waiting."

They turned and ran as fast as they could to the ship, Andy whooping and hollering like a banshee. Inside the ship, he reset the coordinates to Pisgah National Forest two minutes after they left. Seconds later, the machine stopped. Exiting the ship, Andy threw up again.

Julia stood and said, "Did it work?"

Holding his hands on his knees, and breathing hard, Andy smiled. "It worked." He stumbled over to the quilt and collapsed. "That was so freaking cool. Oh my god, I met Leonardo da Vinci."

Charlie joined him on the quilt placing her hand on his thigh. "We both met him. Drink water, Andy. Lots of it before we head back to the house." Charlie punched a button on her watch, and the ship disappeared. "I didn't ask before because I too was caught up in the moment, but did you deactivate ATTRA's GPS device on The Bus?"

Raising a brow, he said, "Yes, darling. Monica has no knowledge of our expedition. I think you need to move the ship closer to the Chalet. There's a meadow on the property less than a quarter mile away. That way we can have quicker access."

"Andy, do the blueprints of Needle-Horn mention any details of the Cloak Shield?"

"Yeah. Why?"

"Monica has an ATTRA watch like mine."

Nodding in thought, he said, "I'll study those pages later and see if I can change the software, but that may mean I'll need to disassemble your watch."

"No, I need the watch. Maybe Ruben has an extra one you can use to conduct an experiment."

He said, "We'll leave the craft here for now, but it needs to be moved closer to the Chalet before the snow. We'll keep an eye on the weather. You think Ruben and his guards are back from Asheville yet? I can't wait to work on his ship too."

Ruben had returned with two immortal guards from the Empyreal Palace in July. The guards were a head taller than Andy, and he'd seen their butterfly wings shimmering during the night as they patrolled the Chalet.

Ruben had taken the immortals for supplies in Asheville. The guards made Ruben and his vehicle unseen to mortals. Julia insisted Ruben pay for the supplies, and he assured her the guards would leave cash in the register after they took any item.

Charlie looked at her watch and said, "By the time we hike back to the Chalet, they should be cooling their heels. Ruben's going to be so jealous we went to see Leo without him."

Julia huffed and said, "Or mad. I hope he found me some clothes. The ones I have are getting tight. Let's head back."

Charlie rubbed Andy's back. "You up for a hike?"

"Yup. My legs are a little weak, but I don't want to be stuck on the mountain in the dark. They say aliens live up here."

Julia snorted and laughed. "Guess the ole timers were right, huh?"

Andy had heard old tales of flying saucers and alien beings living in the mountains. He wondered if it was Charlie's ship that had spurred the stories.

* * *

CLICKING AWAY ON HER KEYBOARD, Monica went over the transcripts from General Agriaous. He had received and assigned jobs to the recent transport of Spinners on Veetreous. Based on the documentation, the colony was thriving.

The settlements had built a water pipeline, and the solar energy panels generated enough power for tools and machinery to build the beautiful New Jerusalem. Soon, the barter system would switch over to currency bearing the image of Queen Monica the First. She giggled to herself.

Chen knocked softly on the glass door of Monica's office. She waved him in. "Yes, Chen?"

"Commander, you asked me to notify you if I had any signals from Ruben's or Charlie's ships. Charlie's ship left Earth and, well…"

"Well, what?" She drummed her fingers on the desk waiting for his reply.

"Well, Commander, the ship disappeared. We thought it could be a glitch in the system, and most of the other ships are accounted for." Chen nervously shifted on his feet, then flinched at her scream.

"It disappeared. How?" She stormed over to Chen glaring into his terror-filled eyes.

Wringing his hands, he said, "There is one possibility. Charlie could've disengaged the GPS tracking system."

"Charlie is a pilot, not a mechanical engineer." Monica shook, and her hands turned into fists. "Andy Clayborn. Charlie Fine is dead. I am going to kill that bitch."

"Commander?"

"What the hell?"

"Ruben's ship isn't giving off signals either." Chen backed his way to the door.

Rage filled Monica, and she pointed to the door. "Get out. Don't come back until you find my ships. Do I make myself clear?"

Chen nodded and turned, nearly sprinting out of her sight.

"Ruben and Charlie, you want to defy me? So be it. I'll find you and your little dog too."

***

RUBEN AND ANDY had refitted the Needle-Horn with the Spinning Time specifications and made a quick expedition to Colonial Williamsburg in 1784 to test the machine. Ruben's great-great-grand-father had lived there after the American Revolutionary War. Thomas Jefferson had hired him as a land surveyor to build roads to the South. It had been one of the most thrilling experiences of Ruben's life.

After returning to the present day, Ruben and Charlie moved the

Needle-horn and The Bus closer to the Chalet before the snow season hit. Once the snow began, the Chalet created a cocoon of warmth for the eclectic group of people: Andy and Julia, Azreal and Chayliel, and Charlie and Ruben. Julia's pregnancy progressed nicely, and for the first time in a long while, Ruben felt like he belonged to a family.

Christmas and New Year's came and went with celebration. January had them playing cards and Monopoly during the day with movie marathons at night. February had unseasonably warm days, and the next plummeting temperatures had them using the chainsaw for more wood.

The weeks of Julia's pregnancy were coming to an end, and with it came a pause, a stillness in the house of uncertainty. Azreal and Chayliel guarded the exterior of the house night and day starting the first of March. More than once Ruben placed Charlie and Julia in the safe place in the bathroom under the stairs due to severe storms and high winds.

The last week of Julia's pregnancy had been perfect. Plenty of sunshine and warmer temps had buttercups blooming and buds on the trees threatening to burst with life.

One morning after breakfast, Julia sat on the little loveseat in Phillip's study talking with Andy. Ruben walked in and sat beside her. He slipped off her shoes and began to massage her swollen feet.

"My ankles are swelling again."

Ruben said, "No more salt in anything. We don't want you to develop pre-eclampsia."

Charlie stepped into the study and sat on the edge of Andy's desk. "You need to drink more water, and don't look at me like that. I get it that you pee every five seconds."

Julia perked up, tilting her head to the side. "So, no walking today?"

"How about a short walk?"

Julia's shoulders slumped, and she released a heavy sigh.

Charlie offered Julia a bemused smile. "Look on the bright side. Every day you're one day closer to holding your baby boy."

Andy swiveled around in his chair. "Do you think she should walk with her ankles that swollen?"

Charlie's smile grew into a smirk. "Yes, walking helps the blood flow. But it's your call, Julia."

Julia lifted her chin. "Okay, I can do it."

Charlie said, "Let's go, chickens. Time waits for no one." She started laughing and playfully popped Andy's head. "Get it?"

Ruben teased, "Weirdo." He enjoyed seeing Charlie happy. The eight months they'd been hiding out together had been the happiest time of his life. Every day Julia came closer to delivery, Ruben knew it meant the time with Julia and Andy would end soon. How? He didn't know. He didn't want to.

Julia stood and extended her hand to Ruben. "Come on, lazy bones. Let's go for a walk. There's a winter storm brewing this afternoon, and I want to get back before it starts."

Andy said, "While my program is saving to the external drive, I'll change into my sweats. Julia, do you need anything?"

"Nope. I'm ready. You all need to slow your pace today. Oh, crap." Julia held onto her belly. "I think I just had a contraction."

With light sarcasm, Charlie added, "You'll do anything to keep from walking. I'm timing you. If you don't have another one anytime soon, it's probably Braxton Hicks. But if you want, I can check your cervix in the labor and delivery room."

Weeks ago, Ruben and Andy had painted the extra bedroom on the second floor a soothing sage while Julia and Charlie transformed it into a labor and delivery room.

Julia waved her hand in the air. "Oh, no. I'm sure I'm fine. To be honest, I'm scared out of my mind at giving birth. The thought of an eight-pound baby coming out of my vagina just gives me the willies. Let me pee, and I'll meet you downstairs."

Ruben shook his head and shivered all over. "God, Julia, stop with the vivid imagery."

The expression on Andy's face changed to one of concern. "Should we take her to the hospital?"

Charlie's arms went around his neck. "I promise I've had extensive medical training regarding many different situations, including delivering a baby. If she has another contraction, I'll check her cervix."

Andy shoulder-bumped Charlie "I trust you, Charlie."

* * *

AFTER LEAVING THE MASTER BATHROOM, Julia took another breath and made her way into the kitchen to grab a bottle of water for the walk. Ruben sat at the bar thumbing through an old issue of *Sports Illustrated*. Charlie and Andy walked down the stairs together.

Stroking the side of her neck, Julia nodded at her new family. She had fantasized over the last eight months as her child grew in her womb about Phillip and her setting up house together, loving each other, buying baby furniture and clothes. He would've fussed over her, and adored her growing belly. Her parents and Sloane would've celebrated in their happiness.

Julia improvised by talking to the baby about Phillip often. Telling him the same bedtime stories Bunny and Big Joe had told her and Sloane. Julia loved her little boy more than anything else in the world. She had unconditional love for the son she would soon deliver and didn't dwell on the what ifs. Julia allowed herself to live in the moment.

Andy and Charlie had bought the baby furniture and baby clothes using a secure site he had set up with the untraceable device from Ruben. They had the stuff delivered two towns over in a rental apartment Charlie found and used as a provisional safe house.

The four of them went out the front door, where Klock waited for them. Julia reached down and rubbed his ears. "Good morning, Klock. You ready for a walk, boy?" He barked and nodded.

Ruben threw up his hand in greetings. "Good morning, we're going on a short walk, and we'll be back soon." Azreal and Chayliel nodded to Ruben.

Pink buds covered the mature cherry trees with their massive knotted trunks in the back garden. The rock water fountain had been turned off before the freeze last fall. A great storm with swirling dark clouds brewed in the distance beyond the snow covered mountain top.

Klock went ahead of their pack, no doubt looking for Monica's enforcers, as Julia followed behind Charlie. Ruben and Andy followed behind her on the narrow path along the mountain trail. With every step, Julia felt like she walked in quicksand.

So, Julia concentrated on breathing, and about a mile into the walk, she stopped, and Ruben bumped into her, nearly knocking her to the ground. He grabbed Julia and said, "What's wrong?"

Hair rose on her nape and arms, and Julia's voice quaked, "My water broke."

Calmness resonated from Charlie as she turned around. "Do you think you can walk? Or do you want Andy and Ruben to carry you?"

Blinking rapidly, Julia said, "I'll walk if I can. We'll get back faster."

Charlie placed a hand on Julia's cheek. "It takes hours before you give birth, sweetie. Most first timers go eight to twenty-four hours in labor, so, don't panic. Remember how we practiced. Concentrate on your breathing."

Julia relaxed a bit, and with a nod, she said, "I'll walk."

By the time Julia reached the house, her contractions were getting more consistent and stronger. It felt as though the baby would just explode through the skin of her belly instead of the birth canal. Andy picked Julia up and carried her to the second-floor delivery room.

The soothing sage walls and cream-colored curtains, with fragrant diffusers of lavender placed around the room, calmed Julia. Andy lowered her onto the bed, and she knew Charlie and Ruben moved about the room getting things together for the baby's arrival, but Julia didn't pay any attention to them. Julia zeroed in on Andy's face, so like his grandfather's. She squeezed his hand and said, "Stay with me, Andy. Don't leave me."

Andy pulled a stool up to the birthing table he'd ordered online. He pushed the hair away from her face and kissed the back of her hand. "I'm not going anywhere, Grannie."

Julia let out a laugh. "Is this whacked? I'm giving birth to your daddy."

Andy's face shone with excitement and tears glazed over his eyes. "I know, right? So, Phillip Andrew Junior will come into the world in the arms of his son. It has a kind of poetic justice to it. I don't remember him as a man, but I'll gaze into his eyes as an infant."

Julia eased a bit. It was as if Phillip was in the room with them. His spiritual presence was so intense that chills ran up her arms like tiny pricks of a needle. That's how Julia's labor began.

Charlie had cleaned Julia up and draped her in sterile linens then checked her cervix. "You've dilated to a five, and we have to make it to a ten."

The bittersweet pain was made bearable by the all-consuming love filling the room.

Ruben began to whistle a soft medley, and Julia asked, "What's the name of that song?"

Ruben walked over to the top of the bed and held her hand. "'Till We Meet Again.' I served in World War I. The song was very popular back then. I used to whistle it when I got nervous before a battle, and it steadied my nerves."

Tears glistened in Julia's eyes. "Sing it to me, please."

Ruben said, "The lyrics were written by Raymond Egan in 1918 during the Great War. Families were being torn apart, losing sons, husbands, and fathers. I can't remember the words. It was a long time ago, but I can whistle it."

Julia nodded, and as he whistled the sad tune, she broke out in a cold sweat. The conversation between Charlie and Andy became background noise as she approached ten centimeters.

Julia lay on her back, and Charlie placed several pillows under her hips while Ruben held her hand. Andy moved a stack of soft towels onto the side table next to Julia. He put a blanket over Julia and had several baby blankets ready to prevent Junior from developing hypothermia.

Charlie had drilled and coached them over the months, preparing them for today, and Julia kept thanking her.

Charlie spoke in a soft voice, "Julia, we're heading into the delivery of your baby. He is in position, so when I tell you to push, honey, you push. I'm ready for him. I can see his head." Charlie laughed, and said, "He has a head full of black hair."

Julia let out a sob and screamed at the same time as Charlie said, "Push, Julia."

Julia pushed and screamed. It felt as if a tiger were clawing his way out of her, not a baby.

"I got him, Julia, I got him. He's beautiful. Look, Andy's going to clean him up a bit before he gives you the baby. I'm going to use this clean string to cut the cord. Then we'll concentrate on the delivery of the placenta."

She had a death grip on Ruben's hand, and he leaned down and kissed her forehead. "You did beautifully. He is a healthy baby boy." A single tear glistened on Ruben's face.

Julia's body shivered and shook from exhaustion. The pain level from one to ten was a freaking ten. But she continued to concentrate on her breathing as she watched Charlie and Andy clean and wrap little Phillip in a blanket to keep him warm. They had warming lights ready if needed.

Andy placed little Phillip in her arms. Smiling with tears rolling down her cheeks, she said, "My beautiful baby boy. Hi, baby, I'm your mama."

Andy looked at Ruben, then down at Julia. "You need to try and breastfeed. Remember what Charlie said, it'll help getting rid of the afterbirth."

Charlie came back to her and said, "Okay, darling, you're doing brilliantly. Here comes the placenta. After this, I'll clean you up and get you both comfortable. I have pain pills if you want one. It won't hurt you or the baby."

Julia shook her head as her baby latched onto her right nipple. "No pain pills. I want to remember everything. Thank you, Charlie, and thank you, Ruben and Andy. He's beautiful, so beautiful." Happy tears rolled down her face.

Charlie placed her hand on Julia's arm. "We're going to clean up the room a bit while you get to know your son. When you feel up to it, I'll help you take a shower. It'll help your milk to come in."

Julia stared at the little miracle she held in her arms. When Junior fell asleep, Julia closed her eyes and prayed to God to protect her baby. A few hours later, Andy took his father in his arms while Charlie helped Julia into the shower. The circle of life completed.

* * *

THE NEXT FEW weeks went by blissfully fast for Julia. All the energy in the house was directed toward her sweet little bundle of joy. Thanks to Charlie's rigorous workouts during her pregnancy, Julia's body returned to normal quick.

March had arrived with storms and severe winds, but the old saying, "in like a lion out like a lamb," held true. The cherry blossom trees were in full bloom, and wildflowers and grasses scattered among the rocky crags. Julia and her baby sat in the back garden with Klock at her feet. The air was much warmer than typical for late March.

Ruben, Azreal, and Chayliel were making a quick run into town for supplies. Andy and Charlie walked hand in hand from the house to the garden.

"Dinner is ready, my lady." Andy bowed to Julia.

"Yum, I stay hungry all the time. Junior's sleeping so peacefully, and I hate to disturb him." Every time Julia looked at her child, her love for him grew and grew so much more than she ever thought possible.

Charlie leaned over and said, "Let me have my little boy." She placed the small baby in her arms, and they walked back to the house, laughing.

Life was too perfect. Julia thought—*the calm before the storm*—and hated when she was right.

* * *

MONICA MET with her team of enforcers at a local motel next to the interstate before heading out to Phillip's Chalet. The team had found Julia a few weeks before the birth of the baby boy. She had given instructions to allow the child to nurse from his biological mother for the first month of his life.

Monica arrived last night with two security specialists that would deactivate any defense guards Ruben had put in place. Upon arriving, Monica learned that Ruben had secured two Empyreal Guards. Kidnapping the child should've been a cakewalk, but with the two immortals, things could get dicey.

They had mapped out a plan to meet in the little grove of trees diagonally across from the property, around one hundred feet from the sensor trip alarms. She looked through a pair of binoculars at the happy family.

Monica had waited decades to have a family, and she was so close to her soon-to-be-son. If all went as planned, Monica and her new son would be back in Lunar City by midnight. A wet nurse and nanny waited to care for her child.

She'd gone over names during Julia's pregnancy. There was no way his name would be Phillip. Not her child. She had decided on Henry Theodore Adams, after her father. Henry would help Monica rule the world. Finally, her dreams were coming true.

As soon as dark fell, they would storm the house. Monica hadn't seen any signs of Ruben, and her Trackers hadn't been successful locating his ship or Charlie's.

Looking at her watch, Monica pressed the button on the side, and her team approached. All of them dressed in black. "Do I need to cover the operation again? Or are we good?"

Stormy's hand pushed the leather jacket away, and she touched her weapons in the holster hanging low on her hips. "I don't know about the rest of these morons, but I've been ready."

"Synchronize your watches, and at my signal, we storm the house." In a few minutes, they'd attack the Chalet. Her blood was pumping. Monica hadn't been on a kill mission in some time. She'd take out Charlie and Ruben first, then Julia. She hadn't decided whether she'd keep Andy or not. He was a brilliant physicist and could prove useful later.

The weapons loaded with the highest grade of Black Beauties were lethal to a mortal. They'd stun an immortal for maybe five or ten minutes, so Monica had a very narrow window of time to get in and get out with the kid.

One by one, Monica watched the lights flicker on in the Chalet. The warm glow of light cast a pretty picture, but not for long. Her wristband lit up three times, which meant the specialists had deactivated the safeguards.

The time had come to take control of her destiny. Monica entered the black Escalade with the rest of the enforcers and drove to the end of the Chalet's driveway.

Exiting the vehicle in silence, Monica circled her hand over her head, and the team broke off into twos. She pulled two weapons and strode purposefully, straight up the hill, in full view of the Chalet. Klock flew off the front steps, heading for her, teeth exposed, growling, and saliva dripping from his jowls.

Klock attacked. Monica shot the dog jumping in midair. He fell to the ground whimpering. She leaned over and spat on him. "I've been waiting a long time, Klock. If you live long enough, give my regards to your master." She hopped over the dog and took the steps two at a time. She shot the lock and kicked the door open and shouted, "Honey, I'm home."

* * *

JULIA WOKE IN A PANIC. Shots outside meant Monica had found them. She grabbed her baby as Charlie burst into the room. Julia threw the baby sling at Charlie and said, "Take him to Phillip. Don't think, Charlie, just take him to his father. Remember, Phillip raises him. The future is now our present. I'll buy you some time."

Visibly shaken, Charlie said, "Damn it. Damn it to hell. Where is Ruben?" She placed the sling over her shoulder and went out the bedroom window with little Phillip.

Julia pushed the dresser in front of the bedroom door to set up a barricade. She heard Monica yelling, "Honey, I'm home."

The enemy overtook the house. Andy shouted, and Julia heard

fighting, glass breaking, and then a dull thud to the ground, shaking the wall she leaned against, and everything went silent. Julia stared without seeing while her body shook uncontrollably. Her heart pounded, her pulse raced, and sweat beaded on her upper lip.

Julia grabbed the baseball bat in the corner and waited for them to break her door down.

Monica yelled, "It's no use, Julia. I have plans, and you have served your purpose. Give me the baby, and I'll let Phillip's grandson live. If not, I'll kill him, and I don't make idle threats."

Bullets pelleted the master bedroom door.

Julia pressed her body next to the wall and raised the baseball bat over her head. She wasn't going down without a fight. Someone big was ramming the door, and after three tries, the door splintered. A tall blond man stuck his head in, and Julia hit him as hard as she could. He fell to the floor, blood oozing from his skull.

Monica sighed and said, "Damn it, Johnnie. What did you go and do that for? Julia, you killed one of the sweetest lays I've ever had. Hey, Zane, Stormy, get over here and move this dresser. Julia, put down your weapon, dear. There's no need for me to kill you, yet."

"I don't believe you, bitch. Once you get my son, I'm dead, and I'd rather go down fighting." Julia held the bat above her head ready to crack the next skull that entered her room.

"My, my, my, don't you have some spunk. No wonder Ruben and Charlie like you. Too bad you must die, but the boy can't have two mothers. It would be too confusing."

Zane broke into Julia's room, and before he tackled her to the ground, Julia broke his wrist with the bat, and it hung loose, bone exposed. He screamed like a crazy person, and kicked Julia in the stomach, making her fly backward crashing onto the floor out of breath.

"Bring her into the living area." Monica spun around and left the bedroom.

Zane held his wrist close to his chest as he dragged Julia out of the room by her hair and dropped her at Monica's feet next to the rock fireplace. "The baby boy is gone. Stormy went after Charlie, and this cunt broke my wrist."

Monica grabbed Julia's hair and jerked her head back until tears spilled from the pain. "Where's Charlie taking the boy? Tell me." Andy sat nearby, a dish towel stuffed in his mouth. Tears leaked from his eyes as another enforcer held a knife to Andy's throat. "You like Andy? Don't' you? I'll cut off his fingers one at a time until you tell me what you've done with my son."

Julia screamed, "He's *my* son." Monica punched her in the face so hard Julia crumbled to her knees and passed out.

* * *

RUBEN KNEW AS SOON as he saw the black Escalade he was too late. A sinking sensation settled in the pit of his stomach. Azreal, Chayliel, and Ruben took off at a dead run to the Chalet. The front door had been busted in, and then Ruben heard a whimper.

Ruben looked down, and rage rolled out of his chest. "Klock, buddy, are you alive?"

Whimpering, Klock said, "It hurts, Boss. I didn't know being shot hurt so much."

Ruben placed his hand on Klock's chest. "I'll be back. Hang on, Klock. I have a bitch to kill."

Ruben exploded onto the scene, with Azreal and Chayliel as his wingmen blasting weapons. He didn't think, he acted.

Monica shouted to Ruben that she'd kill Julia. She gripped Julia by the hair while holding a nine-inch blade at Julia's jugular vein.

Everything went into slow motion as his senses heightened as his kill mode kicked in.

Ruben pulled the trigger and pumped off three rounds into the center of Monica's forehead, blowing her against the wall in a spray of blood and brains.

Azreal and Chayliel were equally successful, killing the other enforcers, including Zane.

Ruben scooped up Julia into his arms and brought her over to the couch as Chayliel helped Andy. "I'll be right back." Ruben quickly scanned the rest of the house for other attackers, and for Charlie. "Julia, honey, where is Charlie? Where's the baby?"

Julia flinched away from Ruben. She didn't recognize him, just sat there shaking her head, her body tensed. Ruben had seen that look before and knew she was in shock. He lowered his voice, "Julia, it's Ruben. Honey, where's the baby?"

Andy held a cold compress to his left side cut by a shard of glass, and his eyes nearly swollen shut from a severe beating. Breathlessly, Andy worked his jaw for a second, then said, "Charlie took the baby to Phillip. You must help her, Ruben. Stormy went after her and the baby. Please, Ruben, help them."

Ruben's chest heaved up and down with the weight of anger and the need for revenge. He knelt before Julia and squeezed her hand. Ruben's voice remained controlled while he reined his emotions. "Julia, I'm leaving Chayliel with you and Andy. I must go, but I'll be back. I promise."

Julia's fingernails bit into her skin, as she stared into nothingness and remained silent.

Ruben's face set in a hard line as he spoke through gritted teeth. "Let's make tracks, Azreal. Time has run out, my brother."

Ruben and Azreal made it to the Needle-Horn in minutes. Seconds later, they arrived in Burkett Falls, the year of our Lord, nineteen hundred and fifty.

CHAPTER 19

1950 Burkett Falls

Phillip and Amelia left the courthouse. He had made plans to take them on a honeymoon at the end of the semester. "Are you sure that's okay with you? We could drive up to Asheville for the night?"

Amelia placed her hand in the crook of his arm. "No, honey, you have work and so do I. We'll take a trip to the beach when the semester ends."

Phillip opened the passenger door for Amelia, and she got in. He made his way to the driver's side, took a deep breath and slipped into the car. They drove down Main Street, passing Big Joe's.

He wouldn't think of Julia today.

Spring had come early, and the warm weather had the flowers and buds on the trees sprouting.

Dusk eased into the night as he pulled in the driveway. He parked in the garage, and Amelia got out of the car. He turned for only a second when Amelia yelped. He wheeled around, and his heart hammered in his chest. A woman with black hair, ashen face, black eyes, and piercings in her nose, mouth, and tongue, had a knife to Amelia's throat.

The crazed-looking woman held Amelia securely in her grip. His mouth went dry as the woman whispered, "Shush. Let's be real quiet. There's someone in your house that I'm looking for, and if you cooperate with me, your lady friend might survive. If not, I guess you'll meet on the other side."

Phillip threw his hands in the air. "Look, you have the wrong house. You can have my wallet. Take my car, but please, let my wife go."

Stormy started cackling. "You got married? No, shit. Well, Julia gave birth to your son. He's inside, and he's coming with me. So, let's move it, bro, real nice and easy."

Phillip's mind went blank as he walked ahead of the deranged woman. He glanced over his shoulder and saw Amelia had tears in her eyes. He prayed for help. Phillip fumbled with the keys and entered in darkness. Palms sweating, he went to switch on the lights when someone grabbed him and propelled him against the far wall.

Stormy entered with Amelia in the foyer. In the darkness, Phillip heard a scuffle, and shots rang out as he pulled himself off the floor and ran and flipped the main light switch.

In the foyer, Amelia and the intruder lay seemingly dead. He stared unblinking as he dropped to his knees and pulled Amelia into his arms, checking for a pulse. The intruder had stuck her knife in the side of Amelia's neck. Blood gushed from her wound, and he cried out in agony, "Oh, God, Oh, God, Amelia." He rocked Amelia back and forth in his arms.

Charlie closed the door and knelt on the floor beside him. She placed her hand on his shoulder. "Phillip, look, you have to call the police. Report Stormy as an intruder that you fought, and she killed your wife, then you shot her. Are you listening?"

Trembling from head to toe, Phillip heard a baby cry. His mind was reeling with an overload of emotions. Terrified, he looked up at Charlie and said, "Is that…my son?"

Tears filled Charlie's eyes, and she replied, "Yes, I'll bring him to you. But you need to call the police. I'll wait until they leave, and then we'll talk, okay?"

A numbness washed over him as he carefully laid Amelia back on the floor. Her blood covered Phillip. He walked into the kitchen and went to the sink to wash his hands, then lifted the telephone receiver on the black rotary phone, and dialed the Sheriff's Department.

Charlie walked in with his infant son sucking on her pinky finger. Tears welled in his eyes as he looked at the baby boy, and she said, "I'm grabbing a clean shirt out of your closet, then I'm taking Junior with me to the store for some formula, and hopefully they'll have diapers and stuff. I need money and the keys to your car. I promise we'll come back."

Phillip reached into his pocket, pulled out his wallet and gave Charlie all his cash. "The keys are in the car." He watched his son leave with Charlie, and shortly after they left, the police arrived.

Phillip answered question after question until they were satisfied. An ambulance from the city morgue took Amelia and the killer. Poor, sweet Amelia. He seemed to bring bad luck to the women in his life.

An hour and a half later, the room had been cleaned, and he'd showered and changed clothes. Phillip sat in the kitchen drinking a cup of coffee waiting on Charlie to return. The doorbell rang, and he jumped. He ran and flung the door open. Ruben and a very tall man stood at the front door, both covered in blood.

Shaking, Phillip said, "Julia? Is she dead too?"

"May we come in, Phillip?"

Phillip motioned them into the kitchen. Ruben's eyes darted about the room, and his face seemed contorted in pain. "What happened here? I saw the police and the ambulance. Where's Charlie and the baby?"

Phillip's nostrils flared, and he shouted, "I got married today. I wasn't married a good hour before some deranged woman killed my wife. Charlie shot the intruder, then took my son and left while I had to deal with the detectives."

Shaking his head, Phillip jabbed his forefinger into Ruben's chest. "You have to make this right, Ruben Callaway. Do you hear me? You do right by Julia. You made me a promise."

The door cracked open, and Charlie came in with a sleeping baby.

She went over and placed the infant in Phillip's arms. "He's named after his daddy, Phillip Andrew Clayborn Junior."

Phillip held his son with trembling hands as tears glazed over his eyes. "He's so small but beautiful, isn't he?"

Charlie gave him a soft look of compassion. "Yes, Phillip, he is." Turning to Ruben, her brows creased with concern. "How's Julia, Andy, and Klock?"

Ruben sucked in air through his teeth. With a scowl, he shook his head slowly and said, "Julia's in shock. Andy is alive but got the shit kicked out of him, and Klock took a bullet for the team. I'll head back soon. If you want to go on, I'll catch up later."

Charlie placed a hand on Phillip's shoulder. "I bought what I could for Junior. But you'll need to call Sloane tonight and tell her what happened. She'll help you care for the boy. It's what Julia wanted. Now, I have to check on my people."

Phillip blinked tears away, and with a quiver in his voice, he said, "Tell Julia I'll do right by our son. I won't let her down again."

Charlie pressed her forehead to his, and said, "Oh, Phillip, you've never let her down." She turned and punched Ruben in the arm. "Drinks on you when the mission is over?"

With a sharp nod, Ruben said, "Yeah, sure."

Azreal uncrossed his massive arms and stepped over to Ruben. "Hey, I'm catching a ride with Charlie. All right?"

Ruben nodded again and watched them leave.

Phillip brought the baby into the little den and sat down. "Are you going to tell me what happened?"

Ruben sat in the chair opposite of Phillip and relayed what had happened since their last meeting. He explained that Andy had developed a time machine using the notes from Phillip's journal. Then he told Phillip about Monica's attack. "Phillip, you're living in a parallel universe. While you may not understand all the details, I will do what is in my power to set this wrong, right. Just know without a shadow of a doubt, Julia loves you and none of this was your fault." Ruben's shoulders slumped, and he dropped his head into his hands.

Phillip gave him a long look of sadness and a tight smile. "Promise if Julia doesn't return to me that you'll take care of her, always?"

"You can bet your life on it." Ruben dragged himself out of the chair. "Don't give up. Have faith, Phillip." He walked out of the house, shutting the door behind him.

* * *

PRESENT DAY CHALET

Julia hadn't moved from the couch since the attack. Chayliel was not of this world with her massive shimmering butterfly wings. She watched Chayliel clean the house and remove the dead bodies and debris with lightning speed.

Chayliel brought Klock in the house and treated his wound. She lovingly cared for the alien dog, who responded by licking her hands repeatedly. The bullet went clean through Klock's muscle, just barely missing his main artery.

Chayliel gently laid Klock on the braided rug in front of the fire. She stepped over to Andy while he slept in the recliner and removed the ice pack, then placed her hands on his eyes until the swelling and bruises were gone. Then she healed his injured side.

Julia watched but never said a word. She had no feelings. None. Physical, mental, and emotional numbness engulfed Julia in despair. Chayliel leaned over her and placed her hands over the marks Monica's punches had left.

Chayliel and Julia locked eyes, and Julia sensed her peace and joy even under the dire circumstances of the day. Chayliel smiled at her and said, "All is well with your soul."

Charlie returned first with Azreal. She walked into the house and went to Julia. Dropping to her knees, she said, "Phillip has your son. He wanted you to know he would take care of him for both of you. Phillip said he wouldn't let you down this time."

Julia supposed she was in a state of shock. She heard Charlie, but she just couldn't move, she couldn't cry. Julia wanted to die, and she didn't think she could bear the loss of a child. Inside her soul, she disappeared through locked doors safely behind a stoic wall of ice.

Ruben came in a few hours later and gave Charlie orders to take Azreal and Chayliel to the Empyreal Palace then instructed her to return to the Chalet.

Andy woke up and stood. "I feel like crap."

Ruben rubbed his neck and took a seat next to Julia, and she noticed his hands trembled. He looked at her, his tears glistening in the moonlight, and he said, "I'm taking you home in the morning. Charlie and I are taking you home. Do you hear me?"

Julia's body stiffened. Ruben had told her stuff like that before. He'd made promises, and she didn't want to hope. "I hear you, Ruben. I'm just not sure I believe you."

"Dammit, woman, I said I was taking you home. That's what you want. Isn't it? That's what you always wanted. Now, get your ass into the shower and go to bed. We're leaving at oh-eight-hundred. I want Charlie to say her goodbyes to Andy, and then we're going on a trip."

Kneeling on the floor next to Klock, Ruben said, "How are you, old friend?"

Klock whined and whimpered. "Chayliel healed me. I no longer hurt, but I'm just dog tired in my bones. Are we going home too, Boss?"

"Soon, Klock, very soon."

Julia listened to Ruben. Dare she hope? A sliver of light crept behind the locked doors. Julia went into the master bathroom and showered. She selected an outfit which would complement the time era where she would travel. Julia curled into the fetal position on the bed. She longed for Phillip, but she missed her baby.

The visible bruises were gone, but the emotional injuries remained. Julia grimaced because she'd taken a human life today. But somewhere back in time, her son was with his father, and that gave her a modicum of comfort before she fell asleep.

* * *

THE NEXT MORNING, Julia stepped into the main room.

Charlie, the lionhearted, kissed Andy as tears wet her cheeks. "I'm going to miss you more than you know."

Andy caressed Charlie's face with the palm of his hand. "Will I ever see you again, Charlie?"

Charlie gave him a wide grin and hugged him tightly. "Count on it."

She went to Julia and squeezed her hand. "Well, it looks like this is it, my dear friend. You know, you're the first real friend I've ever had before."

Ruben glanced at the floor, and then looked up. "Are you ready to spin, my friends?"

Julia nodded. "I've been ready," She turned to Andy and said, "If the Lord is willing, I'll see you again, but I'll be much older. I love you, Andy."

Andy ran over, picked Julia up and spun them around and around. "I love you, Grannie." Then placed her feet back on the floor.

Ruben hugged Andy and slapped his back. "I'll catch you on the flip side. Klock, can you travel, dog?"

Klock barked, "Hell yes, take me to Lunar City. I miss my homies."

* * *

RUBEN PICKED up his pace along the trail to the Needlehorn. Klock ran a few feet ahead of him, and Julia and Charlie trailed slightly behind them. Climbing elevation in the mountains, the temperature dropped, and he said, "Do either of you want my jacket? It's in my pack."

"No. I'm fine. How much further?" Julia walked double-time to keep up with Ruben.

"Just over in the thicket." Ruben closed the gap to where he left the Needle-Horn, pushed up his sleeve and entered the code on his wristband.

The Cloak Shield slid away, and he pressed his thumb on the ID pad, then scanned his eye on the retina recognition screen. The door hissed opened. He smiled and motioned for Julia and Charlie to enter his ship. When this was over, Ruben intended on getting wasted with Charlie at Moonbeams later.

Ruben explained to Julia, "You're only going to get a couple of minutes before Phillip goes into panic mode over your disappearance. He's not going to understand your clothing and neither will your sister. Don't try to explain it. Everything will work out in the end."

Julia replied, "How do you know that?"

Ruben shrugged. "It always does, somehow. You're arriving at the end of a parallel universe loop. Think of jumping rope back at school recess with two people looping the ropes around and around. You remember, Double Dutch? Think of the timing right before you jump into the fray. It's the same principle. As soon as you cross the threshold at the beach, you're going to jump in between the two universe loops. Just as the 1948 loop opens, this parallel universe loop will close, forever."

"It seems like a dream, Ruben. I can't believe that I'm finally going home." Julia brushed her tears away with her fingers.

Entering the Needle-Horn, Charlie strapped herself in, and Ruben strapped in Julia and Klock before climbing into the pilot seat, securing himself. Ruben entered the coordinates and flipped the main control switches. The Needle-Horn hummed with life. He looked out of the window toward the Chalet. "Thanks, Andy, for Spinning Time."

And within seconds they left present day for 1948.

* * *

1948 BURKETT FALLS

The Needle-Horn appeared silently behind the cliffs of Burkett Falls. Ruben helped Julia out of the ship and smiled. "Right around the corner is the man of your dreams." He hugged her, then placed a small Black Beauty on the back of Julia's neck. The variation of the drug disappeared in an hour and the past nine months will be like a bad dream. "This is where we part ways, my little sister."

Julia reached up and kissed him on the lips. Then she hugged and kissed Charlie. "Ruben and Charlie, I don't have the right words to thank you. But, thank you, thank you, and thank you." Julia's eyes brightened, and her face lit up his world one last time.

"Go on now before I change my mind and haul your ass to the moon."

Julia took off toward the Falls but stopped, turned, and blew Ruben and Charlie kisses, then ran to the sandy rock beaches. "Phillip, oh Phillip, I'm here."

From the cover of the forest, Ruben and Charlie watched Julia and Phillip's reunion. Charlie shoulder-bumped him, and he said, "What?"

Charlie lifted her chin, and with a wide grin, she said, "Looks like I have to save your sorry ass again."

Draping an arm around Charlie's shoulders, he smiled. "You like me, don't you?" He tickled her. "Come on, Charlie, say it, say it like you mean it."

Laughing, she rolled out of Ruben's grasp. "I like you, goofus. Are you happy?"

"Almost. Kiss me. That'll make me happy."

"Oh, now you want to kiss. I see how this works. Nope. Moonbeams for drinks and dancing, and then I'll think about kissing you."

* * *

1948 BURKETT FALLS

Julia ran over the sandy stone beach. Diving into the chilly waters, she swam toward Phillip. He met her halfway, pulling her into his arms. Out of breath, his voice quivered, "You just scared about twenty years off my life. I couldn't find you. You—you disappeared. Sloane's gone to your house to call in the cavalry. Oh boy, your mom is going to be mad."

Julia draped her arms around Phillip's neck and kissed him all over his face. "It feels like I haven't seen you in forever."

"Well, we can't have that. Hey, what are you wearing?"

Phillip circled them slowly in the water, he searched her eyes, and she drawled, "Oh, this old thing? I haven't a clue. Hey, Phillip, let's elope."

He chuckled and brushed the hair away from her face. "Let's do it."

Several cars pulled into the field next to the Falls. Sloane, Brooks, Amelia, and Dougy got out of one car. Sam and Ethel stepped out of his truck, and Big Joe and Bunny exited their Cadillac. All of them rushed to the beach, staring at Julia, seemingly in awe at her miraculous appearance.

Tears streaked down Sloane's face as she held onto Brooks. "Julia, you were under the water for at least twenty minutes before I left. What happened?"

Still in Phillip's arms, she leaned her head against his and said, "I'm not sure, exactly. But you were there as an old woman. I missed you all so much."

With an arched brow, Sloane looked up at Brooks. "She must've hit her head."

Bunny ran to the edge of the water, and Big Joe stopped her before she marched right in. Shrugging out of his grasp, Bunny placed her hands on her hips and narrowed her eyes at Julia. "Young lady, you get out of the water right this minute."

Julia threw her head back and laughed. "Oh, Bunny, I've missed you."

* * *

Present day Lunar City

The Needle-Horn locked into place at ATTRA's Gateway, and Ruben looked at Charlie as their harnesses automatically released. "Hey, we'll need to stop by the command center to make an official report before we head to Moonbeams."

"Works for me, but I'm heading to my suite to shower and change before Moonbeams. Do you think they'll conduct a hearing on Monica's death?"

Ruben waved for Charlie to step out of the ship on the walkway deck of the Gateway. "Probably, just for the records. We have the Empyreal Palace backing our mission."

Cheers and whistles greeted Ruben and Charlie as they walked through the Gateway to catch a hovercraft to the Command Center. They looked at each other and shrugged. Ruben hailed a double-seated hovercraft, then he and Charlie entered as the craft closed its clear bubble-like top and hooked into the automated rail system.

"Wonder why they were cheering?"

Ruben chuckled. "News of Monica's death has reached the city. I knew her tyranny had suppressed the people, but looking at their jubilant expressions, the report should be a mere formality."

Inside the Command Center, individuals stood from their workstations, clapping and cheering as Ruben and Charlie passed by. "Ruben, this is getting weird."

Chen ran over to greet them before they entered the elevators to the top floor. "The Lord Supreme came over the public-address system and announced Monica's reign is over. Azreal and Chayliel gave a full report of Monica's attack on Earth. Her treason against the Empyreal Palace and demise is all over the news. You and Charlie are heroes. Prince Aelius is acting Commander until a new one is named. He's in the Commander's suite. I'm to escort you to him."

Ruben straightened his shoulders and reached for Charlie's hand. "We did it. You and I." He kissed the back of her hand and Charlie's face reddened.

"Ruben, we're at work."

Inside the elevators, Ruben said, "What's wrong with me kissing my woman's hand?"

Chen coughed and looked down at the floor, grinning.

Charlie said, "That discussion needs to be tabled until later." But she squeezed Ruben's hand, and he smiled at her and winked.

At the Commander's office, two Empyreal Guards stood at either side of the doorway. Chen looked up at the giants and said, "Prince Aelius is expecting us." The guards moved, and they entered the office suite.

Prince Aelius looked up from behind Monica's old desk and rose. He stepped over and clasped Ruben's hand. "Well done, Ruben. Azreal and Chayliel commended your swift action."

Charlie bowed, and Prince Aelius reached for her hands, holding them in his. "Charlie, you acted very bravely to approach Ruben about Monica's treason. I am proud of your courage. Please, sit down."

Ruben and Charlie sat opposite Prince Aelius, and he proceeded to tell them of the recent events. "The day of Monica's attack, I launched multiple campaigns, here at Lunar City, Veetreous, and Cancri. My armies overtook the enemies, and we were victorious. King Anthobethia of Cancri was executed immediately, but General Agriaous is currently being interrogated at the palace to ensure no other threats exist."

Placing his forearm on the desk, Prince Aelius tented his fingertips and pointed to Ruben. "I would like you to consider becoming the new Commander of Lunar City."

Ruben coughed several times and tried to regain his composure. "Begging your pardon, Prince Aelius, but the past two Commanders were killed. Besides, I love time tracking, and if Charlie agreed, I would like her to be my partner."

Prince Aelius grinned and rubbed his hand over his mouth to suppress his laughter. "Very well, Ruben." He turned to Charlie and asked, "Do you want to work with Ruben?"

"Ah, yes, sir, and at the moment, I'm without a ship. The Needle-Horn is refitted with Andy's Spinning Time specs. The time machine works. In the natural reality of time, will Andy make the discovery again?"

Prince Aelius looked at Ruben and then Charlie. "Yes, Charlie. You and Andy must visit Leonardo and Ruben will visit the colonial Williamsburg. It's part of destiny. Now—how would the two of you like a vacation? Anywhere in the galaxy, all-expenses paid, compliments of the palace for going above and beyond the call of duty."

Ruben reached for Charlie's hand and squeezed. "I can't speak for Charlie, but I would love to go on vacation with her. See, I've fallen in love with Charlie, Prince Aelius, and if she gives me a chance, I'd like to spend the rest of my life with her."

Tears sprang into Charlie's eyes, and she rapidly blinked them away.

Prince Aelius stood and grinned. "Charlie, I believe you have a proposal. What say you?"

Charlie jumped out of the chair, and Ruben stood and caught her in his arms. She looked over her shoulder at Prince Aelius. "Begging your pardon, Prince Aelius, but I've been saving Ruben's ass for years. It's about time he finally noticed that I'm completely crazy about him."

Prince Aelius clapped his hands, and Chen entered the office. "Yes, sire?"

"Chen, if you'll be so kind, we're in need of a bottle of champagne and glasses. We have much to celebrate."

Chen nodded and bowed. "Right away, Your Majesty."

CHAPTER 20

1960 The Chalet

Dancing with Phillip under the twinkling string of lights in the back garden, Julia said, "Phillip, I love the Chalet. What a wonderful birthday surprise."

He pressed his face to hers and inhaled. "You're mine, and I'd give you the moon if I could. It took a lot of effort to keep the Chalet under wraps, but with the help of my dad, your parents, and Sloane, we did it. Looking around at our families and watching our children play is a dream come true."

Julia glanced at little Phil catching fireflies with Sloane's kids. Her parents and Ivey, Phillip's dad, sat in the chairs around a small fire pit, chatting and talking away. Brooks and Sloane walked down the garden trail holding hands, Sloane was pregnant with her third child. She had two little girls, Dawn and Diane. *Life's pretty precious.*

Phillip whispered, "I have one more surprise."

Dipping her chin in, Julia said, "Another surprise?"

He grabbed her hand and said, "Follow me." They ran past Brooks and Sloane into the Chalet through the main room and down the hallway into the master bedroom. Another rather large birthday present sat in the middle of the bed. "Open it. I had Sloane wrap it for me."

Julia sat on the edge of the bed and began tearing into the birthday paper. Her eyes widened with surprise, and happy tears rolled down her cheeks when she saw the painting. "Aw, Phillip, it's me at the Old Dyer Farm the night you ask me to marry you."

"Do you like it?"

"It's beautiful. Just the way I remember it. I know exactly where to hang it."

He chuckled and reached inside the closet for his tool box. "I happen to have a nail and hammer."

Julia lit up with excitement. "There on that wall, so every time I walk into the room, I see it."

Phillip bowed and rolled his hand a couple of times. "Your wish is my command." He measured, then hammered the nail and hung the eighteen-by-thirty-six oil painting.

In the middle of the room, Phillip stood behind Julia, wrapping his arms around her waist. She swiveled around and circled her arms around his waist. "I have a surprise for you too."

"You do?"

"Uh huh. I'm pregnant."

He shut his eyes tight and then hollered, "Yahoo!" He leaned in and kissed her. "You've made me the happiest man in the world. How far along?"

"It's early. I'm still in the first trimester, and I don't want to share with anyone for another couple of weeks. It'll be our little secret. I love you, Phillip."

Julia's blessings in life overwhelmed her with emotion. She closed her eyes and offered a prayer of thanksgiving. Wiping away her tears, she said, "I want to grow old with you."

"Your wish is my command."

* * *

PRESENT DAY, *Boatwright Plantation*

Julia watched the event planners from the new wing of the plantation. Two large tents, thirty round tables, and chairs, with white linen tablecloths, fine china, crystal, and silverware decorated with blue and white centerpieces, scattered about two of the five acres of lawn. Strings of white lights ran from the main house and connected to the tents over the parquet dance floor. The band warmed up their instruments and tested the speaker system.

The plantation gardens filled with mature hollyhocks, pink and red hibiscus and a variety of peonies in pink, red and white reminded Julia of another party, her twenty-first birthday. The old willow oak tree still stood at the end of the gardens. Julia smiled, reminiscing about the night she'd first kissed Phillip. She heard Phillip shuffle into the new master suite.

He went to her, circling his arm around her waist. "You're still the most beautiful girl in the world."

Julia swiveled in his arms, holding onto her walking cane. "How did you know what I was thinking about?"

Phillip chuckled. "Great minds think alike. I've been thinking about that day too. Our first kiss and I knew I wanted to spend the rest of my life with you." He bent down and kissed Julia. "We still got it."

Julia laughed. "How does the dress look? Do you think it's too long? I wanted to wear my comfortable shoes."

Smiling, Phillip took her cane and stretched out her arms. "You're pretty as a picture."

Junior stuck his head in the room and said, "You two ready? Andy and his friends will be here soon. I thought I'd go ahead and place you and Dad at the head table next to Kris. Andy and Denise will sit on the other side of you."

Grabbing her walking cane, she said, "Junior, I'm ready, just one more thing, bring me Grandmother Boatwright's pearls."

Junior walked into the bedroom and picked up the pearls from the dressing table. He placed them around Julia's neck and placed a kiss on her shoulders. "Mom, you know I hate it when you call me Junior. My associates will be here today. Please call me Phillip."

Julia patted Junior's cheek. "Sonny, be glad I can still call you anything. At least, I'm six feet above ground and not below it."

"Mother, don't talk like that. Jensi and Kris are meeting with the party planner and planned for a wheelchair ramp close to our table. If you or Dad gets tired, Belinda is here all day to help us." Junior and his lovely wife, Jensi, had moved into the house with Julia and Phillip and hired a caregiver to help with the daily chores.

"Jensi is too kind, but I plan on dancing with your father. See, I have on my dancing shoes?" Julia held onto Phillip and stuck her foot out, revealing a pair of sandals. They didn't match the formal attire, but the shoes gave her added stability. She looked up at Phillip and said, "Come on, Daddy. Our son is waiting. I can't wait to see Andy and Denise. We're very proud of him, and we know you are too. Dr. Andrew Clayborn. How prestigious, and tenure to boot."

Phillip placed Julia's hand in the crook of his arm. "After you, my love."

Walking down the long corridor into the main part of the house, Julia pictured yesteryear with Bunny and Big Joe, Sam and Ethel, plus her spunky baby sister, Sloane. Oh, the times they had together. All of them had gone on to their heavenly home except Sloane. She had called earlier in the day, declining the invitation due to a health issue, but her kids, Terry, Diane, and Dawn, were coming to celebrate Andy's doctorate. Julia and Sloane had remained best friends throughout their lives. It was still hard to believe they had gotten so old.

After the Burkett Falls incident, the details of which remained hazy to this day, Julia and Phillip eloped to New York to Bunny's dismay. Julia had landed a spot as a writer for a television comedy only to find out two months after her marriage she was pregnant.

Phillip had encouraged Julia to keep the job. But as soon as the show learned of her pregnancy, they discreetly did away with her position. So, she and Phillip moved back to Burkett Falls. Phillip pursued his career and became a well-known theoretical physicist and later authored several books on time travel.

Julia and Phillip's grandson, Andy, had followed in his grandfather's footsteps, and today they celebrated his becoming a theoretical physicist at BFU. Junior had taken over the family insurance business, and Kris was an interior designer.

And Julia became an author too. She wrote about fantastical places and worlds unknown. Spaceships, time travel, and an alien dog named Klock.

Guests filled the backyard with laughter and dancing while Julia and Phillip sat at the head table, their heads pressed together, whispering and laughing like two teenagers. Andy and Denise arrived late and approached the table with another couple.

Andy said, "Papa and Memaw, this is Ruben and Charlie Callaway. Ruben and Charlie just joined the department, and we're working on groundbreaking research regarding time travel. They've read your books."

Ruben stepped over to Julia and kissed the back of her hand just as the music played, *At Last.* Ruben gave Julia a big grin and said, "May I have this dance, Julia?"

Julia tilted her head. There was something very familiar about Ruben and Charlie. She looked at Phillip. "Do you mind, honey?"

With a raised brow, Phillip straightened his spine and replied, "Only if I may dance with Charlie?"

Ruben and Charlie laughed, and they went onto the dance floor joined by Andy and Denise.

Ruben held Julia firmly in his arms and said, "I've got you, Julia."

Julia whispered, "Have we met? You look so familiar. There's something about your eyes that reminds me of..." At that point, Phillip tapped on Ruben's shoulder and said, "May I cut in?"

Recognition lit Julia's face as Charlie left Phillip's arms and embraced Ruben. She leaned over and whispered into Charlie's ear, "I told you Ruben loved you. He just had to figure it out himself."

Charlie threw her head back and laughed. "I've missed you, Julia Boatwright."

Phillip swirled Julia around the dance floor. "What was that all about?"

"Oh, nothing. Charlie reminds me of someone I used to know."

Julia looked up into Phillip's eyes, and she was twenty-one again, in the arms of the man she loved.

Phillip leaned in and tilted her chin with his index finger. "Julia Boatwright Clayborn, I love you beyond the moon and stars.

ABOUT THE AUTHOR

After graduating Middle Tennessee State University, D.F. Jones landed a job as a broadcast consultant at the ABC Affiliate in Nashville, which led her to open an advertising agency. Over the years, she's created many campaigns for clients and still enjoys developing marketing materials.

However, in December of 2010, D. F. Jones became a caregiver for her parents. There's nothing quite like facing mortality to shake up one's life. She began by writing her first novel in fall of 2014.

Writing is a source of creative expression, but it also releases stress for D. F. Jones. Writing takes her to a place where anything is possible, and fiction takes D.F. Jones to a place made of dreams.

D.F. Jones is happily married to the love of her life and best friend, KJ. They have two gorgeous grown sons she loves and adores more than life itself. She loves to laugh, and her husband keeps her in stitches!

D.F. Jones is a fan of the Tennessee Titans, MTSU Blue Raiders, and she enjoys working in her flower gardens.

May love light the way!

For more information
www.DFJonesAuthor.com

BUY THE BOOKS

Signed Paperbacks are available to purchase online through www.DFJonesAuthor.com or order books online through most major booksellers.

Buy links below:
Spinning Time, a time travel romance:
http://a.co/gFeHOvG
Ditch Lane Diaries: One-Volume Collection
http://a.co/hJpquqQ
Ruby's Choice (Ditch Lane Diaries 1)
http://a.co/7vMe51Q
Anna's Way (Ditch Lane Diaries 2)
http://a.co/budztaQ
Sandy's Story (Ditch Lane Diaries 3)
http://a.co/6tC8NE4
Antique Mirror, a Halloween Short Story
http://a.co/hUgWQbo
The Witches of Hant Hollow, Jonathan's Curse
http://a.co/4gmtcWd
Register for my newsletter and *get a free book,* information on

new releases, contests and updates go to
http://dfjonesauthor.com/register-for-updates/

Social Media Links

Facebook: https://Facebook.com/DFJones.author
Twitter: https://twitter.com/Author_DFJones
Instagram: https://Instagram.com/d.f.jones_author

EXCERPT FROM THE WITCHES OF HANT HOLLOW

Prologue
Present Day

Jasmine peered into her dressing table mirror and froze into a state of trance. Her mind's eye watched Jonathan step out of the cabin. Suddenly yanked up into the midnight air, he flew over treetops and neighborhood homes. She connected with his rush of emotions heightened by fear of crashing to the ground.

Not a car or truck in sight on the lonely country roads.

The woods of Hant Hollow rapidly became apparent as she watched him lower over a small clearing that revealed the Doanhart mansion's asymmetrical design and gambrel roof with arched windows illuminating a golden glow on the black and white facade.

He tried to run as soon as his feet hit the ground, but someone grabbed him, digging fingernails into his upper arm, drawing blood. He fought to no avail.

The massive front porch with elaborate classical elements loomed and distorted in Jasmine's view as she watched Jonathan stumble up the steps. His eyes widened as the red double door opened of its own accord.

Bile rose from her stomach, but the knot in her throat pushed it back down.

An unclear voice, neither male or female, laughed at Jonathan. "Sick? Angry? Hurt? Go ahead and tell me what you really think."

An invisible force pushed Jonathan inside making him fall on the foyer's marble floor.

Pushing up on his hands and knees, Jonathan released a deep breath and screamed, "I hate you for stealing my life, for killing my wife, and for manipulating me into doing something you wanted so desperately. But your plans backfired, didn't they? Do you really want to know what I think? I want to wrap my fingers around your scrawny neck and choke you to death."

The sinister laughter echoed in the empty house. "Who said my plans backfired?"

A hooded figure came into Jasmine's view, gripped Jonathan under the arm, and dragged him up the mahogany spiral staircase with an ornate balustrade. On the stairwell landing, portraits of women, centuries old, came to life nodding and whispering to each other as if they knew a secret Jasmine didn't, yet.

Hundreds of candles flickered and floated in the air on the third-floor ballroom. The walls and bookshelves contained antiquities, oddities, and sculptures. The sculptures seemed almost lifelike with terror-filled eyes.

The hooded figure put Jonathan in an ancient Egyptian throne made of ebony and inlaid with gold and precious stones. Glowing ropes mysteriously bound his wrists and ankles securely to the chair.

Jasmine glanced away for only a second when she heard Jonathan shout, "You! It was you this whole time?"

Out of the corner of his eye, Jonathan noticed her, and she screamed.

She shouted, but no vocal sounds came from her lips. The hooded figure spelled her.

Jasmine needed supernatural help. She summoned the Mouijah Stones.

CHAPTER 1

1915 Rockvale, Tennessee

JONATHAN TETHERED his two-horse team to the hitching post and went up the stairs to the general store to pick up supplies and staples for the farm.

He glanced to his right and saw a stunning woman standing next to the fabric bin. Her copper curls hung loosely over her shoulders. She turned slightly lifting her gaze to meet him.

He tipped his Stetson. "Ma'am, I don't believe I've had the pleasure. My name's Jonathan Rogers."

She smiled and lifted her chin. "Everyone in town has surely been hospitable since our arrival. I'm Mae." She extended a gloved hand, and he looked down and for a second thought about kissing it but instead placed his hands over hers and held it a mite too long.

She politely withdrew and raised a brow. "My father is the new bank president. Perhaps, you've heard of him? Anthony Morgan? You should stop by and open an account."

Jonathan chuckled while rubbing the rim of his hat. "I mean no disrespect, but I don't trust bankers with my money."

Mae's mouth gaped open; then she frowned. With a distinct Southern accent, she huffed, "I'll be sure to pass along the information to my father." She turned her back to Jonathan and picked up a bolt of fabric.

He liked Mae straight away but left her to her business while he attended to his shopping list. Once he completed his task, he purposely ignored Mae as he walked toward the door, carrying several boxes of goods.

Out of his peripheral vision, he noticed Mae stared at him with both hands on her hips in apparent vexation as he left the store. He chuckled again and made a mental note to attend the Saturday night dance just in case Mae might be there.

After loading the buckboard, he took off his hat and wiped the sweat from his face with a red and white bandanna. He heard boys shouting and cursing up a storm behind the store.

He ran around back and found three teenage boys throwing rocks and dirt at a young woman.

Jonathan shouted, "Stop it right now, or I'll haul every blasted one of you to Sheriff Watson." He stepped in front of the frightened woman, and she cowered behind him.

One of the boys yelled, "She's a witch. Her grannie put a curse on my daddy's backside, and he broke out with blisters full of pus."

Jonathan narrowed his eyes and said, "Get while the getting's good, boys. Last chance." He pulled out his Colt and fired a round in the air. The boys took off like white lightning and disappeared down the back alley.

He knelt before the crying woman and dried her tears with his fingertips. "It's okay. The boys are gone. By the way, my name's Jonathan, and you must be one of the Doanharts." He noticed the clumps of dirt on her dress and the swelling of her right eye. "If you'd like, I'd be happy to give you a ride home."

"Those boys are mean. Oh, I'm Jasmine—Jasmine Doanhart." Her green catlike eyes widened as she pressed her lips tight with a slight quiver in her chin.

Jonathan tried dusting off her dark blue gored skirt. "Yup, they're mean all right. I'm afraid you're going to have quite a shiner on your right eye. So, how about that ride?"

With a look of fear, she shook her head no. "My grandmother wouldn't like that at all."

"I'll tell you what. I'll give you a ride on my way home, and drop you off just before Hant Hollow. Is this your basket of apples?" He swiftly picked up the shiny red apples scattered on the ground and placed them back into the brown wicker basket.

Jonathan had never been to the Doanhart's house, and for that matter, the people venturing there at night never recalled the location.

"Yes, I was taking the apples and cider to sell at the store when the boys cornered me. They broke the cider bottles and threw rocks at me shouting, 'Witch.'"

Jonathan pushed his hat slightly off his forehead. "I don't believe in witches. People make up things they can't quite put their finger on."

"Why are you so kind to me?"

"That's how my daddy raised me."

"Oh, okay. If you're sure it won't be too much trouble, I'd love that ride." Jasmine reached for the basket as he helped her into the buckboard.

"I've been craving Dutch apple pie so how about I buy the apples from you?"

Jasmine smiled and nodded. "Oh, thank you. But I can't take your money. How about we trade the apples for the ride?"

Jonathan threw his head back and laughed. "You got yourself a deal."

On the road to Hant Hollow, the horse's hooves clip-clopped in a steady rhythm with the jingle jangle of the harness over the occasional whinny and neigh.

He chatted with Jasmine about the new horror film *Dr. Jekyll and Mr. Hyde* with James Cruze opening at the town's nickelodeon. "Have you seen the spooky posters and decorations added to the outside of the building?"

"Oh, no, my grandmother doesn't allow us to attend any of the pictures. I'd love to see one though."

"You've never been to any films? They're wonderful."

She gripped the side of the buckboard as it rolled over the grooves on the dirt road. With a frown, she said, "The people in town shun us. They call us names and cross to the other side of the street when one of my family members approaches. And what happened today isn't the first time one of us has been attacked in town. But they'll sneak to our house in the dead of night for a healing herb when one of theirs is sick or fetch us to help with the delivery of one of their brats."

"That's horrible. Most of the people in town were kind to my father, and still are to me, but after my dad died, I sold our house and bought a small farm in the country not far from Hant Hollow." He didn't mention his weasel of a cousin stealing the family business from him.

"How did your dad die? Oh, I'm sorry, maybe I shouldn't have asked that question."

He didn't want to broach that topic until he found out what happened to his father. He kept investigating even though the town doctor ruled his death as a heart attack.

His dad's cousin, Dale, had been trying to gain control of the family mill and the property that went with it. Dale had something to do with his dad's death—Jonathan felt it in his gut, and one day he'd prove it. One day he'd get the mill back. He didn't want the house. Too many memories, and too many ghosts.

On the edge of Hant Hollow, Jonathan pulled on the reins. "Whoa, Ida. Whoa, Dick." He turned and placed his right arm on the back of the buckboard's seat. "That's a story for another day."

Jasmine burst into laughter. "Your horses' names are Ida and Dick?"

He chuckled. "Yep. I didn't name them. The quarter horses belonged to my father." He pulled on the brake and the horses whinnied and shook their heads. He hopped down and walked around the wagon to help Jasmine.

She held onto his hand and jumped to the ground. "Enjoy the apples, and thanks for sticking up for me."

"No thanks needed. You head along now, and be sure to watch out for those knuckle-headed boys." He paused for a second then asked, "Hey, you want to go to the movie with me?"

Jasmine blushed and briefly glanced to the ground before locking those incredible green eyes with his. His stomach flipped.

She reached up on tiptoe and kissed Jonathan's cheek. "I appreciate the offer, but I have to decline. Although, you're like a knight in one of the Grimm stories."

He took off his hat and placed it on his chest. "Milady." He climbed back into the buckboard and snapped the reins. "Get along. Let's go home." He watched Jasmine disappear into the thicket of Hant Hollow as the horses moved forward along the road.

Shaking his head, he mused over Jasmine.

The Doanharts had never given him any problems. Besides, gossip thrived in a small town, and he never gave the witches rumors any credence.

On the ride home, Jonathan's thoughts returned to his dad's death. The foreman of the mill had worked for their family for twenty-odd years, and he arranged to get a copy of the office key for Jonathan.

He muttered to himself, "I'll leave early on Saturday night and make a stop by the mill before going to the dance. Just maybe, Dale left something behind that will implicate him."

The day his dad died was like any other day in their small town. Except over breakfast, Thomas mentioned he'd met with an attorney to draw up documents naming Jonathan as a full partner. Jonathan worked for his father since he graduated high school. The larger-than-life man had been the epitome of good health and in the prime of his life. A heart attack seemed unlikely.

Dale had lost his shares to the family business in a poker game years ago, and he never forgave Thomas for claiming the debt. Then Dale produced a new will naming him the sole heir to Rogers Mill. Jonathan searched for the deed, but it had mysteriously vanished.

It seemed too coincidental to Jonathan.

Turning the team down the farm road, Jonathan shook off his thoughts about his family and whistled the latest Ziegfeld tune, *"Hello, Frisco."*

The clouds disappeared, and the sun beat down on his face.

Things seemed to be looking up for a change.

He met two beautiful women today.

* * *

Mae watched Jonathan leave the store without even a sideways glance in her direction. Since she'd moved to the town of Rockvale, Mae had plenty of attention from male suitors, but Jonathan Rogers captured her attention by just ignoring her.

Easy on the eyes too.

He wore a long sleeve white shirt rolled up to his elbows. The cut of the shirt complemented his well-defined physique. The mere thought of Jonathan made her cheeks flush.

Mr. Hubern, the storekeeper, approached Mae. "My wife's feeling poorly today, but I'm sure she'll meet with you in the next few days on making new dresses and such. I'd be happy to wrap up the bolts of fabric?"

She handed him the silk and linen. "I'd love to meet with your wife. I hear she's an excellent seamstress. Please charge those to my father and have your wife call on me when she's feeling better. Oh, one more thing, will the new Sears and Roebuck's arrive soon?"

Mr. Hubern placed the fabric bolts behind the counter, took out a ledger, and began to write down the charges. "I 'spect it'll come sometime next week. I'll send a message through the hoot and holler as soon as I get it."

She'd heard of the town's hoot and holler system always opened to two or more parties in point to point communication like Southern Bell in Atlanta. "Wonderful." She paused before leaving and leaned against the counter. "Uh, Mr. Hubern, do you know Jonathan Rogers?"

"Yes, ma'am. Jonathan's a fine fellow. Sad business though. His father owned the sawmill in town. Rumor has it there was some bad blood with his father's cousin, Dale. Poor Jonathan found his daddy deader than a doornail late one night a little over a year ago. Doc Smith said it was a heart attack, but the rumor circulating is Dale had something to do with it. With no proof, the Rogers family feud cost Jonathan the mill. Half the town is still mad over it."

Mae's hand went to her mouth. She'd heard of Dale Rogers because her father had met with him on several occasions. "Oh my, that's awful."

"Are you all right, Miss Morgan? My wife tells me all the time to keep my trap shut and stop sticking my nose in everybody's business, but everybody's business sooner or later ends up at the store." Hubern shrugged, then turned the ledger around for Mae to sign.

She swayed against the counter. "I'm a little light-headed."

Mr. Hubern stepped over to the soda fountain and poured her a glass of lemonade. "Why don't you take a seat and have a drink of lemonade?"

Mae sipped the drink. "Thank you, but I'll be okay once I get outside. It's stifling hot in the store. How do you stand it?" She bent over to sign the bill.

He laughed. "Aw, I'm used to it. I've been working in the store most of my life."

She handed him the empty glass. "Well, tell Missus Hubern that I hope she feels better real soon. Good day, Mr. Hubern."

"Good day to you."

Outside in the blazing sun, Mae opened her parasol and walked along the flagstone sidewalk. Her thoughts turned to Jonathan. She wondered if he might come to the Saturday night dance, and pictured herself in his big strong arms.

She blushed from the heat of desire licking improper thoughts in her mind of the well-built farmer.

Oh, Mae Morgan, it isn't proper for a lady to have such sinful thoughts about a man.

She giggled.

Shaking her head, she opened the bank door and went inside looking for her father. She glanced to his office, and two men dressed in suits sat in front of his cherry desk. He looked up and smiled, and she returned a silent greeting.

Mae glanced at the Seth Thomas clock hanging on the back wall, and under it sat a lush potted palm plant. She beamed with pride at her father's ability to bring in a new Protectograph check writer sitting on the teller's counter alongside a Webster pencil sharpener.

She noticed a tall, thin man dressed in elegant Edwardian style leaning against a walnut conference table looking at her as if she wore only knickers. She glanced away from his impertinent stare.

Several newspapers lay out on a side table next to two straight back chairs. Mae picked one up, and the headline read, *Lusitania Sunk by Submarine, 1300 Dead.*

Mae averted her eyes. The threat of war loomed over America. She placed the newspaper back on the table.

The tall gentleman stepped over and slightly bowed. "Hello, Miss Morgan. I'm Dale Rogers, an associate of your father. He's in a meeting. Would you like to sit and wait with me?"

"My father speaks highly of you, but if he's busy, it's nothing that can't wait until dinner." He reached for her hand, and she took a step back.

He asked, "Do you like the house? Have you settled in?"

"I have a few things left to unpack, but the house is beautiful. Now, who did you say were the prior owners? They took such good care of the place."

"My cousin, Thomas, and his son, Jonathan."

Mae's heart started racing. She lived in Jonathan's house. "Why did they sell?"

"Oh, my cousin died suddenly. His son decided to sell the house and purchased a place out in the country."

"And his mother? What happened to her?"

"She died in childbirth when Jonathan was small. Why are you so interested?"

"Older houses have such character, and I believe that comes from the people who lived there."

"So, you believe in ghosts?"

She tilted her head to the side. "I believe in the Holy Ghost so it seems to me there would be other ghosts too."

"You're a delight. Would you like for me to give Anthony a message?"

"Not really. I'll see Dad at dinner. Good day, sir." Before she turned, Dale grabbed her hand, bent over, and placed a kiss on it.

The nerve of the man.

If he weren't a business associate, she'd smack his smarmy face. She withdrew her hand and quickly left the bank.

She sensed more to the Rogers family drama than Dale let on, and she intended to find out what.

Chapter 2

Jasmine ran into the hollow and quickly shapeshifted into a calico cat. She clawed her way up to the top of the cedar tree and watched

Jonathan drive away in his wagon. His kindness and gallantry touched her heart.

Jasmine could've used magic to stop the boys, but Grandmother Iris had forbidden spellcasting in town.

She stayed in the tree until Jonathan disappeared from her sight; then she made her way home. Jasmine shifted back into her human form and stopped briefly to catch her breath.

The boys hated her, and she didn't even know them. They wanted to kill her. She read their thoughts. They might have succeeded if Jonathan hadn't intervened.

What would her grandmother do to the boys if she found out?

Iris didn't take kindly to mortals hurting her family after the murders of Aunt Silver and Cousin Aster.

Jasmine walked along the path. To the left of the house, Iris worked in the herb and vegetable garden wearing a wide-brim hat, long sleeve shirt and a wide skirt hitting at the ankles. Jasmine didn't know the exact age of her grandmother, but she didn't look a day past twenty-one, a timeless beauty with light auburn hair, cobalt blue eyes and full lips. Her peachy skin held no imperfections.

Jasmine's mother, Isidore, Aunt Peony, and Aunt Silver had different fathers. Heck, she'd never met her dad. The Witches of Hant Hollow thought loving and living with a mate meant weakness.

She'd only seen them with males during the Solstice Festivals, holiday parties, and the occasional ball. Except for Lavender, her best friend, and first cousin. She loved men, wizards, werewolves, and vampires. She didn't discriminate.

Thinking of Lavender made her smile.

Jasmine's eyes widened as Iris made an incision in her forefinger with a paring knife, then walked the garden rows allowing droplets of blood to splat into the earth.

Why was she using blood?

Jasmine made a mental note to research the use of blood in the garden during her spell, potions, and charm study time in their library. All types of books filled their library including books on light and dark magic.

She glanced down and tried dusting off her clothes once more, then ran up the porch stairs into the front foyer nearly knocking her mother down.

Isidore held her face. "What happened?"

She fell into her mother's arms and hugged her tightly. "Oh, townies again. This time a group of teenage boys tried to stone me to death, but this kind man named Jonathan saved me. He stood between the boys and me. He protected me with his life."

"A little comfrey root will fix you right up." Isidore let out a deep sigh and caressed Jasmine's cheek before pulling her into the bright yellow kitchen. "You know you aren't allowed to make friends with the mortals. We can't trust them under any circumstance. One day, they're nice to your face, and the next day, they're stoning you or worse." She pressed the herbal paste on Jasmine's eye and held it there with a cold washcloth. "Hold the compress while I make you a treat."

Lavender stepped into the kitchen and gasped. "Jasmine, who did this to you? Let me know, and they'll wish they'd never been born."

Jasmine grinned. "Oh, I'll be okay. It isn't the first time, and I'm sure it won't be the last." She repeated the story of the attack and meeting Jonathan. She omitted that he'd given her a ride home.

Lavender twirled her long white-blond hair and secured it in place with magic. "Jonathan is incredibly good-looking. Well done, Jasmine."

Isidore frowned. "Let's not encourage her, please. You know mortals are off limits. We have much to do, and so little time left to do it in. The summer festival is only a couple of weeks away."

"But mortals are so much fun to play with."

Isidore shook her head. "You are incorrigible."

"Yeah, but you love me."

Jasmine held the cloth against her eye as she shifted her position in the chair. She loved the kitchen. It was one of her favorite places in the house whether they cooked food or prepared potions.

The kitchen had bright yellow walls, tall cedar cabinets, and a large stone fireplace the length of the back wall that was big enough to roast a pig or contain several large black kettle pots. Twelve-foot arched bay windows let in loads of natural lighting in the day, and stars and moonlight streamed in at night.

Isidore sat a plate of tea cakes and a pitcher of milk on the table. "After you finish your treats, I need you to start washing the vegetables to prepare for canning. Iris is hiring servants for the celebration, but she wants to use our recipes."

Lavender rolled her eyes. "Why can't we just use magic? It's much faster, and it tastes the same."

"Magic has a time and place but expends much energy. You may not enjoy the practice of spellcasting later if you spend your energy on menial tasks now." She turned to Jasmine while wiping her hands off with a dish towel. "You've been named the fortune teller for the summer festival."

Jasmine's face lit up. "I can't believe it. Really?" She had a gift in foretelling the future and only used tarot cards and tea leaves as props for the mortals.

Her mom nodded and smiled.

Lavender said, "Aunt Esiey, tell us about the old ones."

"You're stalling, precious. But if you promise to help me the rest of the afternoon, I'll tell you the story, again."

"Promise."

Isidore continued washing the vegetables without looking up. "Once upon a time, there was a group of influential and talented women descended from the Celtics. The women fought against the underworld of darkness with the divine powers from the Goddess of Light. Our leader, Dreena, the Lady of Light, passed down the knowledge and gifts from one generation to another. The Doanharts trained with the best of the ancient ones and that's why our library is full of books and documents. Some of the sacred scrolls predate the Babylonian area."

Jasmine removed the compress. "I met Dreena last year. She doesn't age either, and she's incredibly beautiful. I hear she's coming to the celebration."

Isidore brought the vegetables over to the fireplace and scraped them into the boiling pot. "Yes, and she's staying with us. So, that's why we must finish canning and gathering the food stores. The house will be full of guests."

Jasmine went over to the well and drew a pail of water, then placed it on the wood-burning stove to boil.

Lavender said, "Come on, Aunt Esiey, finish the story. You're getting to the good part."

"Well, let me see, where was I? Oh yes, in the beginning, the mortals living in our community held our wise women and our powers sacred. Until one day, a group of men arrived wearing long black robes, black caps, and they had long beards. The men proclaimed to the community that the wise women's magic came from the devil. The men called the women, witches, and made the people scared of the women they'd known all their lives. The men blamed the wise women for every sickness and misfortune in the community."

The mantel over the fireplace held jars of herbs and spices. Isidore chose carefully from each jar, sprinkling the contents into the kettle as she continued the story. "Many of the gifted women, that had saved many lives in the community, were tortured and killed while the other wise women took the sacred documents and fled to the four corners of the world to escape the wrath of the black-robed men. Those men are why we're called witches. Personally, I wear the witch name as a badge of honor to those that sacrificed their lives so that we could live."

Jasmine stirred one of the black kettle pots. "But our magic comes from the light, not the darkness."

Isidore glanced up and said, "Well, yes and no. That's when the two factions of our people formed. The first group of wise women remains faithful to Dreena, the reigning Lady of Light, and the second group follows Urslina, who formed a separate group of witches using the dark arts. To this day, the Lady of Light and the Queen of the Dark Night are constantly at odds. We come together during the winter and summer solstice celebrations to reconcile."

Jasmine said, "But both sides want to control the magic."

Isidore slowly stirred the pot, scraping the sides. "Yes, that is unfortunate. Just remember, once a witch calls upon Urslina and the dark powers, they rarely return to the light. Don't open the door to evil unless you want it to come in. Iris teaches us from the Book of Light, but she practices the dark arts, and its power remains within her."

Jasmine shuddered. "No doubt. She scares me to death sometimes."

"Me too, and her foul moods are ghastly."

"Girls, you're disrespectful."

Lavender shrugged. "Well, it's the truth."

"I believe Iris had a chance of returning to the light once. I think she loved Jonathan's father. Thomas almost succeeded in destroying the darkness within her, but unfortunately, in the end, he only made the darkness grow."

"My Jonathan?" Jasmine asked in shock.

Lavender laughed and playfully shoved Jasmine. Mimicking Jasmine's voice, she said,

"My Jonathan?"

Jasmine zapped Lavender in the behind, and she yelped.

Jasmine asked, "How? What did he do?"

"He married Jonathan's mother."

Jasmine said, "Well, then, let's not tell Iris about me meeting him today."

Isidore smiled. "It's probably wise. Why don't you and Lavender go on to the library and start studying the Book of Spells? You never know when Iris will give you a test."

"I thought we were canning vegetables."

"We are, but I have to parboil them a couple of times and then allow the vegetables to cool. I'll call you when I need help."

"All right. There's something I want to look up anyway."

Isidore nodded, and then Jasmine and Lavender raced down the wide hallway.

At the door of the library, Lavender looked both ways and whispered, "Don't tell. I'm meeting Brody in the glen. He's trekking the terrain for the layout of the festival. I do love a man in the Mage Alliance uniform." She popped out of sight.

Jasmine shook her head and entered the library. She loved the smell of old books. Each book released a different scent and the chemicals within the pages carried messages to her brain. She'd read most of them.

Jasmine.

Her ears pricked at the sound of her name.

Jasmine.

She turned and followed the sound to the oldest section of the library where the forbidden hand-written books on delicate papyrus, rolled scrolls, and ancient leather-bound books filled the top tier of the bookshelves.

She glanced over her shoulder and wiggled her finger to lock the library door and then floated to the second landing. Her fingers scanned across the books searching for the one calling out to her.

Jasmine.

The hair on the nape of her neck rose. Light shimmered through the windows catching the dust particles dancing in the air.

She closed her eyes and concentrated on the sound of her name.

Jasmine.

Holding her hand's palms up, she said, "Come to me and let me see the book that beckons me." She peeked through one eye, then opened the other. No book appeared, but behind the scrolls, a golden light glimmered.

Iris would kill her if she caught Jasmine sifting through the archaic texts. The ancient manuscripts were the oldest in the library and forbidden to all, except Iris.

As the scrolls parted, what looked like an antique jewelry box with mother-of-pearl inlay opened to her.

Pick up the golden jeweled stone.

Her fingers trembled as she pulled the box to the edge of the wooden shelf and opened the lid. She found two round golden sun discs each encrusted with large ruby stone similar in shape and size engraved with what appeared to be hieroglyphics. But they weren't Egyptian. She'd studied Egyptian hieroglyphics, and her grandmother owned several ancient Egyptian pieces.

Part of her told Jasmine to put the box back, but her curiosity got the better of her.

She picked up the disc and faded from the library into a room bathed in warm sunlight. The incandesce filled the dense air.

No sky. No ground.

"I am the Goddess of Light, and you're holding the Mouijah Stones."

Jasmine wanted to throw herself at the feet of the light, but nothing existed except the sound of her voice. So, she bowed her head and lowered her eyes.

"You don't need to fear me. I'm here to warn you of an encompassing darkness. One that will try to claim your soul. But you will not let it. I'm here to help you. I have always been here. I understand you feel strange, but it will pass. Light and Darkness have coexisted for many millennia. You cannot have one without the other. The Lord Darkness, you call death, comes for each being. But you do not have to give him your soul."

Jasmine rocked back and forth in a weightless state. She worried for a second she might vomit on the Goddess. Headiness and heaviness nearly took her, but somehow, she managed to stay alert.

Tongue-tied, Jasmine wanted to ask questions, but what?

"Are you flesh or spirit?' It sounded better in her mind than when she asked the question.

"I am both. I understand you're overwhelmed. Open your ears that you may hear. There are two discs. One is to call me, and the other is to call The Lord Darkness. When you need guidance, I am here. No one will ever know of our conversations, especially not your grandmother. But remember, if you ever call on the Lord Darkness, he will expect payment. He will expect a soul."

She nodded. "I-I'm not quite sure what to ask except, why me?"

"You have a generous heart, and you seek to help and not harm."

She frowned. "How did the discs end up in our library?"

"Your grandmother stole them for Urslina. She was called to keep them safe, but she is changing, and I no longer trust her."

"How am I to help? What do you want from me?"

"You will know how to help and what I want when the time is right."

The light faded and once again Jasmine stood in library holding the sun disc. She placed it back in the box and the box melted into the scrolls.

Did she want the responsibility of caring for the Mouijah Stones?

She spoke softly. "I will try and honor you, Goddess of Light."

Her chest tightened as the realization struck her that she'd been called to offset her grandmother's darkness.

An invisible line drawn in the sand with two witches living in the same house wielding the enormous powers of the Light and Dark magic.

THE WITCHES OF HANT HOLLOW: Jonathan's Curse
by D.F. Jones
Link: http://a.co/dSvpsOZ

Made in the USA
Middletown, DE
17 January 2020